Pushing pas~~~~ ~~~~ stumbled over the threshold, her chilled body drawing her like a moth to the flames dancing on the hearth.

In her dazed and exhausted mind, images swirled before her eyes: the rain-swept road. Her stiff cold fingers. Her empty purse.

She felt as if she were swaying in a high wind. The disapproval on the face of the tall man by the hearth was the last thing she saw before the images dissolved and she slipped into blackness.

Consternation tempering his irritation, Ned hastened to catch the girl before her head hit the wooden floor. As he gathered her up, glancing about him to determine where to deposit his soggy burden, he realized his first impression had been wrong.

Before she fainted, he'd noted little more than large dark eyes, a determined little chin and the fact that she was dripping all over the carpet. But though her body was short and slender, this was no girl he held in his arms, but a woman.

His sleepy body roused abruptly to full attention.

* * *

From Waif to Gentleman's Wife
Harlequin® Historical #964—October 2009

Praise for Julia Justiss

A Most Unconventional Match

"Justiss captures the true essence of the Regency period…
The characters come to life with all the proper mannerisms
and dialogue as they waltz around each other in a 'most
unconventional' courtship."
—*Romantic Times BOOKreviews*

Rogue's Lady

"With characters you care about, clever banter,
a roguish hero and a captivating heroine, Justiss has
written a charming and sensual love story."
—*Romantic Times BOOKreviews*

The Untamed Heiress

"Justiss rivals Georgette Heyer in the beloved
The Grand Sophy (1972) by creating a riveting young
woman of character and good humor…The horrific nature
of Helena's childhood adds complexity and depth to this
historical romance, and unexpected plot twists and layers
also increase the reader's enjoyment."
—*Booklist*

The Courtesan

"With its intelligent, compelling characters, this is a very
well-written, emotional and intensely charged read."
—*Romantic Times BOOKreviews*, Top Pick

My Lady's Pleasure

"Another entertaining, uniquely plotted Regency-era novel…
top-notch writing and a perfect ending make this one
easy to recommend."
—*Romantic Times BOOKreviews*

My Lady's Trust

"With this exceptional Regency-era romance,
Justiss adds another fine feather to her writing cap."
—*Publishers Weekly*

JULIA JUSTISS

FROM
Waif to
GENTLEMAN'S
Wife

HARLEQUIN®

TORONTO • NEW YORK • LONDON
AMSTERDAM • PARIS • SYDNEY • HAMBURG
STOCKHOLM • ATHENS • TOKYO • MILAN • MADRID
PRAGUE • WARSAW • BUDAPEST • AUCKLAND

To my children,
who, like Elizabeth's David, bring me joy

Recycling programs
for this product may
not exist in your area.

ISBN-13: 978-0-373-29564-7

FROM WAIF TO GENTLEMAN'S WIFE

Chapter One

South-west England—spring 1817

Making sure little Susan, who suffered from nightmares, had finally settled into a deep sleep, Joanna Merrill gave the child's silky hair a gentle pat and slipped from her charge's side.

'Thank'ee, ma'am, and I be sorry to have intruded on your evening,' the nursemaid Hannah whispered, still rocking Susan's younger sister in the schoolroom just beyond the little girl's bed. 'But I was fair at my wit's end, what with this one wailing and Miss Susan all afret. Ye've got the touch that soothes that little mite. Better get downstairs now, afor you miss your tea.'

Having escaped another interminable dinner under the lecherous eye of Lord Masters, her employer's husband, Joanna had no intention of pouring tea for the family, despite her mistress's instruction that she return to do so after calming Miss Susan.

'No, Hannah, I'm feeling weary. I believe I will just return to my room and read.'

'Very well, miss. Goodnight to you…and be careful.'

Joanna had no need of the nursemaid's cryptic warning.

Avoiding Lord Master's unwanted advances was becoming so great a challenge that, much as she enjoyed the peace of the countryside and her active young charges, Joanna knew she would soon be forced to seek another position, thereby confronting head-on the concern that had prevented her from giving notice within a week of her employers' arrival in the country—the suspicion that Lord Masters, loath to allow the current object of his wandering eye to escape, would somehow prevent his wife from giving her the necessary references.

How things had changed in the fortnight since her long-absent employers' return from London, she thought with a sigh as she tiptoed across the schoolroom. When a friend of her late husband's family had recommended her for this governess's position almost a year ago, she'd thought it the answer to her prayers, devastated as she'd been after losing first her babe and then her darling Thomas. Having neither strength nor funds to seek out Papa, still a chaplain with the East India Company, and unwilling to throw herself on her elder brother Greville's charity, or abase herself by begging assistance from Thomas's family, who had made clear their disapproval of his marrying the daughter of a untitled country gentleman, she'd been happy to trade the noise and dirt of London for the rural beauty of this remote corner of southwest Hampshire.

Instructing two small girls, at once sweet and demanding, filled her days with an endless activity that left her little time to brood. She'd found a measure of tranquillity that dulled the pain of having to surrender her dreams of building a family and a future with Thomas. A fragile peace that had been shattered within a few days of the arrival of Lady Masters, whom she'd met once the day of her interview, and Lord Masters, whom Joanna had never seen, back at his ancestral estate.

As she paused on the threshold, peering cautiously into the corridor, she recalled with a bitter smile how charming she'd thought Lord Masters at their first meeting. Appearing not at all high in the instep, he'd paused to chat with the new employee, enquiring about her family and even claiming friendship with her distant and high-born relation, the Marquess of Englemere, who employed her brother Greville to manage one of his small properties. After she informed Lord Masters how remote was her kinship to this cousin she'd never met and confessed how removed she'd always lived from London society, she expected the Viscount would soon abandon his politeness to a mere governess.

Instead, he'd continued to seek her out, paying her flattering attention as he chatted about literature, art, music and the theatre under the guise of discussing what he considered important for his daughters' education. Lulled into complacency, she'd noticed nothing untoward until the fourth evening after his arrival…when he'd cornered her alone in the library after dinner.

Still loath to step into the shadowy corridor, she lingered a moment longer, a shudder rippling through her as she recalled that infamous night. Something about his lordship's gaze, which had seemed to hover with unseemly interest on her bosom, had made her immediately uneasy. The quantity of wine he'd drunk at dinner glazing his eyes, he'd tried to persuade her to remain in the library and talk to him. She'd kept the big desk between them as he entreated her, then walked quickly away, holding the book she'd chosen before her chest like a shield.

Heart thumping like a drum beating the advance, she'd almost managed to escape before, closing the distance between them, he'd reached out and run his fingers over her bottom. The sound of his laughter when she knocked his hand away and scurried out, slamming the door behind her, had chilled her to the core.

Locked inside her room, heart still thrumming in alarm, she'd considered complaining at once to Lady Masters. But what would she do if her employer didn't believe her?

Lord Masters was a Viscount and her employer's husband. She was a soldier's widow, her father an insignificant clergyman currently out of England, the brother she'd not seen in years employed on an estate far away. Who would support her if Lord Masters denied her charges, as he was almost certain to do?

Vowing to remain ever vigilant while she considered the wisest course of action, since that evening she'd kept her chamber door locked and her eyes watchful.

As she would tonight.

Taking a deep breath, she exited the schoolroom and walked swiftly through dimly lit space towards her room. She'd almost reached that sanctuary when a figure materialised from the shadows further down the hall and strode towards her.

'Lord Masters,' she said coolly, despite the dismay that sent her pulse racing. 'I have the headache a little. Kindly let Lady Masters know I will not take tea this evening.'

'Ah, then I must eschew tea as well...and tend you. Have you a fever?'

She sidestepped his attempt to lay a hand on her forehead. 'Just a headache, my lord, which solitude and quiet will soon cure. I'm sure your wife, waiting for you below, is most impatient for your return.'

'She's had hers; she can wait,' he said carelessly, his gaze roving her figure with such blatant relish that she felt besmirched. 'Whereas you, little fox... It's been a long time, hasn't it? Years since that soldier-boy husband of yours sent you back to England? You must be eager...panting for it.'

As he spoke, Joanna had backed away from him towards her chamber until the fingertips she'd extended behind her touched the door latch. Advancing as she retreated, Lord Masters now put both hands on either side of the door frame, corralling her against the door's solid mahogany panel as he breathed alcoholic fumes into her face.

If she darted into her room, could she close the door quickly enough to prevent him from following? Lock it before he could use his greater strength to force it back open?

She might be smaller and weaker, but she'd not give the bastard the satisfaction of knowing how much he frightened her. Summoning her best governess voice, she said repressively, 'Lord Masters, I find your…attentions most distasteful. Pray recall that you were born a gentleman and abandon them at once.'

Instead, the Viscount chuckled. 'What a prim little pet you are! Have I ruffled your sleek russet fur? By heaven, you make me mad to soothe you…to tear off that drab dress and feel the silk of your skin under my fingers.'

Alarm extinguishing any further desire to reason with him, Joanna ducked under his outstretched arm and tried to dash away. Laughing in earnest now, he caught her easily, then pinned her against the door and assaulted her with a kiss, his tongue probing her firmly closed lips.

Furious as well as afraid, despite the limited space between them, Joanna struck at him with as much power as she could muster and bit his tongue.

With a yelp of pain, he slammed her into the door, trapping her arms behind her. Covering her mouth with one hand before she could cry out, he wrapped his other arm around her, binding her to him with a punishing grip that left her wriggling to free herself as ineffectually as a worm on a hook.

'Like it rough, do you?' he panted, his beetle-black eyes glistening with excitement. 'Well, I can accommodate! By God, I'll have you now, you little vixen.'

Clutching her against him, he kicked open her chamber door. While she continued to struggle, desperately seeking to injure or delay him, he dragged her across the room, threw her backwards on to the bed and climbed atop her, holding her in place with the bulk of his body. With one hand he started dragging up her skirts.

Barely able to breath from the weight on her chest, spurred by panic when she felt his hardness pressed against her, Joanna managed to free one arm. Striking out blindly, she pummelled Lord Master's head and bit at the hand covering her mouth.

Despite her efforts, he'd slid his fingers up to her thighs when a shrill female voice cried, 'Mrs Merrill! What are you doing?'

After a startled instant of immobility, her attacker lurched away from her. Gasping for breath after the removal of his smothering weight, Joanna scrambled to a sitting position on the bed.

Her expression tight and affronted, Lady Masters said, 'What is the meaning of this outrage?'

'Now, Lizzie, don't go off into a pelter,' Lord Masters said, his tone cajoling. 'That auburn-haired witch has been throwing herself at me ever since we arrived. There's only so much temptation a man can withstand.'

Lady Master's look turned contemptuous. 'In some cases, 'tis very little indeed.'

'Temptation!' Joanna croaked furiously, finally able to find her voice. 'I gave you no encouragement whatsoever! Indeed, I did everything in my power to discourage your unwelcome advances.'

'Discourage, hah!' Masters responded. 'Just look at her, my love. That flaming hair coming loose and her gown awry, cheeks flushed and bosom heaving—why, the hot-blooded wench even bit me!' He gestured with his bloody hand to his equally bloody lip.

Lady Masters closed her eyes and took a deep, shuddering breath. Now that the danger had passed, Joanna felt a surge of pity for Lady Masters. How awful to be tied for life to a lecher who embarrassed one by trying to debauch one's governess under one's very nose! She'd bet her tiny sum of savings this wasn't the first time, either.

Opening her eyes a moment later, Lady Masters said quietly, 'My lord, you will let me handle this, please?'

'If you wish, my love.' Giving a smile to his wife—and throwing Joanna the surly glance of a spoiled child denied the treat he'd been anticipating—Lord Masters ambled out.

'Lady Masters, I assure you—'

'Please, Mrs Merrill, do not try to explain. Under these circumstances, I can hardly continue to allow a woman of your…appetites to supervise my children. I must demand that you leave this house at once.'

The charge was so unexpected—and so blatantly untrue—that for a moment, Joanna could only stare at her employer in astonishment. Her sympathy for the woman evaporating, she said, 'But, Lady Masters, surely you can't blame—'

'Mrs Merrill, I've already said I shall not entertain any excuses. I will be charitable enough to have a groom bring round a gig to convey you to the village in half an hour, but do not test my indulgence by remaining under my roof a minute longer.'

'Now?' Joanna asked incredulously. ''Tis already full dark! And what of my salary for this quarter?'

'The lateness of the hour is your own concern. As for your salary—' Lady Masters looked her up and down '—I expect you'll soon find a way to earn whatever you need.'

And so, an incoherent blur of time later, her mind still reeling in shock and fury, Joanna found herself deposited at the public house in the village by a surly groom who dropped her without a word, whipped his horse back to a trot and disappeared into the darkness on the long journey back to the manor.

Unwilling to wake the sleeping inhabitants of the inn, unsure yet what story the woman the villagers knew to be governess at the Masters estate could or should tell them about her unexpected appearance, Joanna slipped into the barn. Only the soft wickers of several equine inhabitants greeted her as she found a thick pile of straw and sank down on to it.

Struggling to resist the fear and despair threatening to overcome her, she considered her few possessions—a hurriedly packed bandbox of underthings, shoes and gowns along with the clothes and cloak she wore—and her hoard of coins, which was pitifully small.

Without references or any current prospects of further employment, how would she survive without succumbing to the fate the monstrously unfair Lady Masters had predicted?

After a moment of blind panic, a reassuring thought calmed her. She'd go to her brother, Greville Anders.

He'd left the army after Waterloo, she'd learned in the last message she'd had from him, a bitter diatribe against the aristocratic patronage system that had denied him the promotion he felt should have been his after that great battle. Always an indifferent correspondent, he'd sent her nothing since. For all she knew, he might have a wife and a hopeful family at the snug estate he now managed for their more illustrious cousin. He'd not journeyed to London to console her after she had sent word of Thomas's death and, not wanting at that time to inconvenience him, she'd taken the employment offered by Lady Masters without further thought.

But, married or single, Greville was the only close family she possessed still in England. Surely he would take her in until she figured out what to do next.

Encouraged by that thought, she settled back into the soft hay with a sigh. Tomorrow she would expend her small savings to purchase coach fare to Blenhem Hill.

'So, Ned, what do you think I should do?'

The next afternoon, Sir Edward Austin Greaves raised his gaze from swirling the brandy the sun was illumining to burnished bronze and looked thoughtfully at his friend Nicholas

Stanhope, Marquess of Englemere, who sat across from him in Englemere's library. 'What is happening at the property now?'

After sipping from his own glass, Nicky shook his head. 'I can't be certain, not without inspecting the place personally. Frankly, if it were not for the unrest in the countryside and the general distress occurring even at some of my own holdings, I'd be inclined to think Martin exaggerated. After he retired as my agent, I gave over the management of Blenhem Hill to a distant cousin who approached me about employment after Waterloo. Thought it was the least I could do for one of our brave men, and as he'd served in Wellington's commissary corps, I assumed he would be capable. Not so, according to Martin, who despite his advanced years still has a sharp mind and a keen eye.'

'How bad did Martin say conditions are?' Ned asked, a ready sympathy rising in him. Except for a few very rich landowners or those with properties as well tended as his, the drop in prices at the end of the war had wreaked havoc with the agrarian economy.

Nicky grimaced. 'Wretched enough that Martin urged me to immediately discharge my cousin and his agent, another veteran with whom he'd served. Which I did, leaving me now at a standstill. Blenhem Hill is a damnably long distance from any of my other properties. Though I hate to leave Sarah and our son to make an extended journey, I'd already been intending to visit to view operations at the small stocking mill I had constructed—something Hal recommended.'

'A local manufactury that would offer supplementary income for tenant families to offset the drop in crop prices?' Ned asked. When Nicky nodded, Ned continued, 'I talked with several estate owners who are doing that. An excellent notion.'

'So Hal thought, now that better looms have been designed. You know Hal—' Nicky grinned as he mentioned their mutual friend Hal Waterman, a big bluff man with a passion for in-

vestment and a fascination with inventions '—always enamoured of the latest gadget. At any rate, I'd planned just a
quick stay at Blenhem Hill, but if the distress is as general as
Martin reported, I owe it to the tenants to give the place a
thorough inspection. And since my expertise is in finance
rather than agriculture, I wanted your recommendations on
how best to proceed.'

Ned was mulling over his answer when a knock sounded
at the door, followed by the entry of a graceful, golden-haired
lady. Warmth and brightness entered with her, Ned thought,
like sun on the fields after a spring rain.

'Ned, Nicky, I'm sorry to interrupt, but—'

His eyes lighting, Nicky jumped up and strode over to kiss
his wife's cheek. 'Seeing you is always a pleasure, sweeting.
Isn't it, Ned?'

'Always,' Ned affirmed, the glow her presence kindled in
his own heart tainted by an envy he could not quite subdue.
He'd been drawn to Sarah Wellingford the moment they'd
met. Had his good friend Nicky not already established a
claim on her, he'd have pursued her himself.

'Thank you, kind sirs,' she replied with a twinkle, making
them both an exaggerated curtsy. 'Nicky, Aubrey won't settle
for his nap until you kiss him goodnight. Ned, can you spare
him for a few moments?'

'Of course.' Turning to Nicky, Ned said, 'Go see your son.
I'll wait here, making inroads on your brandy and contemplating solutions.'

'The demands of fatherhood,' Nicky said with a sigh Ned
didn't believe for a moment, knowing Nicky adored his little
boy as much as he loved his wife. 'I'll be back shortly.' His
wife on his arm, Englemere walked out.

Ned watched them leave together, trying to suppress another swell of envy.

Barred from courting the one woman he'd ever cared for,

a countrywoman who might love and esteem a simple gentleman farmer like himself, would Ned ever find another lady Sarah's equal? Bitterness stirred in his gut. After his recent disillusionment over Amanda, he'd be much less likely to believe it if he ever again encountered one who appeared to be as worthy of his loyalty and affection as his friend's wife.

Unwillingly his mind caught on the image of the vivacious, charming Amanda. He thought he'd found the lady he'd been seeking when her father, Lord Bronning, a fellow agricultural enthusiast he'd met years ago at the annual meeting at Holkham, had invited him to visit his estate after last autumn's meeting. Ned had been immediately taken with the bright gold hair, mischievous blue eyes and sparkling wit of Bronning's country-born, country-bred daughter. Nor had she discouraged him, he recalled, his lip curling.

Oh, no, she'd immediately come forwards to monopolise his attention. Insisting to her papa that she be his guide on walks and drives around her father's property, she'd impressed him with her knowledge of the estate and entertained him with her needle-sharp commentary.

His scowl deepened. She'd also fired him to a simmering passion long denied, with the subtle brushes of her fingers against his body, her deliberate, stroking touches to his hands and arms and shoulders, her jutting bosom and moistened lips. Lonely after having lost the company of his two best friends, one happily wed to a girl Ned cherished and the other, Hal Waterman, occupied with his investments in the north, he'd let lust and neediness persuade him what he felt for Amanda was love. And offered for her hand.

Thank a kind Providence he'd first made a formal application to Lord Bronning! To his own chagrin and that gentleman's embarrassment, her father confessed apologetically that his Amanda, terrible flirt that she was, had vowed to him she would marry none but a wealthy gentleman of high title who, since she'd had enough of rural living, resided for as much of the year as possible in London. Pretty as his little scamp was, Lord Bronning added with fatherly pride, he had no doubt she would accomplish that goal when his sister introduced her in town next Season.

Grateful to at least have been spared the humiliation of having the lady refuse him to his face, Ned had swiftly hied himself home. And vowed in his turn that, being neither as rich as Hal nor as high-born as Nicky, he would be cautious indeed before ever again casting his bruised heart into the matrimonial ring.

Dismissing with irritation that painful episode, he forced his thoughts back to Nicky's problem. Though Ned wasn't accounted truly wealthy, his assets tied up as they were in land rather than coin, he did well enough, and managing land was a passion that had never disappointed him. From the first time he'd met like-minded individuals at Coke of Norfolk's Holkham Hall meeting, he'd devoted all his time and energy to implementing the ideas discussed there and persuading his tenants to adopt the latest and most efficient agricultural techniques.

But even advanced agricultural practices weren't always enough to stave off disaster in these hard times, he mused, frowning. The cost of the enclosures essential to modernise agriculture had fallen most heavily on those least able to bear them, the poor farmers who held little beyond their plots of ground in the old commons and wastes. With the drastic fall in the price of wheat and corn, even a well-managed small property could fall into difficulties. The fate of those on a poorly managed one could be grim indeed.

Nicky was right; it was the duty of the local landowner to help his tenants prosper and see that those forced to sell their small plots found employment at a reasonable wage. He was right about the difficulty of the endeavour, too. Rectifying the effects of a long period of mismanagement under current conditions would pose a difficult challenge even for one of Ned's experience and expertise.

By heaven, right now he could use a challenge, something to distract him from the lingering bitterness over Amanda and keep the loneliness at bay.

The idea flashed into mind just as Nicky walked back in.

'You'd had time to mull over the situation,' Nicky said, pouring himself another fingerful of brandy. 'What advice do you offer?'

'Sell Blenhem Hill,' Ned replied. 'It's too far away for you to oversee properly, forcing you to depend on an estate agent of uncertain expertise, and it's reputed to be in poor condition anyway.'

'Sell it?' Nicky echoed. 'Now? With land and crop prices falling like a duck full of shot, who would be fool enough to purchase a failing agricultural property in the restive Midlands?'

Ned smiled. 'I would.'

Chapter Two

If one means to try a new crop, best to start broadcasting the seed, Ned had always thought. Which was why he found himself ten days later jolting along in Nicky's crested travelling carriage down the rutted lane to Blenhem Hill.

Trusting the legal niceties of the sale to the expertise of their respective solicitors, Ned had proposed to Nicholas that he take over the management of the property immediately. His friend agreed, and, upon learning that Ned, who had already completed preparations for spring planting on his several holdings in Kent, meant to go to Blenhem directly from London, Englemere insisted he borrow his travelling carriage so as to make the journey in greater comfort.

Despite the daunting description of what probably awaited him at Blenhem Hill, with the coach now so near its destination, a rising excitement buoyed Ned's spirits. He might be hopeless at the capricious game of love, but one constant he knew to his bones—the feel of richly scented loam between his fingers, waiting for one of skill and patience to nourish it, tend it, woo from it a bounty of tasseled corn or waving wheat.

Land in good heart was honest, rewarding one's care with a harvest that varied only according to the vagaries of the weather. Soil did not look upon you sweetly one day, offering up a fine stand of wheat or beans or corn, and the next, turn to weeds and bramble. Even poor ground, thin and rocky or soggy with clay, could be improved through the use of well-tested techniques. Yes, a man knew where he stood with his land. It was never fickle like a woman's smile or changeable like a lady's whim.

He also relished the opportunity to work with the tenants, both at Blenhem and in the surrounding neighbourhood. Farmers, especially in lean times, were often loath to change practices that had been handed down for generations. Coaxing them to try different methods that Ned knew would yield healthier soil and better harvests, thereby increasing their income and security, would bring him a satisfaction far greater than a mere increase to the rent rolls and a chest full of coins in his estate office.

At that moment, the vehicle bounced into another pothole and came down hard, almost throwing him off his seat. Catching himself with a grimace, Ned reflected that perhaps travelling by horseback, as he'd initially intended, would have been more comfortable than the barouche after all, despite the soaking rain in which they'd set out from London.

He was about to signal the coachman to halt and call for his horse, being led behind the coach by his groom, when the explosion of a pistol discharged at close range blasted his ears.

Before the reverberations stopped ringing, Ned plastered himself against the squabs, seeking the thin protection of the coach wall as he peered out of the window. 'John! Harrison!' he called to the coachman and his valet, riding on the box beside the driver. 'Are you all right?'

Scanning the surrounding forest through the small coach window to try to determine from whence had come the shot, as he awaited a reply, Ned scrabbled for his own pistol, left negligently in a corner of the coach after their stop at the last inn. But who could have imagined they would encounter highwaymen here, on this isolated lane far from any town?

'Winged Mr Harrison,' the coachman called back.

Before Ned could enquire any further, a small party of masked men led by a rider on horseback emerged from the thick woods to the left.

'Nay, don't reach for yer blunderbuss,' their mounted leader cautioned John Coachman. 'If'n we'd wished to kill ye, ye'd be dead. Our quarrel's not with you, but with that fine gent cowering inside.'

Raising his pistol, the man fired, blasting a hole through the centre of the crested door. The ball whizzed past Ned's knees and buried itself into the opposite door panel. 'That's for the vote and General Ludd. Death to mill owners and tyrants!'

'Aye, hurrah for General Ludd and death to tyrants!' his companions cheered, waving their arms in the air.

Out of the corner of his eye, Ned saw one of the band raise his pistol and sight it. Not sure whether the man meant to target him or the unarmed servants sitting exposed on the box, Ned quickly levelled his own weapon and fired.

The gunman cried out and grabbed his shoulder, dropping his pistol, which discharged as it hit the ground, sending a stray ball whining into the cluster of men. While the leader's horse reared in panic, the group scattered.

Controlling his mount, the leader rode over to his injured follower, steadying him before he could fall. Looking back over his shoulder at Ned, he snarled, 'You'll pay for this!'

'Not if you swing for it first,' Ned retorted as the leader signalled another of the group to pull along the injured man, then trotted after his followers back into the thick greenery from which they'd emerged.

While the sounds of their passage through the woods receded, Ned tossed down his empty pistol and jumped out of the coach. 'Harrison, how badly are you hurt?'

He looked up to see the valet clutching his left wrist, grimacing as the coachman inspected it. 'Grazed only, Sir Edward,' he replied through gritted teeth.

'Lost a bit of blood, but the ball didn't penetrate the bone,' the coachman announced. 'Bless me, Sir Edward, I be powerful sorry! Caught me napping, me old musket too far away even to grab afore they halted us. What's the world coming to, when honest folk can't travel a country road without being set upon? 'Tis a blessing they left you yer purse without murdering us all!'

'They weren't after my purse,' Ned replied, leaning into the coach to retrieve a flask of brandy and hand it up to Harrison. 'Drink,' he instructed the valet, who had gone white about the lips and looked definitely unsteady. 'It will ease the burn and help settle your head.'

The groom, who'd succeeded in quieting Ned's frightened horse, ran up. 'Sure enough they would'a robbed us, Sir Edward, if'n you hadn't scared them off.'

Ned shook his head. 'There were five of them, by my count, and probably they had more weapons. They must know I would have handed over whatever they asked for to prevent further bloodshed. Besides, they were cheering for "General Ludd".'

'General Ludd?' Harrison repeated. 'You mean…they were Luddites? I thought all that nonsense ceased after the arrests and hangings in 1814.'

'There's been a revival of frame-breaking attacks since Waterloo. We're not so far from Nottingham, which has always been in the thick of it,' Ned replied, frowning.

'Thugs and vermin is what I call 'em,' the coachman pronounced. 'Should be hung or transported, the lot of 'em. As I expect they will be, once you report this to the nearest magistrate!'

'Whoever they were, I believe they've got safely away,' Ned said. 'Richard—' he turned to the groom '—help Har-

rison to that fallen log.' He gestured towards the wood's edge.
'You and John walk the horses while he recovers himself
before we must jostle him the rest of the way to Blenhem Hill.'

After a token protest that he was all right, the valet let himself
be assisted to the ground, where he walked on wobbly legs to
sit on the mossy tree trunk. Leaving the man sipping at the
brandy flask, Ned paced the road, pondering what to do next.

Though he'd heard of the unrest and Nicky had specifically
mentioned it, Ned had never truly expected to encounter any
difficulties. Indignation over the unprovoked attack and the
injury to his valet prompted him to proceed directly, as John
Coachman advised, to the local magistrate. But was that the
wisest course of action?

His agreement with Nicky was so recent that no one at
Blenhem Hill or the surrounding area knew he'd acquired the
property. He was neither expected, nor would anyone recognise him when he arrived. Indeed, even Nicky's former
manager didn't know about him, for he carried Nicky's note
of introduction to Mr Martin in his pocket.

During their discussions he had focused on the agricultural problems at Blenhem. With the shock of the attack to
prompt his memory, he now recalled that Nicky also owned
a controlling interest in one of the local cotton mills.

Had the Englemere crest been recognised when they
stopped at the inn in Kirkwell? It seemed rather a stretch of
coincidence to presume the attack on a carriage belonging to
the nobleman known to own both the cotton mill at Dutch-
field and the estate at Blenhem Hill, occurring on the seldom-
travelled road leading to that property, could be just the
random act of local hooligans. Especially given the slogans
being shouted by the perpetrators.

Last summer, a renewed series of Luddite uprisings had
swept through East Anglia. The mob had smashed frames in
a mill at Loughborough and though this time none of the pro-

prietors had been killed, Ned vividly recalled that two owners had been murdered in a previous wave of violence.

Even if the attack hadn't targeted Nicky personally, the fact that such a move had been made against a crested coach indicated that, at a minimum, a strong sense of disaffection prevailed in the area. If the people around Blenhem Hill were suffering and desperate, as Martin had indicated, the attackers might well be local men. Having Ned ride in demanding justice of the magistrate and threatening transportation to the perpetrators—perhaps sons and husbands, brothers and sweethearts of his own tenants—would hardly gain him the confidence and co-operation he needed to restore prosperity to Blenhem.

Or discover the true purpose behind the attack.

A course of action occurred to him, expeditious if unprecedented. Mr Martin and the staff at Blenhem Hill were not expecting Sir Edward Austin Greaves; however, they would be anticipating the arrival of a new estate agent.

Though an agent might be the younger son of gentry, as a working man rather than an owner there was less of a difference in station between him and the tenants on his estate. Such a man would be more likely to inspire trust and elicit candid opinions about Blenhem—and any agitation in the neighbourhood—than an unknown new owner of aristocratic birth. No matter how sympathetic or friendly a face Ned presented to them, simple 'Mr Greaves' would probably be able to learn a good deal more about these people and their circumstances than the more elevated 'Sir Edward'.

He would do it, he decided. An estate agent having little need for a valet, he'd send Harrison home to Kent to recover and John Coachman and the groom back to Nicky with a report of what had happened.

The decision made, an ironic amusement tempered his anger and frustration. This 'challenge' was turning out to be even more interesting than he'd anticipated.

* * *

An hour later, the carriage turned down the gravelled drive leading to the front door of Blenhem Hill. Or at least, what had once been a gravelled drive, now mostly given over to the weeds that flourished between the wagon tracks.

Mr Martin had not underestimated the dire condition of the property. Indeed, there was so much wrong that Ned hardly knew where to begin. With every neglected field and tumbledown dwelling they had passed, Ned's ire had increased.

No wonder the local citizenry were restive! If he were a tenant on one of those farms, he'd be ready to don a mask and shoot someone himself. Nicky shouldn't have simply fired his previous manager, Ned concluded, struggling to control his outrage, he should have had him flogged on the village green.

His angry gaze swept over the manor house as they approached, then checked in surprise. Unlike the vistas he'd just passed—bracken-filled fields and dilapidated cottages roofed in mouldering thatch, many of which seemed in imminent danger of collapsing altogether—this dwelling seemed to be in good repair.

The coach pulled up with a squeal of brakes and a jingle of harness. Ned hopped out—but no one emerged from the manor to greet the new arrivals. Not until he had raised his fisted hand to knock at the broad hickory-planked door did it swing open.

An older man he presumed to be the butler stood upon the threshold. After glancing at the carriage, its crest visible on the undamaged door nearest them, the man bowed. 'How may I help you, my lord?'

With a warning glance to his servants, who had only reluctantly agreed to the plan their employer had outlined to them before resuming their travels, Ned extended his hand. 'Myles, isn't it? Lord Englemere sent me. I'm Ned Greaves, the new estate manager.'

* * *

An hour later as he walked through the deepening dusk
from the manor to the stables to confer with Harrison and
John Coachman, Ned noted the first benefit that had derived
from his altered status. Sir Edward must have summoned
the men to the estate office, perhaps causing speculation and
risking the possibility that they might be overheard by
eavesdropping servants. Mr Greaves could simply go to
their quarters. There was a curious and rather liberating
freedom in ambling across the stableyard almost unnoticed,
he reflected.

Not a flicker of surprise had crossed Myles's face when
Ned had informed the butler he needed to consult with Lord
Englemere's grooms and coachman on the repair of his
vehicle, the damage to which and the wounding of Harrison
he'd fobbed off as an accident with the coachman's pistol that
had occurred on the road.

Of course, the butler's demeanour had been wooden since
his arrival. It was impossible to discern whether this senior
member of the household sympathised with or detested the
man who had previously held the position Ned had assumed,
whether he welcomed or resented the arrival of a replacement.

In the same polite but impersonal tone with which he'd
answered the door, Myles had asked Ned if he wished his
baggage to be stowed in the largest guest chamber, where the
previous agent had been installed. Upon Ned's assent, he
directed a footman to fetch Ned's things, informed him of the
hours when the household normally breakfasted and dined,
and bowed himself out.

Myles was a sapling he'd have to water carefully and dili-
gently cultivate if he was going to find out what he needed
about the previous direction of the estate, Ned mused.

He found John Coachman, Richard and Harrison in the loft
above the tack room where they'd been given accommoda-

tions for the night. The two horsemen were chatting while Harrison, an affronted expression on his face, picked a piece of straw from his coat with his good hand.

'How does the arm?' Ned asked, pitching his voice low.

'Richard fetched water so I've washed and dressed it,' John Coachman replied. 'Long as he don't take fever, he should heal quick.'

Ned gave his valet a sympathetic glance. 'I dare say you're not sure what is more painful, eh, Harrison? The wrist or being compelled to pose as a groom.'

'Are you sure you want to continue with this…scheme?' Harrison replied, pausing, Ned suspected, to swallow an adjective like 'caper-witted'.

'It do go against the grain, not reporting the attack,' the coachman added. 'An outrage, it is, good Christian folk being attacked in full daylight! Dastardly ruffians ought to be prosecuted.'

'What would you have me tell the magistrate?' Ned said. 'That our coach was accosted by five masked, armed men who shouted slogans, fired their weapons wildly, winging one of our party before fleeing into the woods? We couldn't even give a good description of the perpetrators.'

'Recognise the horse, if'n I seen it again,' Richard spoke up.

'Even if we identified the horse, we'd have no proof its owner was involved. It wouldn't be the first time a mount was "borrowed" from his pasture. No, I shall not report the incident. I'll let the attackers wonder *why* there was no report. Let them speculate that they intimidated us, or that the magistrate did not deem the incident of sufficient import to investigate. Such conclusions may make them bolder and more likely to do something for which I can lay charges.'

'Are you sure you want us to leave?' Richard asked. 'We could be three more pairs of eyes watching out, Sir—I mean, Mr Greaves,' he corrected at Ned's sharp look.

'No, 'tis better that you all go, lest one of you slip up and address me with proper honours. I shall discover much more quickly what is going on here if I can mingle among the farmers more or less unnoticed.'

As the three servants exchanged glances over that dubious notion, Ned added, 'Come now, who would not more easily confide something to a man near his own station? The sooner I uncover what has transpired here, the sooner other good Christian souls can travel the roads in safety.'

That being unanswerable, Harrison said, 'As you wish, sir, but if you do not leave here with your linen grey and your coats frayed, I shall be much surprised.'

Ned grinned. 'You think me too high in the instep to care for myself? I'll have you know I'm quite capable of tying my own cravats, shaving and dressing respectably. And if the laundry maid's skills are not adequate, I shall engage another one.'

Sobering, he continued, 'I appreciate your desire to be of assistance, all of you, but you can serve better elsewhere. Lord Englemere must have his coach returned—and repaired—and should be made aware of what has transpired. Harrison should rest and let that arm heal.'

John Coachman nodded. 'If'n that's the way you want the game played out, Sir—Mr Greaves—then I reckon we must do it your way.'

Ned nodded. 'Very good. I shall count on the loyalty and discretion of you all. Harrison, do you think you will feel up to travelling tomorrow? '

'Aye, sir. Reckon I'll go to my sister in Kent. She's been after me for a while to come visit. But how long do you expect to remain in this…interesting situation?'

'I cannot be sure. I'll send word when I wish to recall you. In the meantime, I've a letter for Lord Englemere. See that he gets it immediately upon your return, and all of you, please say nothing about what happened here to anyone else.'

The three men nodded. 'Best you watch your back, sir,' Harrison added.

'I shall,' Ned said soberly. 'On my guard as I am, I don't intend to be surprised by anything else that happens here.'

The following day, Ned went to meet Mr Martin, introducing himself as the replacement estate agent dispatched by Lord Englemere. Greeting him warmly, the old man immediately offered to give Ned a tour of the estate and introduce him to those of the tenants who'd not been driven off by the dwindling price of harvests and the steadily increasing rents.

Ned's initial good humour diminished with every mile they drove. Fully half the farms were abandoned, the former tenants having left to seek work at the mills in Manchester, Nottingham and Derby. It pained him more than finding gorse in a fine stand of wheat to see so much land lying fallow.

He was more shocked still when Martin led him to the 'mill' Nicky had supposedly set up. The empty, roofless two-storey stone building stood silhouetted against the sky in a small clearing near a well, lacking not only a roof, but also doors, window frames, stairs to reach the second floor—and knitting looms.

Worst of all, though, were the thin frames and gaunt faces of the tenants and the tales they related of the greed and abuse of authority practised by Barksdale, Greville Ander's supervisor.

Making a note of the names, needs and conditions of each tenant family, Ned thanked the workers for their candour and left with promises of seeds for planting, repairs to their dwellings and new and better farm tools. Though from most he received at least a nod of agreement, more telling than all the tales of mismanagement were the blank looks with which most received his promises, mute testaments of their disbelief and hopelessness.

Unlike at his own estates, where visiting a tenant usually ended with them sharing a mug of home-brewed, though none of Blenhem Hill's people were openly hostile, only one offered him any hospitality. Elderly Dame Cuthbert begged them to honour her by accepting a mug of cider.

The old woman, Martin told him as they followed her into her tiny cottage, had been raised on Blenhem land, married a Blenhem farmer, and had a grown son who'd recently abandoned the property to seek work in the city.

Though the exterior of the dwelling looked as dilapidated as the other Blenhem cottages, the dirt-floored interior was tidy, the rough wooden table clean and the hearth freshly swept. But Ned noted with a troubled glance the dampness on the back wall where the rotted thatch must have let the rain in. The old woman herself was far too thin and frail, her eyes large in her emaciated face, veins visible beneath the translucent skin of her parchment-wrinkled hands.

After pouring cider into two earthenware mugs, she offered them a bite of cheese to accompany the beverage. Having already realised with a shock that there appeared to be nothing but the one jug of cider and a single round of cheese in her small larder, Ned sent a sharp look to Martin, who politely refused.

Already angered, dismayed and distressed at the condition of Blenhem and its tenants, Ned left the cottage with an ache in his gut. 'How does she manage with her son gone?' he asked Martin abruptly as they climbed back into the gig.

'I help out some, and the Reverend sends her cheese and ale when he can,' Martin replied. 'Poor Dame Cuthbert was another reason I was so glad to see Lord Englemere had sent you! Barksdale threatened to evict her after her son left—cast her out of the only home she's ever known with no place to go. 'Twas what drove me to write that letter to his lordship and tell him how things stood here. Praise heaven, he sent Anders and his bully boy packing before Barksdale could make good on his threat.'

'No wonder she offers you half her victuals.'

Martin shrugged. 'Only tried to do what was right. Biddy Cuthbert's a kind soul—good to the bone, no matter what life hands her.'

After returning Martin to his cottage, Ned drove back to the manor, his head filled with facts and faces, his mind simmering with projects and potential remedies. While he planned and figured, his heart ached for the misery and hopelessness of the people he'd visited. He'd see the gaunt face of Dame Cuthbert in his dreams tonight, he thought, his soul still haunted by the image of the old woman on the brink of starvation, offering him the last of her cheese.

After the abject poverty he'd witnessed, as he strode into the manor house he was struck anew by the superior condition of that dwelling. The stone exterior and timbered roof had been recently cleaned and repaired. Within, polished floors shone, fresh paint covered the walls, window panes gleamed, and curtains and upholstery were fashioned from new, finely woven cloth. Though by no means grand, the furnishings of the morning room, dining room, salon and guest bedchamber were stylish and of the highest quality.

Greville Anders certainly had not suffered with the rest of the estate at the downturn in agricultural prices.

A recurring refrain in the tales he'd heard today was the cruelty, indifference and avarice of Anders's assistant, Barksdale. Ned had first thought that perhaps Nicky's cousin had left to his agent the distasteful wrangling over crop production and rents so Anders might play the magnanimous gentleman when he rode about the estate. However, it appeared that Anders had turned the day-to-day operations of the estate entirely over to his subordinate, for the tenants reported that they had seldom even seen Mr Anders.

Had Nicky's cousin been aware of the suffering of Blenhem's people? Or had he been content to take the money Barksdale extracted from them, neither knowing nor caring about their fate as long as his own home was in good repair, his own rooms elegantly furnished, his own belly well filled?

Ideas and emotions still churning in him, Ned consumed rapidly and in silence the meal Myles served him in solitary state in the dining room, burning with impatience to move on to the estate office so he might compare the estate books Nicky had given him with those kept at Blenhem.

As he cleared away the dinner service, Myles said, 'I expect, after riding about the estate today, you must be fatigued. Shall I bring brandy to the morning room or will you be retiring immediately?'

'Retiring?' Ned echoed. 'Indeed not! I shall probably sit up late. Please have an extra brace of candles sent to the study.'

By the time Ned arrived in that room shortly afterwards, the books he'd brought with him had been neatly aligned on the desk along with the additional candelabra and a flask of spirits.

Myles wasn't such a bad sort, despite his taciturn ways, Ned concluded as he took his seat.

Several hours of contemplation later, Ned paused to avail himself of the spirits, both angry and perplexed after his perusal of the records. Nicky's books, filled with figures that must have been copied by his London secretary from reports sent by Anders, were detailed, neat and orderly. But the Blenhem Hill ledgers not only did not match Nicky's entries, the numbers varied from nearly illegible to incoherent.

Many expenses were listed simply under general categories like 'manor house' and 'home farms', tallied in columns that were sometimes incorrectly added—or not totalled at all. The monthly summaries were penned in a different hand entirely.

Exasperated, when the butler entered to refresh his brandy flask, Ned said, 'I know this isn't your purview, but would you happen to know who made the entries in the estate books?

They appear to be in two different hands.' He pointed to the open ledger.

After studying the page, the butler said, 'The figures that are hard to read, here—' he touched the page '—were penned by Mr Anders. The smaller, neater ones here—' he indicated the summaries '—were written by Mr Barksdale.'

As Ned had deduced. Grimly satisfied to have this supposition confirmed by someone familiar with both men, he said, 'Mr Anders did not keep the books solely by himself, then? He allowed Barksdale access?'

'To them and everything else at Blenhem,' Myles replied acerbically.

'Damnable way to handle the property for which *he* was responsible,' Ned burst out, finally losing his grip on his temper after all the indignities he'd witnessed that day.

To Ned's surprise, Myles's impassive face creased into a slight smile. 'Indeed, sir. Overall Mr Anders weren't a bad sort. Gave himself airs, always reminding everyone he was Lord Englemere's cousin and puffing off about his service with Wellington. Though if he did as little in the army as he did here, 'tis a wonder he wasn't cashiered out! About the only time he exerted himself was when he ordered some doxy sent out from town. Otherwise, he left everything to Barksdale.'

Myles's smile evaporated. 'That one wasn't lazy a bit. Kept a hand in the business of everyone and everything. Had a mean streak in him, too.'

Ned struggled to keep his jaw from dropping. Myles had just opened up like fertile ground under a sharp plough, offering more words in that one speech than Ned had got out of him in the nearly two days he'd been at Blenhem.

Had Myles been subjecting him to some sort of scrutiny which he had successfully passed?

Hoping that was the case and the butler's candour meant

the beginning of a useful working partnership, Ned said, 'Thank you for the information, Myles. I shall very much appreciate hearing anything you, the staff, or the tenants can tell me about what has been happening here. I mean to make things right, I promise.'

Myles studied him silently for a moment. 'I believe you do, Mr Greaves. Let me say then how glad I am that Lord Englemere sent you.'

After refilling the flask, Myles withdrew and Ned went back to his work.

By midnight, his rage had revived. The best he could make out, the harvests on every farm had steadily decreased. Yet rents had been raised, sometimes sharply, at every renewal since Anders took over control of the property. The shoddy state of the accounting in the Blenhem books made it impossible to determine exactly what expenses and income had been. The account sent to Nicky in London must have been a pure fabrication.

In sum, the estate books at Blenhem were completely useless. He would have to begin with the last figures Martin had compiled, then ride the property and consult with each tenant about every detail relating to the farms' operations before he could make any useful estimates of income and expenses for the current year.

As for the mill, there were no figures whatsoever in any of the ledgers detailing what had happened to the funds Nicky had dispatched for the construction and equipping of that enterprise.

If he could have got his hands on Greville Anders and his henchman at that moment, Ned would have chained them to a plough and sent them out into the darkness to break ground on every bramble-infested field at Blenhem.

Slowly his anger fizzled into fatigue as he downed the last of the spirits. He was snuffing the candles in preparation to retire when he heard raised voices emanating from the front hall, followed by the sounds of scuffling.

He'd risen from his chair to investigate when, after a knock at the door, Myles stepped in, his countenance rigid with disapproval.

'There is a Young Person to see you, sir. I tried to turn her away, the hour being late and her coming unannounced, but she insists she must speak to you.'

To Ned's astonishment, the slim, slight figure of a girl pushed past Myles and tumbled into the room.

Chapter Three

The evening was already far advanced when Joanna Merrill climbed stiffly down from the farmer's cart in which she'd hired a ride after missing the stage-coach run to Hazelwick, the village closest to Blenhem Hill. She'd hoped to arrive there early enough to be able to send word to her brother to come and fetch her before dark, but once again, circumstances had conspired against her.

It had been a disaster of a fortnight. When she had left the Masters estate at Selbourne Abbey, she'd expected to spend no more than a few days on the road, a week at most. Her small stock of coins would stretch for coach fare and perhaps a few modest dinners, as long as she caught every stage on time and spent most of the day travelling.

Instead, during each segment of the journey some accident or disaster had brought her progress to a halt. From a horse pulling up lame on the first stage, to a broken axle on the next, to the wild driving of a drunken Corinthian who'd forced the mail coach off the road into a ditch, she'd ended up each time too late to make her connections and had been forced to spend extra nights on the road.

After splurging on accommodations the first few nights,

bespeaking a chamber had become impossible, but even for a dry place under the stable roof she'd been forced to part with a few more precious pence. Her stomach rumbling at the savoury smell of stew emanating from the Hart and Hare, Hazelwick's inn, while she doled out her last coin to the farmer who'd given her space in the back of his wagon, she tried not to recall how long it had been since she'd eaten.

Though he'd agreed with reluctance to convey her to Hazelwick, that taciturn gentleman had flatly refused to bring her to her final destination. She hoped to wheedle someone at the inn into performing that task, on promise of payment when she arrived at Blenhem Hill.

The prospects of convincing someone to do so had been fair when the trip could be completed in daylight. Now that darkness had fallen, her chances were fast diminishing.

Somehow, she must make it happen. With her purse emptied of its last coin, she could afford neither dinner nor accommodations for the night.

'Need lodgings, miss?' The innkeeper of the Hart and Hare walked over to greet her as she entered the taproom. 'The missus has a right fine stew on…' As his practised gaze took in her dusty, travel-stained apparel, single bandbox and solitary state, he stopped short and his welcoming smile faded.

No respectable gentlewoman travelled with so little luggage, unaccompanied by a maid or companion to lend her countenance. She felt her cheeks flush with chagrin at what he must be thinking of her character even as he said, 'The Hart and Hare be an honest house. I don't let rooms to the likes of—'

'I don't require a room,' she interrupted. 'I need transport to Blenhem Hill. I have business with the manager there.'

'I wager you do, missy,' the innkeeper replied, his tone scornful. 'Well, I expect if ye've coin to pay, Will in the stables might be able to take you, even with night fallen, for I'd as lief not have you standing about the place.'

Though she felt her flush deepen, she tried to infuse her voice with authority. 'I do not intend to pay in advance. Your man will reimbursed after I am safely conveyed to Blenhem Hill.'

The innkeeper shook his head impatiently. 'I'm not sending out the boy and my gig without I get payment first. 'Tis the way we've always done it, bad enough business that it is, and I ain't about to change the arrangement now.'

Joanna worked hard to keep desperation from leaking into her voice. 'You will be well paid, I assure you. Twice the usual rate.'

She had no idea what the innkeeper normally charged to transport items to Blenhem Hill and could only hope her brother wouldn't be furious with her for cavalierly doubling the price. But with her strength, her funds and her spirits exhausted, she absolutely must get to Blenhem Hill tonight.

'Double the rate! Must think pretty highly of yer charms,' the innkeeper said snidely. 'But the answer's still "no". If you've not got the ready, take yourself off before the wife comes in and gives you a jawing. Go on, off with you!'

The man approached, waving his arms in a shooing motion. Affronted by his insinuation that she was a woman of low repute bent on enticing her own brother, Joanna hesitated, torn between standing her ground to argue and the risk of having him drag her bodily out of his establishment.

'I'll see her out,' a feminine voice said.

Joanna jerked her attention from the advancing innkeeper towards a girl who tossed her apron down on the bar.

'Very well, Mary, but you step right back. There be *paying* customers to tend,' the innkeeper said, giving Joanna one last scornful glance.

The barmaid motioned her to the door. Her momentary courage failing, her tired brain unable to reason out what she must do next, Joanna gave in and followed.

'Not a bad man, but none too bright,' the girl said as they

stepped into the evening chill. 'Otherwise he would have seen in a blink you're no doxy. Have business out at Blenhem Hill, do you?'

Heartened by the first kindness she'd encountered in her long travels, Joanna said, 'Yes. And I very much need to find transport there tonight.'

'Can't help you with that, but I can tell you how to get there. See the road that forks by the forge? Follow that straight on and it'll take you to Blenhem Hill. Not above five miles or so, and there'll be some moon tonight.'

Five miles. Tired as she was, it might as well be five hundred. But it appeared that if she meant to get to Blenhem Hill tonight, her feet would have to take her there.

'Thank you, Mary,' Joanna replied. 'When I come to town next, I'll bring you a coin for your kindness.'

The girl shrugged. 'Hard for a woman travelling alone to keep trouble from finding her. Stay to the road and you can't miss it, but have a care. If you hear anyone approaching by horseback or cart, you duck into the woods right quick until they go by. Best of luck to you.'

Five miles. She could keep her feet moving for five more miles. Taking a deep breath, Joanna grasped her bandbox and set off.

With the fall of night, the wind picked up, chilling her despite her travelling cloak. So desperately tired she could scarcely think, she plodded along, keeping her eye on the road ahead and concentrating only on placing one numbed foot after the other.

Once, she stumbled into an unseen pothole and fell, losing her grip on the bandbox, which rolled away from her over the side of the road. Almost she was tempted to lay her head down into the mud and give up.

Papa toiled away in the fetid heat of India, she tried to rally herself, ministering to the army and the members of John

Company, far from home and all things familiar. Her brother had followed Wellington through the dirt and misery of Waterloo. Her own dear Thomas had braved the baking summers and monsoons of India, proudly serving his nation. All she need do was walk a few more miles along an English lane. Mustering all the will she possessed, she forced herself to stagger upright and collected her bandbox.

She fixed her mind on the image of Greville receiving her warmly, distracting herself from her present misery by painting mental pictures in her head of the estate he managed for Lord Englemere. There'd be a neat sturdy manor house, fields ploughed and newly planted in corn, tenant cottages with thick roofs of fragrant thatch.

Maybe he'd have a wife to welcome her, children, even. She imagined dawdling a chubby toddler on her knee, filling the emptiness in her soul by nurturing a girl like little Susan, instructing her in her letters and numbers and the sewing of samplers. Perhaps, after she had rested and recovered, Greville or his wife would know of a genteel family who might have another position for her.

She must find something else. She'd no more be a burden upon her brother than she would consider contacting her late husband's family for assistance. Thomas's father had made it quite clear upon their last painful meeting that the Merrill family wanted nothing further to do with the woman who, he insinuated, had used some potion of the east to bewitch a young man far from home into a most unsuitable match.

Her heart twisted again, remembering the coldness on Lord Merrill's face, more hurtful still since she could see her dear Thomas's features echoed in his sire's countenance. The snug bungalow she'd shared in India with Papa, where she and Thomas had met and fallen in love, had been her last real home. Not since she'd lost their unborn child and Thomas insisted she leave him and the malevolent fevers of India for the healthier clime of England had she felt there was a place she truly belonged.

Ironic that she'd swiftly recovered after the miscarriage, while it was Thomas who had succumbed to a fever. Alone in her London lodgings, she'd patiently awaited his return. He'd been dead for weeks by the time the news reached her.

A surge of grief swept through her, bringing her dangerously close once again to despair.

With Lord Walters having at the last moment cavalierly awarded the living on his estate, promised to Papa when the current incumbent retired, to some distant connection, the joyous reunion she'd looked forward to when Papa and the rest of her family returned from India had never happened. Anticipating their reunion had been her sole comfort as she'd struggled to cope with the enormity of Thomas's death. The loss of that consolation was yet one more charge she could lay at the feet of a venal, uncaring aristocracy, she thought resentfully.

And as if her spirits were not already low enough, the moon dipped behind a bank of clouds and it began to rain.

She wouldn't think any more of sad things, she told herself, straining through the gloom to follow the dim road and keep her feet moving while rain dripped off the brim of her bonnet and soaked through her cloak.

She'd think of Greville, his genial smile, his easygoing temperament. He'd always been a charmer, if a bit slow to bestir himself. But having served with Wellington, a notorious taskmaster, would surely have cured him of his lazy ways. The army would be the making of him, Papa always said.

A sudden flow of icy water dripped from an overhanging tree down her neck, shocking her back to the present. It seemed she'd been walking for hours, days, her whole existence. Her feet and fingers beyond numb, she forced herself onwards through sheer will-power, knowing if she missed one step she might lose her balance and fall. This time, she'd not be able to rise again.

She'd begun to fear that this would indeed be her fate when finally, in the distance, she perceived a faint glimmer of light.

Blenhem Hill! She must be approaching Greville's manor at last.

Now that the moment of reunion had almost arrived, her heart jolted with a gladness tempered by anxiety.

What if Greville were not happy that she'd sought him out uninvited? Certainly she must look a sight, her sopping skirts muddy, her cloak and bonnet soaked through.

Still, regardless of what her brother thought about her un-solicited midnight arrival, surely he would take her in? With a shiver, she made her clumsy-cold feet pick up the pace until, a few moments later, she stood before the front door and knocked, wincing at the pain to her frozen knuckles.

She waited, but when no response was forthcoming, she knocked again. It was late enough that she might have believed everyone within already abed, but for the light still glowing through one of the windows. She'd almost decided to try rapping on that when at last the door swung open.

A man in butler's attire gazed out at her, the mismatched buttons on his waistcoat suggesting that he had indeed been abed and only hastily re-donned his clothing.

'Good evening, sir,' she said. 'I know it is late, but I should like to see your master, please.'

For a silent moment the man looked her up and down. Then, without a word, he moved to close the door on her.

'Just a minute!' she cried. 'I demand to see the manager!'

'The manager?' he said finally. 'And who would that be?'

Did he think she'd wandered aimlessly across the country-side with no definite destination? 'Mr Greville Anders, of course,' she snapped back. 'Please tell him that Mrs Merrill has arrived and wishes to see him at once. He will receive me, I assure you.'

'It be Mr Anders you're wanting?'

'Yes,' she replied impatiently. 'And I warn you, he will be most displeased when I tell him you forced his only sister to stand forever in the doorway before admitting her.'

'His *sister*, are you?' the man asked with a sly look. 'When did he send for you?'

Though her brain was muddled with cold and fatigue, she thought it was probably best not to admit that she hadn't been sent for. 'That's not your concern,' she replied. 'All I require is that you convey me to him at once.'

'Must have miscalculated the date,' she heard him mutter before he said in a louder voice, 'Nothing here for you, miss. Best go back where you come from.'

'Go b-back?' she repeated, her voice breaking as alarm jolted through her. Desperately summoning up her best governess tone, she said firmly, 'At this hour of the night? You must be mad! Why are you keeping me here on the threshold, nattering on in this stupid manner? Just inform Mr Anders I have arrived.' Ducking around him, she darted into the hall.

And stopped on a sigh. Ah, how heavenly it was to get out of the wind and cold!

The butler-person, mouth pursed in disapproval, stomped after her. 'Haven't ever laid hands on a woman and don't expect to start, so I suppose, being a good Christian, I'll let you dry off and sleep in the kitchen. But you must be gone first thing in the morning.'

Anger filtering into her desperation, Joanna crossed her arms. 'Have you heard nothing that I've said, my good man? I am not going anywhere until I've seen the manager. If you force me out, I will simply come back.'

For a moment they stared at each other, nearly nose to nose. Finally the butler nodded. 'Very well, I'll fetch you to the manager. Follow me.'

Eagerness and trepidation stirred in her again as he led her on. He halted, she realised, before the door that opened into the room whose lights she'd glimpsed from the road, the lights that had led her to the manor.

Greville's room! Illumined as if he'd meant to send a beacon of hope and welcome out to her in the darkness.

As the butler opened the door, warmth and the faint scent of wine wafted out. Her stomach growling at the hint of sustenance, her numb fingers and toes luxuriating at the caress of heated air, she scarcely heard the butler announcing her.

At last, she would see Greville and all would be well again. Pushing past the butler, she stumbled over the threshold, her chilled body drawing her like a moth to the flames dancing on the hearth. After the misery of the rain and chill, the temperature of the room made her feel light-headed and giddy, almost as if she might swoon.

Only then did she look up into the face of the tall man who'd risen from his chair behind the desk.

A man who was frowning at her.

A man who was not Greville.

'Wh-who are you?' she gasped.

'Who did you expect?' he asked, his faintly hostile gaze running with insulting familiarity over her figure.

'G-Greville,' she stuttered again. 'Greville Anders. This is Blenhem Hill manor, is it not? He—he manages that estate for Lord Englemere.'

'Not any longer,' the tall man said curtly. 'Lord Englemere discharged Mr Anders. Almost a month ago.'

For a moment she blinked stupidly at him. 'Greville…isn't here?'

'No.' His implacable gaze held her motionless, mesmerising her like a python regarding its prey.

Greville. Discharged. Not here. In her dazed and exhausted mind, syllables detached themselves from words and meaning, echoing down into her empty belly, up into her dizzy head. Images swirled before her eyes: the rain-swept road, her stiff cold fingers, her empty purse.

She felt as if she were swaying in a high wind. The disapproval on the face of the tall man by the hearth was the last thing she saw before the images dissolved and she slipped into blackness.

Chapter Four

Constellation tempering his irritation, Ned hastened to catch the girl before her head hit the wooden floor. As he gathered her up, glancing about him to determine where to deposit his soggy burden, he realised his first impression had been wrong.

Before she fainted, he'd noted little more than large dark eyes, a determined little chin and the fact that she was dripping all over the carpet. But though her body was short and slender, this was no girl he held in his arms, but a woman. The firm soft mound of her breasts pressed into him as he cradled her inert form, while a lingering hint of some exotic perfume mingled with the scent of rain and sodden wool.

His sleepy body roused abruptly to full attention.

Muttering a curse at that distraction, Ned turned to Myles, who was motioning him to lay the senseless girl—nay, woman—on the couch. 'Who the devil is she?'

'Said she was Mr Anders's sister,' Myles said, pouring a glass of brandy while Ned seated himself beside her, rubbing her hands to try to revive her. 'At first I thought she be another of Anders's women, but none of 'em ever arrived this late and soaked through.'

Abandoning his thus-far ineffectual efforts chaffing her

hands, Ned delivered a smart slap to her cheek. Her slack body tensed and she gasped, her eyes flying open.

She gazed up at him, her dazed look barely focused, seeming completely unaware of where she was and with whom. Just as Ned noticed the chill emanating from her and realised how icy were the hands he'd tried to chafe, she began to shiver, violent tremors that set her teeth chattering.

'She must be frozen through,' he muttered. 'Myles, hand me that glass, please,' he asked, nodding towards the brandy before looking back at the woman still reclining in his arms. 'Miss…Mrs—' Ned looked to the butler.

'Mrs Merrill,' Myles supplied.

'Do not be alarmed, Mrs Merrill,' Ned said. 'You are at Blenhem Hill. I'm Mr Greaves, Lord Englemere's estate agent. Here, have a sip of this brandy to warm you.'

He coaxed her lips—plump, in a pretty bow of a mouth, he noticed unwillingly—open and poured some brandy in. After choking a bit, she swallowed, her fingers coming up beside his to steady the glass. The tremors eased, then stopped.

He inspected her as she sipped, her hand absurdly small and delicate beside his. That pointed chin was set in a heart-shaped face with a pert nose and large dark eyes of a hue impossible to determine in the shadowy firelight. A soggy bonnet masked her hair, but her travelling cloak had fallen open when he'd set her down, revealing a graceful arc of neck and shoulders above full, rounded breasts. Chilled she certainly was, for even through her gown, he could see the peaked nipples.

His mouth watered to taste them.

He stifled a groan as his body hardened further. A fine cosy armful, if she was indeed Anders's fancy woman. All sweetness and curves with a subtly intriguing scent, fresh as a new-mown hay meadow, that tickled his nose over the aromas of mud and damp.

Ned could think of a number of ways to warm her more effectively and much more pleasurably than brandy. Unleashed like hounds eager for the hunt, his thoughts tumbled over themselves, conjuring up images of firm white thighs straddling his, those small hands stroking and teasing as she coaxed him within, bare slender legs locked around his waist as she rocked him hilt-deep.

Heat flooded him and sweat broke out on his brow. Damn, he should have lingered in London long enough to visit Mrs McAllen's Emporium. It had been way too long since he'd bedded a woman.

With a ferocious will, he jerked his lascivious thoughts to a halt and leashed them. She might be a doxy, but 'twas just as likely she was Anders's sister. Which meant she was Nicky's cousin, however distant. Regardless of what her brother had done, Nicky would expect Ned to treat any connection of his like a lady.

At that moment she pushed the glass away.

'You told Myles you were looking for Mr Anders—your brother?' Ned said.

She nodded, her eyes finally turning alert.

'How did you happen to arrive here alone in the middle of the night? Soaked as you are, you must have driven in an open gig. Is there a driver waiting? Can I have Myles fetch your things?'

Opening her lips, she hesitated, looking stricken. 'I…I don't have a gig,' she said after a moment. 'There's no driver. I…walked.'

'You walked from *Hazelwick*?' Ned asked incredulously. 'Alone, in the dark?'

Ignoring that query, she placed a hand on his arm. 'Did…did I hear you aright? Greville…isn't here?'

Whoever she was, she must have been desperate to come so far on foot, at night and through the rain. Despite his loathing for what Anders had done, Ned couldn't help feeling a certain sympathy for her. 'No. I'm sorry, ma'am.'

She swallowed hard. 'Do you know his direction?'

Ned looked over at Myles, who shook his head. 'No, ma'am.'

Two fat tears welled up in her eyes before she clapped her hands over them. 'Merciful Lord,' she whispered brokenly into her fingers, 'what am I to do?'

For a moment he watched as she struggled for control. Admiration stirred in his chest as, with a ragged breath, she mastered her emotions and swallowed the tears.

'Nothing tonight,' Ned said, infinitely grateful for her courage. He'd rather battle a plague of rabbits in the kitchen garden than deal with a woman in the midst of a weeping jag. 'Myles, rouse Mrs Winston and see if she can turn up some dry clothes for Mrs Merrill.' Looking back to the woman, he said, 'Did you have dinner before you…left Hazelwick?'

'I…no.' she admitted.

No wonder she looked fragile enough to shatter, walking all that way on no sustenance. Studying her suddenly downturned face, Ned would bet that wasn't the first meal she'd missed on her travels. 'See if Mrs Winston can heat up some of the stew from dinner,' he told Myles.

She looked up at him then, eyes huge in her drawn face, her lips pressed firmly together.

Lush, plump lips he'd like to kiss, he realised irritably as she cleared her throat.

'You've been very kind. I don't know how I can thank you—'

Ned lifted a hand, silencing her while he absolutely forbade himself to think of the many and delectable ways she might show her appreciation. 'We'll speak of it in the morning, after you're warm, dry and rested. Ah, here is Mrs Winston.' He looked over at the housekeeper. 'We've an unexpected visitor, as you see.'

'Aye, sir,' the housekeeper said, giving Mrs Merrill a hard scrutiny before, reluctantly, she curtsied.

Mrs Merrill sat up abruptly and swung her feet back to the floor. Ned felt the loss of her curves against his body with an inward sigh of regret as she rose to return the housekeeper's curtsy.

Ned stood up as well. 'Mrs Winston will fit you out with some dry things and see that you're nourished before you retire. I shall see you at breakfast. Goodnight, Mrs Merrill.'

She offered him a nod from that pointed little chin, then dropped a curtsy graceful enough to please a patroness at Almack's. If she was a fancy woman, she'd been well trained.

'Goodnight, Mr Greaves. Mrs Winston, I'm indebted for your kindness.'

Thoughtfully he watched her follow the housekeeper—who must be thinking who knows what to be charged with caring for a half-drowned woman arriving unannounced in the middle of the night. What catastrophe had befallen her that she'd come here alone, on foot, probably penniless? he wondered.

As Anders's sister, she'd been a lady born, if not a highly ranked one. No gentlewoman of good reputation would travel as she had.

Maybe she *was* Anders's doxy, his lustful imagination suggested hopefully.

Perhaps, he returned, though she had that indefinable look of quality about her bearing and carriage.

Since, as he'd told her, there was nothing more to be done tonight, he might as well go to bed. Absently he walked around the room, snuffing out the remaining candles.

Somehow, knowing the delectable Mrs Merrill dozed somewhere under his roof, he didn't think he was going to get much sleep.

* * *

After tossing restlessly, Ned rose the next morning with a feeling of expectation swelling his chest. Considering the mountain of work awaiting him on the dilapidated farms at Blenhem, as he surfaced to consciousness he was wondering why such a sense of excitement exhilarated him when he remembered—Mrs Merrill. This morning he would hear her story and sort out what was to be done with her.

After dressing with care—for he ought to garb himself as a gentleman when there was a lady present—he inspected himself in the glass. Even Harrison couldn't find fault with his appearance this morning.

Ah, Ned Greaves, what a handsome bloke you are, he thought with a chuckle. Not rich like Hal nor sporting as fancy as title as Nicky, but a fine figure of a man. Maybe fine enough to entice his unexpected guest into his bed if she should prove to be less than a lady.

He hastened to the small salon where Myles brought his breakfast. He'd just taken his first sip of coffee when the door opened and, in a soft rustle of skirts, Mrs Merrill walked in.

He rose, intending to greet her, and the words died on his tongue.

Those great dark eyes under expressive arched brows were green, he realised—the deep green of the velvety moss beside a woodland brook that invited one to sit and listen to its throaty chatter. And her hair! Hidden last night by the bonnet, haloed now by the morning sun, it was an intricate arrangement of auburn braids that glowed bright as a copper penny.

Though the soft green morning gown had a modest neckline, the scrap of ribbon under the high waist nonetheless managed to emphasise her breasts. For a petite lady, the top of whose head would scarcely touch his chin, they were deliciously full.

His hands curled into fists, itching with the desire to cup them.

One by one he catalogued her other charms: graceful curve of neck and shoulders, slender arms, narrow wrists, those delicate small hands.

Warm, dry and dressed, he found her even more alluring than he had by firelight.

'Good morning, Mr Greaves,' she said at last, startling him into realising he'd been evaluating her as blatantly as if she were Haymarket ware in a theatre box.

Maybe she is, a little voice murmured in his ear.

Well, probably she isn't, he growled back. 'To you, too, Mrs Merrill,' he replied. 'Please help yourself to the dishes on the sideboard. Should you like coffee?'

'Yes, thank you.'

Ned nodded at Myles to pour and waited for her to fill a plate. She sat, taking small delicate bites as if she were savouring each mouthful…while he savoured the play of those tempting lips against her teeth and tongue. Ah, the wickedness he could imagine inciting them to!

Thanks to years of ingrained breeding, he needed but a tiny portion of his brain to carry on a polite conversation. However, her open, apparently honest answers to his slightly disjointed questions about her home, her growing up with her brother, her sojourn in India—that must be the origin of the exotic spicy scent that clung to her—and subsequent marriage slowly began to curb the ravening lust in his brain with the unhappy conviction that she most probably was exactly what she represented herself to be: Greville Anders's sister, thus Nicky's cousin, thus beyond the touch of his lecherous imagination.

That still did not explain how she'd ended up dripping on his doorstep at midnight.

Regardless, he'd better stop contemplating naked assignations in the moonlight and start thinking of and reacting to her as a lady, he concluded, squelching a niggle of disappointment.

He waited until they had both finished their meal, asked Myles to pour them each another cup and dismissed him. Now to discover what she'd been about.

'So, Mrs Merrill, how did you come to arrive at Blenhem Hill last night?'

She gave him a pained smile, a slight flush colouring her fair skin. 'Humiliating as the details are, after your hospitality to a total stranger, I suppose I owe you the truth.'

'As you wish.'

She looked away, a troubled expression on her face. He sat silent, reining in his impatient curiosity and waiting for her to continue.

'My husband was a soldier, as I already told you,' she began at last. 'About a year after our marriage in India I—fell ill. Fearing for my health, he insisted that I return to England. Later I learned that he himself had succumbed to a fever. As…as his family never reconciled themselves to our marriage and I had not the funds to voyage back to India and my father, I was pleased to accept a position as a governess. My employers, Lord and Lady Masters, spend most of the year in London or visiting the country estates of their friends, while their daughters reside at Selbourne Abbey in Hampshire.'

Hampshire—gently rolling hills, corn, cattle and sheep, he thought. 'A lovely county,' he interjected.

She looked up. 'It is indeed. I was very happy there. Until…until my employers returned.'

Her flush deepened. 'There's no genteel way to express it. Lord Masters pursues every female within reach, whether they encourage his interest or not. I most certainly did *not* encourage him, but he…he kept after me anyway. Despite my continual vigilance, he managed to corner me in my chamber, where Lady Masters discovered us in a…compromising position. She expelled me from the house that very night.'

Twisting her hands together, her face averted, she continued in a low voice, 'With little money and no references, I could think of nothing else to do but come here to Greville. Encountering delays at every turn, by the time I reached Blenhem Hill my resources were exhausted. So…I walked from Hazelwick. And now you know the whole.'

Her cheeks still rosy, she lowered her eyes and studied her hands, as if she couldn't bear to look at him and perhaps see censure in his eyes.

If it was a performance, it was masterful. She appeared every inch a wronged and virtuous lady. Except…except for those plump, bite-me lips and those lush, fondle-me breasts.

Even if her story were true, Ned felt a stir of sympathy for Lord Masters. Here was a tasty morsel to dangle in front of a rake.

Only a bit, however, for he considered a man who preyed upon women, particularly a woman dependent upon him, to be beneath contempt.

Had Lord Masters preyed upon Mrs Merrill? Or was this gentlewoman with the body of a temptress a temptress indeed? Either way, what was he to do about her?

If she had been dismissed for wantonness, he could understand her deciding to throw herself on her brother's mercy until some more promising pigeon came along. Her shock at discovering Anders was no longer at Blenhem was genuine enough that Ned felt certain her sudden appearance had not been part of some devious scheme devised by the two of them.

If she were in fact Greville Anders's sister, and it appeared she was, then she was also cousin to Lord Englemere. Though she appeared despairing of her future, Ned knew that Nicky would never turn away a connection of his—and warm-hearted Sarah would probably delight in helping her settle somewhere.

But he couldn't in good conscience send on to them a woman who might be a doxy.

How could he tell for sure?

At the moment, she was entirely dependent on *him*. Suddenly a means to test her veracity occurred to him—a scheme that revived his lustful thoughts with a guilty zing of excitement.

With her brother beyond reach and only Ned at hand, if her morals were less than they should be, she would probably, with only a token protest, be amenable to accepting an arrangement that would be profitable for her and pleasurable for them both.

Not that he really intended to make her his mistress, but if he made advances that she accepted, he would know not to burden Nicky with responsibility for her welfare.

In such a case, a plump purse with coach fare to London and enough to live on until she found herself a new protector would be sufficient to fulfil whatever obligations Nicky might owe her.

She still sat, silent and head bowed, as if in deep contemplation. As he gazed at her loveliness, his body protested against the decision not to avail himself of her charms, should she respond to his lures.

Impatiently he dismissed that weakness. Upon occasion he'd taken his ease with ladies of the profession, but he'd never set up a mistress, being neither venal enough to corrupt an innocent, rich enough to tempt the discriminating palate of a courtesan or willing to settle for a woman of broad experience. Though he didn't insist on planting his seed in virgin soil, neither did he wish to farm for any length of time what had previously been common ground.

Indeed, he'd always hoped—although as yet that desire had not come to fruition—that eventually he might permanently sate all his carnal desires in a wife's embrace. Though after his most recent foray into the briar-filled field of courtship, he intended to stick to husbandry of the agricultural sort for the foreseeable future!

Even so, he had to shut his ears to the wheedling argument that said if she were of easy virtue, there was no harm in taking her for a quick tumble before he sent her on her way.

Since Mrs Merrill was obviously still lost in thought about her future, he might as well make a move immediately and determine it for them both. Another guilty little thrill zipped through him, settling into a hardness in his loins.

But how did one lead a lady astray? He'd never in his life played the rake and wasn't sure he could pull off the role. Though fortunately for his purpose, he had no need to feign his desire for her.

When he did advance, would she offer him her lips—or slap his face?

Chapter Five

$\sim\!\!\sim\!\!\sim\!\!\sim$

If she studied her hands long enough, perhaps this whole nightmare would go away. Too exhausted last night to do more than gobble down some soup and fall into the bed to which the distinctly disapproving housekeeper had led her, Joanna had awakened rested and buoyed by a sense of optimism that somehow, things would work out for the best.

Having just related to Mr Greaves the whole tawdry tale of how she'd come to appear on his doorstep, however, brought back to mind just how deplorable her situation was.

Did he even believe her? Arriving as she had, she could hardly blame him if, like the innkeeper in Hazelwick, he thought her a woman of loose morals, her protestations of innocence in the matter of Lord Masters entirely false.

Still, though he'd been understandably annoyed when she stormed into his room last night, dripping mud all over his Turkey carpet, he'd nonetheless treated her as if she were in fact Greville's sister, entitled to the respect due a gentlewoman.

Except…she *had* caught him inspecting her, a gleam of appreciation in his eyes. Oddly enough, despite her recent experience, knowing he found her attractive had not made her uncomfortable or uneasy. Unlike Lord Master's slack-jawed ogling, Mr Greaves's heated yet respectful scrutiny had sent a little tingle of anticipation through her, reminding her as it had of the desire she'd read in Thomas's expression while they'd been courting.

Mr Greaves was worthy of appreciative glances himself. She'd been too distressed last night to fully notice, but this morning at breakfast she'd been immediately struck by what a tall, broad-shouldered figure of a man he was. Though emanating an aura of power and authority—useful qualities in an estate agent, she presumed—he didn't seem overbearing or arrogant. His manners were impeccable; he'd waited until she'd taken her seat, her plate filled, before beginning on his own meal, watching to make sure her coffee cup was kept full.

Even Papa had not been that solicitous.

A little smile played at her lips. He was certainly handsomer than Papa! Thick, wavy dark hair, one lock of which insisted on curling over his brow no matter how many times he raked it back with his fingers. Honey-brown eyes that watched her intently as he listened. A noble nose and those finely chiseled lips…

She had a sudden vision of that mouth slanted over hers and a heated bolt of sensation sizzled through her.

Goodness! she thought, shocked and suddenly overwarm. She'd not experienced such a powerful physical response since leaving Thomas in India. Were Mr Greaves privy to her thoughts just now, he'd believe her wanton for sure.

Clutching her fingers more tightly together, she put her mind back to trying to decide what to do next. Oh, that she might throw herself on Mr Greaves's mercy, lay her problem at his feet and appeal for his help in coming up with a solution to her dilemma!

But, of course, that was impossible. He was merely a kind but chance-met stranger who happened to be inhabiting the house Greville had vacated.

Why had Greville been summarily discharged? she wondered suddenly. The manor house, she'd noticed since rising this morning, was beautifully managed, the servants skilled and respectful, the house itself gleaming with polish and paint, furniture and curtains well made and of fine quality. By Mr Greaves's own account, he was but recently come to Blenhem Hill, so its excellent condition must be attributed to Greville's management.

Was Lord Englemere capricious, carelessly discharging her brother on a whim, as thoughtless of the well-being of those beneath him as Lord Masters? It certainly appeared that Greville had been turned off in almost as much unseemly haste as she had been harried out of Selbourne Abbey.

Maybe those upstart colonials in the New World had been right to throw off rule by privilege.

But the character of Lord Englemere wasn't her most immediate concern. Damping down her indignation on her own and her brother's behalf, Joanna had turned her mind once again to unearthing a solution to her present dilemma when she glanced up to see Mr Greaves quietly watching her.

Heavens, what an ill-bred savage he must think her! Feeling the flush rise on her face, she said hastily, 'Excuse me, sir! How impolite of me to sit here wool-gathering. But you mustn't think I mean to burden you with my problems. Thanks to your kind hospitality, I'm well nourished and rested, and as soon as the remainder of my garments are dry enough to pack, I shall be on my way.'

'Where do you mean to go?' And how? the slight rise of his eyebrows said. Since she'd been honest about her current circumstances, he must know she had no money.

'To London, I suppose. 'Tis the easiest route by post and, once there, I may be able to discover Greville's whereabouts from Papa's solicitor.' Which would be an excellent plan, if she but possessed the funds to travel there and maintain herself once she arrived.

He nodded. 'Why not join me in the estate office? Perhaps in the account books your brother may have left some hint of where he meant to go when he left Blenhem.'

Her spirits leapt at that ray of hope. 'I hadn't considered that! If you would not mind, I should be very grateful for the opportunity to look through them.'

They rose and he led her to the estate office, pulled a chair up to his desk, and set the ledgers before her.

But as she flipped through page after page of Greville's nearly illegible scrawl, her sparkle of excitement dimmed. Hanging on to her last hope, she kept at it, inspecting every entry, but when she arrived at the last page of the last book, she knew no more about her brother's probable whereabouts than she had when they'd entered the room.

She struggled to keep despair from swamping her. Forcing a smile, she said, 'Well, it was worth trying. Thank you for allowing me to make the attempt. I suppose I should get to that packing now.'

On numb feet, she rose to drag the chair back, trying to keep her fingers from shaking. Preoccupied with combating the fear and dismay clawing its way into her gut, she only dimly heard Mr Greaves offer his assistance before he took the chair's heavier side and walked with her to set it in position by the window.

What am I to do now? she asked herself over and over, her mind running back and forth like a mouse cornered by a cat…life being the cat that was about to devour this mouse, she thought, swallowing an hysterical giggle.

She could apply for work at the posting inn, though the chances that they would take her on weren't good. Possessing only the skills of a gentlewoman or a governess, where could she find employment?

Was she doomed to suffer the fate to which Lady Masters had consigned her after all?

Suddenly she realised that, though they'd set the chair down, Mr Greaves remained beside her…very close beside her. As he was nearly a head taller, she had to angle her face up to give him a questioning look—and encountered a heated gaze that scorched her to her stays.

'You don't really need to leave,' he said softly, his intent gaze never leaving her eyes. 'You've no money for coach fare—and no way to earn any in the village. Why not stay here, write to your father's solicitor and request him to advance you funds on your father's account? Or, if you prefer, we might come to…another arrangement.'

Though half an hour previously she had burned at the thought of kissing him, as he towered over her now, desire in his eyes, she felt only a blind panic.

He did believe her a doxy! She raised her hands as if to ward him off—though she knew despairingly that if he was bent on taking her, he could do so, for she'd never be able to fight him off and there was no one here to rescue her.

'P-please, Mr Greaves,' she stuttered, hot tears of shame dripping down her cheeks. 'I'm n-not what you think.'

She must have closed her eyes, bracing herself, but suddenly instead of the warmth of him pressed against her, she felt a chill. She snapped her eyes open, astounded to discover that he'd re-treated several steps away her. A flush on his handsome face, he was drawing a handkerchief out of his waistcoat.

Handing it to her, he said, 'Pray forgive me, Mrs Merrill! I know my behaviour was unconscionable, but I needed to de-termine if your character was as you presented it or not.'

'You needed to determine…' she echoed, relief, disbelief and confusion making her hot, then cold, then dizzy.

He seized her arm—but gently, protectively—and eased her to the sofa. 'Sit, I beg you!' he said, urging her down on its edge. 'Don't want you swooning on me again. I've been considering plans for your future—which do not, I assure you, include having you assume a horizontal position for me or anyone else. However, to implement them I needed to know with absolute assurance that you are in fact the lady of blameless character you've just shown yourself to be.'

She blotted her eyes and handed him back his handkerchief. 'You mean,' she asked incredulously, 'you were... *testing* me?'

His cheeks reddened again. 'Well...yes,' he admitted.

She was torn between shrieking with laughter—and slapping him for scaring her so. 'And here I'd been thinking what an exemplary gentleman you were! You are a brigand, sir! A bully and a brigand!' she fumed.

'You are quite justified in abusing me. I assure you, I believe that a man who takes advantage of an unwilling lady is a cur who deserves to be horsewhipped. I don't have a whip handy, but you may strike me if you like.' He angled his face towards her.

'You should be more careful what you offer,' she said tartly. 'I grappled with my brother growing up and could plant you a facer that would leave you bruised for a week. Indeed, had I not been so cast down by the dreadful events of the last few days, I should have done so when you made your insulting offer.'

'Please, don't remind me!' he groaned. 'I deserve that fate and more. Although if I were truly a brigand, I'd not have let you go,' he added.

His tone was light—but a heated *something* flared between them that she felt right down to her bones. Only this time, she was not afraid.

She had been right on both accounts, it seemed. He did desire her. But Mr Greaves was no Lord Masters, plundering where he would.

He was truly the gentleman she'd thought him—if a devious one! A man with whom, except for that single moment he'd towered over her, she felt *safe*, even though she was virtually alone with him in his house, with neither friends nor family to defend her.

'Would you like a glass of wine?' he asked, recalling her.

'You think I require something to settle my nerves?'

'I don't know about you, but I do, and it wouldn't be polite to drink alone. Though at this moment you probably don't believe me, I've never before tried to debauch a gentlewoman. 'Twas a deucedly disturbing experience.'

She chuckled, sure his levity was meant to set her at ease. 'Very well, I'll take a glass. To be polite, so you may settle *your* nerves.'

After he poured the wine and took a chair a respectful distance away, she said, 'What are these plans you mentioned? Though it is indeed kind of you to be concerned, I have no claim upon you. There is no reason whatsoever for you to concern yourself with my predicament.'

'Perhaps *I* have no claim on you, but there is another, much more important than me, who does. I was given to understand that your brother is Lord Englemere's cousin?'

When she nodded, he continued, 'Which, of course, makes *you* his cousin as well. I am certain that, once he is apprised of your situation, Lord Englemere will wish to assist you.'

All the indignation she'd previously felt on her brother's behalf returned in a rush. 'Indeed? And whatever could have led you to that astounding conclusion? Need I remind you that Lord Englemere recently discharged my brother from a position he no doubt counted on filling for the rest of his days? My brother, who served his country valiantly at Waterloo?'

Once begun, she couldn't seem to stop. 'Oh, you don't know him,' she rushed on, 'but I assure you, Greville possesses the most agreeable and obliging of temperaments. I cannot imagine anyone being vexed with him! He was the kindest elder brother a girl could wish for.'

'And look around you!' she demanded, her tone strident as

she gestured towards the spotless, orderly room. 'How could any reasonable employer fault Greville's management of this house? I begin to believe that all gentlemen of high rank are as venal as Lord Masters! In any event, if Lord Englemere had no compunction about summarily discharging my brother, why should he trouble himself about my fate? Nor do I wish him to. I would as soon throw myself on the charity of the man who ruined my brother's career as I would play the doxy for him.'

Her tirade over, suddenly she realised poor Mr Greaves was just sitting there staring at her, surprise and dismay on his face. Heavens, what had possessed her to run on in such a fashion?

'I beg you will excuse me,' she began again quietly, embarrassed by her outburst. 'Truly, I am not normally so intemperate. Perhaps the events of this last week have disordered my sensibilities more than I'd thought.'

'Perhaps,' Mr Greaves said drily. 'I recommend the wine. 'Tis a fine vintage.'

Not until she'd obediently swallowed a sip did it occur to her that the personage she'd just roundly abused was Mr Greaves's employer, the man to whom he owed his position and his loyalty. 'Excuse me as well for insulting your patron,' she added hastily. 'Admittedly I know nothing of the circumstances surrounding Greville's discharge. Lord Englemere awarded you this post and you may well think highly of him.'

Looking troubled, Mr Greaves opened his lips, closed them, then finally said, 'I am…sorry for your brother's circumstances. Though at present my regard for Lord Englemere may seem inexplicable, yes, I do esteem him very highly.'

'I'm sure you have your reasons. Let's simply agree to speak no more of him.'

'Then you absolutely would not consent to my contacting the Marquess on your behalf?'

'I want nothing to do with him,' she said flatly.

'I see.' Mr Greaves sipped his wine, looking thoughtful.

After a moment, he said, 'Very well, then, we shall have to come up with another plan.'

That reminder of her grim and still unresolved circumstances abruptly drained the high spirits engendered by their verbal sparring. 'Coming up with a solution is my task,' she emphasised again, as if to armour herself against the temptation to rely on him. 'Though I do appreciate your concern.'

He nodded absently, setting down his glass and gazing into the distance, his brow creased in concentration. Determined to enjoy the last few moments of his company before she must pack her things and say goodbye, Joanna pushed the worry from her mind and contented herself with simply sipping her wine and watching the play of thoughts over his handsome face.

Odd, she thought with a little pang, realising how much she was going to miss someone whom this time yesterday she had not even known existed.

Suddenly Mr Greaves straightened. 'I have it!' he announced, triumph on his face. 'You recently worked as a governess, correct?'

'Yes. Though I'd never been formally employed as one before, I have three younger sisters. My mother having died after the youngest's birth, I taught them all as they grew up.'

He nodded. 'Then perhaps I have a situation for you. One of my aims here is to establish a school for the children of the tenants and the village. As enclosures continue, fewer and fewer of them will end up becoming farmers. Even if they remain on the land, knowing how to read, write and do sums will help them with their accounts, while a rudimentary knowledge of science will make them better farmers. If they must or choose to leave to look for work in town, possessing such skills will enable them to more easily find employment.'

She gave him a speculative look. 'Just how long has establishing a school here been one of your aims?'

''Tis a worthy aspiration,' he replied, not answering her question.

'Are you sure?' she said softly, sudden emotion flooding her. She would bet her few remaining worldly possessions that a school for the village children was an idea he'd come up with but a moment ago. His kindness in proposing to create a respectable position that would allow her to extract herself honourably from her current predicament brought a lump to her throat.

'I'm sure. I have to confess, I've been here but two days and have done nothing as yet towards the establishment of a school. You would be doing me—and the children around Blenhem, of course—a great favour in organising and initiating such an enterprise.'

Would she enjoy running a school of her own? Was she even capable of it? But how much harder could it be than teaching her sisters or the little daughters of Lady Masters?

She'd have children to care about and instruct, to surround her with their chatter and tears and laughter. That wouldn't fully assuage the anguish of knowing she would never cradle a child of her own…but it would be a useful way to employ her time while she worked out what to do next.

A useful and honourable way.

It wasn't as if she had someone or something more pressing awaiting her elsewhere.

While she sat, considering, he rushed on, 'If you aren't sure yet what you mean to do, you could just get the school started and teach until another mistress is found. The position would allow you to accumulate funds while you attempt to contact your brother or your family in India and consider what you wish to do permanently.'

Despite his assurances, she knew any service she performed for the school and its children didn't compare to the one he did her in offering respectable employment to the indigent female who'd landed at his doorstep. Whatever else befell her, she would always consider Mr Greaves the kindest, most thoughtful gentleman she'd ever met.

'Thank you, Mr Greaves.' She smiled a bit. 'I accept *this* offer.'

To her amusement, he flushed again at this reminder of his rakish behaviour. 'You are most welcome, Mrs Merrill. By the way, you haven't enquired about the salary.'

She smiled ruefully. 'I'm not in a very good position to bargain, am I?'

He grinned. 'Excellent. Then I shall pay you twice what you were getting from Lady Masters.'

'Twice?' she echoed, startled. One reason she'd so quickly accepted her former post was because the situation paid considerably more than a governess normally earned—Lady Masters, perhaps, having had difficulty finding a qualified individual who was willing to work on an estate in such a remote part of Hampshire…or tolerate her vile husband. 'You truly wish to offer that much?'

'You shall be instructing quite a few more children than you did as a governess.'

That was true, she acknowledged. Then the thought struck her that perhaps, moved by her plight and that of her brother, Mr Greaves had decided to strike back for them by chousing his employer out of a hefty sum to set up his school.

She was smiling at the idea when the humiliating realisation struck her that, employed or not, at the moment she was still homeless and without funds. 'I'm afraid I shall have to beg an advance on that enormous salary. I must find lodgings and purchase some necessities.'

He waved a hand. 'No reason for that. You can lodge here. We'll probably set up the school in one of the old cottages nearest Hazelwick, once workmen have time to repair and furnish it.'

Lodge—under his roof? Unbidden, the image of his lips taking hers invaded her head. She felt a blush mount her cheeks. 'It wouldn't be…proper.'

He raised his brows. 'Not proper? Why? You resided in the same dwelling as your employers in Hampshire. Had Lord Masters conducted himself as a gentleman, no one, yourself included, would have thought there was anything improper about it.'

He was quite right. She wasn't an unmarried—or even married—lady of quality any longer, but a servant who did not have a reputation to safeguard. Nor would she be joining the household of a single gentleman. Though she suspected Mr Greaves, like herself, was gentry-born, he too had become simply an employee, albeit the most important one at this estate.

Though to her, she thought with a thrill of warmth in her breast, not even a duke could have conducted himself more nobly. She would be both thankful and proud to work for him. She'd just have to keep her lustful imaginings to herself.

But as she was about to agree, one other objection occurred to her. 'What of Lord Englemere? I doubt he'd be happy about housing the sister of the man he just sent packing.'

Mr Greaves gave her a smile that looked positively conspiratorial, strengthening her conviction that he'd deliberately offered her an outrageous salary as a recompense for Lord Englemere's dismissal of her brother. 'You needn't worry about Lord Englemere. I have the charge of Blenhem Hill now. So—have we a bargain?' He offered his hand.

She took it, feeling a little tingle where their fingers linked. 'A bargain. No more little "tests", though! From now on, we shall deal with each other honestly.'

Chapter Six

After he'd sent Mrs Merrill back to her chamber to begin preparing lists of what they would need to set up a school, Ned poured himself another glass of wine and sank into his chair behind the desk.

Though she seemed to think he'd been joking, he'd not exaggerated when he'd claimed he'd found pretending to make advances to her disturbing. First, because as he stood near her, her luscious breasts brushing his chest, her tempting lips parted in surprise, he was consumed by desire so intense and compelling that even after seeing the fear on her face, he'd had to battle himself to step away.

Quite a lowering realisation for one who'd always considered himself impeccably honourable. What a damnable fool lust could make of a man!

Even now, thinking back on it, his hands trembled at the violence of his conflicting emotions. He'd felt like the veriest beast in nature for frightening Mrs Merrill—even while still wanting her more than his next breath.

He blew out a breath now. At least he *had* resisted. Not that he wanted her any less, but if he ever felt the velvet touch of

Mrs Merrill's lips against his, it would be because she wanted the kiss as much as he did.

An unlikely occurrence, given that she'd nearly been attacked by her last employer and frightened half out of her wits by him.

Though he wasn't very proud of his behaviour on the seduction front, he was pleased he'd hit upon the notion of engaging her to create a school. Though, as she suspected, he'd not yet begun planning one at Blenhem Hill, he was a firm believer in the value of education. He'd seen first-hand the good results he'd described to her after setting up a school on his holdings in Kent.

Establishing such a venture was not as easy as it might seem, though, he'd discovered. Finding a building and furnishings were the least of the problems. Some backward-thinking individuals, both yeoman and gentry, felt that farm children had no need of book learning, nor anything else that took them out of the fields.

It was a project he would have to work on with her, both to refurbish a building and to persuade the local inhabitants to allow their children to attend. He found the idea of collaborating closely with her appealing indeed.

He was also pleased to have struck upon a way, short of bodily restraint, to prevent her from leaving Blenhem Hill still destitute and in desperate need of immediate employment. If not in Hazelwick, almost certainly somewhere along the way to London some unscrupulous rogue, leering at those plump lips and that alluring figure and discovering her wholly alone and without resources, would have tricked or forced her into the position Lord Masters had envisioned for her.

Ned's lip curled. If he ever encountered her unlamented former employer, he'd plant him a facer before kicking him down the street. No woman should be preyed upon, regardless of her station, but for a person of title to abuse his wealth and power in such a way infuriated him. A man like that—he'd not dignify him with the title of 'gentleman', regardless of his rank—ought to be crushed underfoot like a maggot on a corn stalk.

How providential his idea to present himself as plain 'Mr Greaves' had turned out to be! If Mrs Merrill had met him as 'Sir Edward', owner of the estate, Ned was nearly certain she would have refused to remain at the manor. Not only would she have considered it improper, at the moment she obviously did not have a very high opinion of titled gentlemen.

Of course, *he* knew the truth and it really *wasn't* proper. But he'd been surprised by the strength of his desire to persuade her to stay, not just so she would be protected from potential debauchers—or even because he still wanted her himself, badly as he did.

Quite simply, he liked her. When he considered how terrifying it must have been to find herself alone, penniless, unprotected, without property, husband or position and no means to earn any, he could not help but admire her courage and endurance. Walking five miles alone through the rain! By heaven, she had fortitude!

He chuckled when he recalled her tart responses after she realised he'd not truly been trying to seduce her. Plant him a facer, would she? He looked forward to more demonstrations of that spirit.

Although he had to squirm when he recalled her declaration that they might now deal with each other honestly. She'd presented him with a perfect opening to confess he was not who he appeared. But though he was certain she had no connection to the attack on the road, he had not yet begun to uncover the truth behind that incident. The reasons for him to remain simply 'Mr Greaves' were as compelling now as they'd been when he'd first conceived of the notion.

Nor had he told her the truth about her brother or defended Nicky from her censure. Of course, simple 'Mr Greaves' could hardly claim to know a Marquess intimately enough to vouch for his character. Distraught as she already was, he didn't think it would have been a kindness to speak contemptuously of the brother she so obviously admired. Nor was it likely, given her memories of Anders, that she would have believed Ned's testimony anyway.

She *had* noticed how well the manor was kept. Having grown up in a parsonage rather than on an agricultural estate, she might not recognise the wretched condition of the fields, but as they went about the estate in the process of setting up the school, she would surely observe the harsh contrast between the comfort of the manor house and the poverty and misery of the tenants and their dwellings.

With time and a discerning eye, there'd be no need for him to disparage her brother; her own observations would lead her to draw a more accurate conclusion about the reasons behind Anders's dismissal.

Smiling as he recalled the determined look on her face as she left the room to go and prepare her lists, he raised his glass once more to the new mistress of Blenhem Hill's first school. He was looking forward to bandying words with her every day over breakfast and dinner, to riding about the estate together as they conferred over the creation of the school and the recruiting of its pupils. Though while they did, he'd have to keep the lust within firmly leashed—unless Mrs Merrill herself chose to loose it.

'To you, my intrepid Mrs Merrill,' he said and drained the glass.

A fortnight later, wearing one of the cook's voluminous aprons to protect her oldest gown, Joanna worked at cleaning out the inside of the gutted wreck of an old stone cottage. Located just off the lane to Hazelwick, adjacent to the village yet readily accessible from most of the farms on the estate, it would, Mr Greaves believed, be the best location for the new school.

Outside, some workmen from the village were assembling thatch to replace the roof. Tomorrow or the next day, he'd told her, stonemasons would arrive to repair the walls, while, as soon as they finished the interior work on the stocking-mill project Mr Greaves was directing, estate carpenters would come here to begin constructing doors, window frames, desks and benches for the school.

She wiped her grubby hands on the apron and peered at the sky. Judging from the position of the sun, it was well after noon. Cook had packed her a basket of ham, bread and cheese to sustain her for the day. Though she was hungry, she'd delayed opening it, hoping, as he had the last two days, that Mr Greaves might pause in his work to come by and share it with her.

Otherwise she seldom saw him during the day, which he spent riding about the estate with its former manager, old Mr Martin, assessing the needs of the tenants and preparing for the spring planting. After completing her planning lists, she'd spent two days lounging in the morning room reading books he'd lent her. After viewing the building he'd selected as the schoolhouse, she'd argued him into letting her come and begin cleaning it. She was unaccustomed to being idle, she'd told him, and not afraid of a little hard work.

Becoming actively involved in the project also gave her something else to discuss with him over breakfast and dinner. Though he was far too prone to encourage her to speak while he listened, that intent expression on his face that made one think he found whatever one was discoursing about the most fascinating topic in the world.

After a year with only children and housemaids to talk to, she'd been all too easy to encourage, she thought ruefully, especially by a gentleman as attractive and attentive as Mr Greaves. After merely a week, he knew nearly everything about her, from birth to her sojourn in India. Having never travelled outside of England, he'd been especially eager to have her describe in detail the people, culture and happenings in that faraway land. They'd whiled away every evening after dinner in the small salon while she related stories of everyday life there interspersed with the tales and legends about the exotic land in which her husband and father had served and that she'd come to love.

The subtle, sensual *something* that sparked between them whenever they were together doubtless also played a part in her desire to linger after dinner. Being with him made her realise just how much she'd missed a man's companionship. She found herself revelling in the simple pleasure of hearing his deep-toned voice, engaging his lively wit…observing the leashed power of his body.

Several times she'd caught her gaze lingering on the play of his lips or wandering down his torso from the strong shoulders to the flat stomach to the moulded front of his breeches. Fortunately, though she sensed he found her attractive as well, he treated her with such respect and restraint that she had no fear he would interpret her appreciation as an invitation to make advances she was not yet sure she wished to encourage.

Admiring his intelligence as much as his sensual appeal, she'd tried to prompt him to tell her about his own life. However, he'd proved surprisingly reticent, turning aside her questions with non-committal responses. Not wishing to pry, after several rebuffs she'd not inquired further. Perhaps, she mused, he'd suffered some sorrow or disappointment he did not wish to share. Which made her all the more curious—and admiring, for if life had treated him harshly, he had emerged from the experience with his optimism, kindness and courtesy intact.

Or perhaps when it came to his own personal affairs, he was just an unusually private person.

Only when she asked him about his work on the estate did his eyes light up and his face grow animated. Though she knew next to nothing about farm management, she loved to listen as he talked about his plans for breaking new ground, rotating crops, instituting improved planting techniques and working with the tenants to rebuild and refurbish their cottages. Then there was the mill project to provide supplemental employment for the farmers or those of their families who preferred to work elsewhere than in the fields. As she drove a trap back and forth to work on the schoolhouse, she'd begun to observe details about the countryside and the farm workers she would never have noticed previously.

From his talk of improvements and her own observations, it did appear that the tenants were a rather ragged lot, their dwellings in poor repair and many of their fields overgrown. The distressing thought occurred to her that perhaps Greville hadn't done as good a job at managing the agricultural part of his duties as she'd assumed, though she was still not ready to excuse Lord Englemere for summarily dismissing him.

She was carrying out another armload of rotted wood framing when over her shoulder, she saw the figure of a man approaching from behind the cottage. Though she'd not heard the hoofbeats of his horse approaching, it must be Mr Greaves, she thought in delight.

Dumping the debris and scrubbing her hands on her apron, she quickly smoothed back under her bonnet the wisps of hair that had escaped their braids and turned to greet him, a welcoming smile on her lips.

She saw immediately that the thin, rangy man limping towards her was not Blenhem Hill's manager. Her disappointment changed to compassion, though, when she realised that in addition to the limp, the newcomer was missing one arm.

As he approached, he doffed his hat with his remaining hand—although that, too, lacked a thumb. 'Excuse me, ma'am. Tanner, the stonemason in the village, told me they were building a new school here. Would you be the mistress?'

Trying not to let her distress over his injuries show on her face, she said, 'Yes, I am. Can I help you?'

He nodded. 'If you would, I'd like to engage you to write a letter for me. As you can imagine,' he said with a bitter twist of his lip, 'my penmanship isn't what it used to be.'

'I would be honoured. Were you in the army? My husband served with the Penrith Rifles in India.'

His dull eyes brightened. 'A rifleman, is he? My unit was the 95th. Fought with them all through the Peninsula and then at Waterloo. Sergeant Jesse Russell, ma'am.'

'Pleased to meet you, Sergeant,' Joanna said, curtsying. 'I'm Mrs Merrill. I should be happy to pen a missive for you, but I'm afraid I don't have ink or paper with me. If you'd like to accompany me back to Blenhem Hill manor, I could fetch some from my room.'

His eyes widened. 'You live at the manor?'

Was he insinuating there was some impropriety in that? Stiffening at his apparent disapproval, she said, 'Lodging was provided as part of the conditions of my employment, since there isn't yet adequate housing here at the school.'

Perhaps he must have noted the defensiveness of her tone, for he replied, 'Only right you should be offered quarters. I'm just surprised, is all. Wouldn't think the puffed-up toff who owns the estate would concern himself about housing for a schoolmistress.'

Secretly sharing that opinion, Joanna smiled. 'Actually, it was the estate manager who provided it.'

'Mr Greaves, is it?' At her nod, he continued, 'Heard good things about him from Tanner. Seems to know land and how to manage it.'

'He has a great concern for the people who work the land, too,' she replied. ''Twas his idea to establish the school.'

'Good someone is thinking of the people's welfare,' he muttered. 'But, no, ma'am, there's no need to use your things.

I brought paper, ink and pen with me.' He gestured to the leather bag slung over his good shoulder. 'If you've time, we could do the letter now.'

Though a little surprised that an army sergeant would be carrying such costly writing items, she nodded. 'Let me just fetch something to write on. There's a bench in the cottage, but 'tis too dark inside to write properly.'

'I'll get it, ma'am,' Sergeant Russell said. 'Can't shoulder a rifle or write any more, but I'm not totally helpless.'

'Of course not,' she said softly, compassion for his injuries twisting her heart again. While he dragged the bench out of the dim cottage, she extracted quill, paper, ink and a knife from his bag.

After all was in readiness, she looked up at him. 'You may begin now.'

'The letter's to Lord Evers of Eversly Park, Dorset,' he instructed.

Your lordship,

Being, as I previously informed you, no longer fit to take up the post of secretary you had promised me upon my leaving the army, I write instead to ask that you advance me passage money to the Americas. I pledge to repay this sum within a year, with whatever interest you consider appropriate. Please reply to me care of the Hart and Hare in the village of Hazelwick. Yours etcetera, Jesse Russell.

While he watched, she carefully scribed the missive. 'You were to work as his lordship's secretary? You must have been well schooled.'

He smiled. 'My parents were crofters—skilled weavers in Nottingham. Earned a good wage in the old days, when Nottingham workmanship was famous throughout England. I wasn't interested in the weaving trade, wanted something different. So they sent me to school. One of the masters recommended me to Lord Evers. But for a Polish lancer at Waterloo, I'd have had a fine job. But no one in England wants a crippled old soldier.'

His nonchalant tone held an undertone of bitterness. 'I'm so sorry,' she said softly. 'But America! Is your family not concerned about your going so far away?'

''Tis partly to help them that I want to go. A few years back, rich men came to Nottingham and set up factories, making stockings on machine looms any untrained fool could operate. Though the quality of their work far surpassed the factory-made hose, my kin could no longer sell enough to maintain their business. Had to go work for the factory owner for a pittance of what they used to earn, losing their independence as well as their livelihood. Finally sold their house, but even so, they can barely feed the family.'

While she shook her head in sympathy, he continued, 'I want better for myself than to toil in a factory, but even if there were land to be had, most of the farmers hereabouts barely raise enough to meet their rents. America offers a new start, where every man has a vote and "The Land is the People's Farm". As it should be. Not like here, where the nobs control everything and always will—until they're forced out,' he finished darkly.

Though Joanna found it deplorable that a soldier who'd suffered as grievously for his country as the sergeant should be shunted aside like damaged refuse after the war's end, the angry fervour of his last words made her uneasy. Before she could decide what, if anything, to reply, the sergeant's expression lightened and he smiled again.

'Thank you, ma'am. Here's a copper for your efforts.' He pulled a coin from his pocket.

'Goodness, no, I can't take your money!' she protested, waving it away. 'My husband was a soldier, too, remember.'

'You write in a fine hand,' he said, inspecting the finished document. 'I bet your man looks forwards to reading your letters—in India he is, you said?'

A rush of sadness filled her, as it always did when she thought of Thomas. 'My husband died several years ago,' she said softly.

'Excuse me, ma'am. Right sorry for your loss. I'll be heading back to town now, but if I need more letters written, would you be willing to do them?'

'I'd consider it a privilege to assist a man who has served the nation as valiantly as you have, Sergeant Russell,' she replied.

A dull flush stained his cheeks and he stood straighter, like a soldier going on parade. 'Thank you, ma'am, but I did no different than any of the men I served with, many of whom are now faring no better than I. Well, good day to you, and good luck with your school.'

'Good day to you, Sergeant Russell.'

She watched thoughtfully as he limped back in the direction of Hazelwick. Living as she had for the last ten years, first in India, then in London, then in a remote corner of Hampshire, she knew almost nothing about cloth making and factories. Aside from her observations of the ragged farmers and idle fields at Blenhem Hill, she knew little more about the state of agriculture. She vaguely remembered reading something in the London journals about unrest and the threat of violence. Surely there was no chance of that here?

Still, if valiant men like Sergeant Russell were being pushed aside, ignored or made to feel useless, if honest yeoman who'd always prided themselves on their independence were forced from their small businesses or their lands, the well-being of their families sacrificed to the greed of wealthy landowners and factory owners, even someone as uninformed about the politics of the nation as she was could see how dangerous the situation might become.

Troubled, she walked slowly back into the cottage. Though she hadn't much appetite for eating alone, she ought to make an attempt to consume her provisions, lest she seem unappreciative of Cook's efforts. She was unpacking the basket when she heard the sounds of a rider approaching.

She hurried back to peer out the door. Her worry dissolved in a giddy little rush of excitement as she confirmed that this time, the gentleman approaching the cottage was indeed Mr Greaves.

She paused to watch him ride up. Upright posture, hands just taut on the reins, powerful thighs controlling his mount…yes, he was an admirable horseman. An idea of how else he might employ those hips and thighs invaded her mind.

Her thoughts coalesced in a series of searing images: a shadowy bedchamber; a strong, broad-shouldered, brown-haired man brushing one lock of hair from his brow as he looked down at her, his tawny eyes molten with desire; her lover crooning sweet words to her as he thrust himself deep into her willing warmth. A tremor shook her to the core, flooding her with wetness.

She'd been told a widow buried her sensual desires with her husband and, for more than two years, she'd believed it to be true. But with the gradual increase in her preoccupation with Mr Greaves, Joanna was less surprised this time to have her body demonstrate those desires had not in fact been lost forever. It appeared they'd just been slumbering…waiting, perhaps, for the right man to reawaken her to pleasure?

How disconcerting and inconvenient to have that awakening occur now!

But as she returned his smile, a wicked little voice whispered that perhaps here and now was in fact very convenient…and Mr Greaves the perfect man for the task.

Chapter Seven

He really ought not to stop…but after working with the tenants to prepare new ground for planting on the nearby Wilkers farm, Ned hadn't been able to keep himself from riding to the schoolhouse…just as he had the other two days Mrs Merrill had been working there.

In addition to the sensual pull that irresistibly drew him to her, every day he liked her more. Instead of spending dull evenings poring over agricultural tracts, after dinner he walked her to the salon and coaxed her to tell him about herself and her life in India. With her expressive hands and warm velvet voice, she was entrancing, a natural storyteller as gifted as a Scheherazade.

She made him hear the roar of the great beasts and the beating sticks of the trackers during a tiger hunt, the rattle and hiss of a snake battling a mongoose. Feel the dip and sway of the *howdah* strapped high atop an elephant's back, the heavy summer air stirred by a servant-boy with a plumed fan. See the mud-brown of villages brightened by the brilliant pattern of ladies in their multi-coloured saris, experience the swirling dust of the markets with their babble of voices and scent of dung, marigolds and spices.

If she enthralled her students half as much as she fascinated him, they would have to drag the children back to their farms every night.

Of course, keeping her talking was a good way to avoid having to talk himself. He hoped his reticence to discuss his own history and background hadn't offended her, she who trustingly offered up her life to him with an openness he'd refrained from reciprocating.

But the necessity for secrecy wouldn't last forever. Once he'd uncovered the reasons for the attack on Nicky's carriage and the extent of Luddite activity in the area, he would safely be able to divulge his identity. Intelligent and reasonable as she was, she would surely understand why the deception had been necessary.

Though he had to admit, he was glad that revealing the truth had to be put off. Hopefully, before then she would come to understand why her brother had been sacked and the painful memories of the lecherous Lord Masters would begin to fade. A lessening of her current distaste for *ton* gentlemen along with some time for her to grow to like him for himself, and perhaps she would not then hold his title against him.

He certainly hoped so. He didn't know what she would ultimately decide to do about her future, but he was already finding it difficult to imagine Blenhem Hill without her industrious, witty presence. If she agreed to stay on after establishing the school, he might have to remain here for longer than he'd initially expected.

He'd always thought his ideal helpmeet would be a countrywoman as steeped in knowledge and love of the land as he was. He was beginning to think an enchanting storyteller who could bring the gift of knowledge to the children of his tenants might be an even better match.

An enchanting storyteller who engaged his mind and made his senses sing every time he saw her, as he did now as he rode up to the cottage.

He couldn't help smiling as he approached. Silhouetted in the doorway of the old cottage, fine strands of hair escaping her bonnet to gleam auburn in the sunlight, she looked as warm and appealing as the glow of the bonfire at the end of a successful harvest. How lovely she was, her face flushed from her exertions, her green eyes bright, those lush, smiling lips slightly parted, as if she were thinking wicked thoughts.

Of course, he was the one with the lustful imagination, he acknowledged with a sigh. He couldn't seem to look at her without envisioning rapid breathing and tangled sheets. Something about her made the breath seize in his throat and all the blood in his body rush straight to his loins.

She kept him forever on the knife's edge between liking and longing, respect and desire. He wouldn't allow himself even to contemplate the nature of the feelings—if any—he might be arousing in her.

It was enough for now that they were growing to be friends— good friends who enjoyed each other's company, could anticipate each other's thoughts and share each other's amusements.

Ned Greaves, you're a liar, he told himself as he dismounted and walked towards her. When it comes to the beauteous Mrs Merrill, in the treacherous ground between affection and lust, you're mired deeper than an ox in a bog, no matter how many times you tell yourself that you're not ready to expose your heart to the danger of a woman's fickle fancy.

'Dare I hope there's a bite left of Cook's bread and ham?' he asked, struggling to pry his thoughts away from the idea of pulling her into his arms. But, oh, how he wished he might lean down to kiss the luscious lips she now raised to him!

'You are in luck,' she said, taking the arm he offered her and walking him into the dim cottage while the skin beneath the fingers she rested on his wrist smoked and burned. 'Let's fetch the basket and bring it out into the sunlight. As it happens, I haven't yet consumed a crumb.'

'Indeed! Late as it is? You've been entirely too diligent, then. Although you've made immense progress,' he noted, looking around the interior of the cottage. The bits and pieces of rotting rushes, old straw, broken crockery and other debris had been carried off, the floor swept, the cobwebs cleaned from the walls and roofing. 'Everything looks ready for the arrival of the masons and carpenters. Perhaps tomorrow you can rest.'

'I'd rather come here and observe the workmen. Or perhaps, if you have time, you could ride with me to visit the tenants and introduce me to the children.'

He nodded. 'An excellent notion. I've about finished my consultations with all the tenants on the placement and planting of the crops. Although I'm afraid it may require a deal of convincing to get some of them to allow their children to come to school. Many of the older folk are suspicious of education, thinking we mean to instil wild ideas in the children's heads or make them believe themselves above working the fields.'

'They will respect your opinion,' she said, picking up the basket and strolling back outside with him. 'Already the folk hereabout are impressed with your knowledge and concern. In fact, 'tis why you are lucky enough to be able to claim half Cook's good bread and ham. Apparently there's already talk in the village about the school, for I had a visitor who made me postpone my luncheon.'

'Father of a prospective student?' he asked, spreading out a cloth on the rough bench one of the workmen must have set out for her.

'No. A former soldier,' she replied as she unpacked the provisions. 'Poor man, he lost an arm and part of his remaining hand at Waterloo. He wished me to write a letter for him.'

Ned shook his head, a ready sympathy welling up. ''Twas a dreadful battle. If his injuries were that severe, he's probably lucky to be alive.' The food spread out between them, he motioned her to sit. 'He's found work in the village, then?'

Mrs Merrill frowned. 'No. In fact…' She hesitated a minute, then said, 'I must say, his situation leaves me rather troubled. Though the letter was personal, he didn't forbid me to divulge its contents.'

'If you don't feel you would be violating a confidence, please tell me about it,' he invited, tearing off a hunk of the bread.

'He had me write to the nobleman who was to engage him as his secretary—before his war injuries made such an occupation impossible. He wished that gentleman to advance him passage to the Americas, where I believe he hoped to find some good land to settle.'

Ned nodded. 'I've heard there is rich land to be had for a fair price.'

'I suppose so. What disturbed me, though, was the way he described it. As if America was to be preferred over England, it being a place where—how did he put it?—"where every man has a vote and 'The Land is the People's Farm'".'

His mind alerted and his whole body tensed, as if he'd just heard again the explosion of the pistol outside his coach on the road to Blenhem Hill. Finally snapped out the sensual haze that seemed to settle over his brain every time she opened her lips, he repeated, '"The Land is the People's Farm"? He said that exactly?'

'Yes, I believe so. Are those words significant?'

'They could be. That phrase, worded in just that manner, is a slogan often repeated by the members of the Society of Spencean Philanthropists. A radical group, some of whom seek not just to reform government by extending the vote, but to overthrow it entirely. Did he mention meeting with others of similar views?'

She looked even more troubled. 'No. However, he did say something about how in England those who hold power through birth or great fortune control everything and always will—until they are "forced out", I believe he worded it. It…it sounded rather extreme to me.'

In his mind Ned replayed the afternoon of the attack. Were any of the armed and masked men possessed of only one arm? Ned didn't think so; even in the tumult of the moment, he would have noted a man who had suffered that drastic an injury. But perhaps there was a radical group hereabouts to which the young soldier belonged.

He had certainly echoed their rhetoric.

While Ned remained silent, Mrs Merrill continued, 'I confess I know almost nothing of the politics, but even in my ignorance, I recognise that such talk could be dangerous. Men of wealth and influence would surely act quickly to demand the arrest—or worse—of anyone who seemed to advocate their overthrow. Still, when a man who has sacrificed as much for his nation as Sergeant Russell is pushed aside—or craftsmen are robbed of their businesses by the establishment of large industries—how can one fault these men for protesting?'

Ned hesitated, trying to decide how much to reveal to her. Though he understood her sympathy for the labourers' distress—indeed, he shared it—he did not wish to encourage her involvement in what might be a very perilous cause. And he knew her character well enough now to know she was incapable of dissembling.

If he warned her about the attack on him, even without revealing his identity—which he hoped not to do until she could evaluate him for himself and not his name—as honest and straightforward as she was, if questioned, she might inadvertently reveal something of the matter—perhaps even putting herself into danger. Until Ned had more answers than he now possessed, he'd prefer that no hint of the attack emerge.

Telling her nothing about it would probably be safest, he concluded. 'Talk of open resistance is certainly unwise. You were right to warn me. Though I feel for the soldier's situation, stirring up a hornet's nest of protest would only lead to repression—the hangings and deportations after the uprisings a few years ago should have taught everyone that.'

'I find it deplorable poor wretches should be hanged or transported simply for protesting against injustice,' she retorted hotly. 'And what of soldiers like Sergeant Russell, wounded or maimed in the service of their country, now facing an uncertain future while the government they fought to preserve does nothing to help? One is hard-pressed not to approve of the Sergeant's desire to relocate to a nation where ability and individual effort, not an accident of birth, determine a man's worth!'

Knowing how she had suffered at the hands of a man of birth, Ned tried to skirt that delicate issue. 'The way the returning soldiers have been treated is a disgrace,' he said, trying to turn the subject. 'My—' he barely caught himself before saying 'my friend Nicky' '—ah, friends tell me that some in Parliament have argued for providing assistance to the veterans, perhaps having the government employ on the roads and canal systems those who came home to find their farms or their jobs gone.'

She nodded eagerly. 'Indeed, that exact thing happened to Sergeant Russell's family! They were skilled weavers in Nottingham, he told me, who lost their positions when factories were built in the area.'

Which made it even more likely the young soldier might be involved with Luddites—and have few scruples about using force to achieve his aims, Ned thought, his concern deepening.

'The legislation was not approved?' Mrs Merrill enquired, recalling his attention.

'No, unfortunately. Conservatives argued that the government employing former soldiers or trying to alleviate the distress of displaced farmers or factory workers, by interfering with freedom of trade and the individual's liberty to choose a position himself, would end up only exacerbating the distress.'

'All well and fine to talk of freedom of choice when one has alternatives,' Mrs Merrill said bitterly. 'But when want is staring one in the face…I can understand why some might feel forced to more drastic measures. Did the more conservative men not see that by giving desperate people no hope, they might bring about exactly the sort of unrest they wished to avoid?'

Ned imagined she was recalling her own predicament, stripped of her position by her aristocratic employer with little cash and no place to go. How could she help but sympathise with the radicals? He must keep watch, to make sure no one played upon those sympathies to her detriment.

'Some men of power and influence, keenly aware of the difficult situation in the countryside, are actively working to improve conditions. But I agree, there is still much to be done. One can only hope that in the interim, no such violent disaffection develops. Should you hear anything further, I would appreciate it if you alerted me. If there are murky doings afoot, I want to be able to protect Blenhem Hill's people.'

'I know you would do anything to protect those under your care,' she avowed, looking up at him with an expression he hoped was respect and admiration.

'Especially the pretty ladies under my care,' he said, smiling at her. How he would like to protect her…and more, he thought, all discussion of politics fading as his mind fired with the images of what he might do for and to her.

'Am I…under your care?' she asked softly, leaning towards him, her face uplifted, her full moist lips almost inviting a kiss.

Under him—ah, that would be a fine position, he thought, digging his nails into his palms to resist the innocent allure of those lips.

A virtuous matron who'd loved her husband, she couldn't know what her subtle scent and the proximity of that lush, pouting mouth did to him.

But he'd vowed to her that he didn't pursue women under

his protection, as she was, and he meant to keep that promise. Even if it meant he had to take a dip in the icy brook every night to cool the fevered imaginings engendered by the knowledge that she slept down the hall, only a few dozen steps from his bedchamber.

Wrapped in a soft linen night rail—or clothed only in her auburn hair? Enough! He stifled a groan and hauled back on the reins of imagination. He could use an icy dip right now.

'Absolutely,' he affirmed, moving away from her. 'Now, shall you have some of this ham before I devour it all? Since you've finished your work here, I can escort you back to the manor before heading on to the Anderson farm.'

She sat back too, an odd look—he'd almost call it disappointment—in her eyes. But then, she kept his senses in such a continual uproar that he'd hardly be able to tell a duck from a goose, much less guess the tenor of her thoughts.

Perhaps, rather than wondering if she was willing to be kissed, he'd do better to put some distance between them. 'While you finish up and pack the basket, I'll speak to the workmen and hitch the horse to the trap.'

'If that is what you desire,' she murmured, turning her face away.

If she only knew what he desired! No—better that she did not. Reluctantly he rose and made himself walk away from her.

Protect his tenants from becoming involved in dangerous mischief indeed, he thought, disgusted with himself. Just the hint that Mrs Merrill might be ripe for kissing and his concern about the disturbing report she'd just given him had gone clean out of his head.

He'd better remind himself again of the reason he was masquerading as his own estate agent. After he'd escorted Mrs Merrill home and stopped by the Anderson farm, he'd go into town and see what he could discover about one Sergeant Russell.

* * *

The sky was darkening and it was not yet dinnertime when Ned pulled up his mount before the Hart and Hare in the village of Hazelwick. The information Mrs Merrill had given him today had spurred him to make immediately the visit he'd been planning for several days.

He'd always found it a wise practice for the estate owner to pay frequent visits to the public house in the villages near his properties. 'Twas here that the country people gathered to lift a tankard of home-brewed, gossip, and glean news about the country roundabout as well from more distant metropolises from the travellers stopping at the coaching inn.

In addition to which, it was the practice of the Society of Spencean Philanthropists to meet in small groups at local public houses. If Hazelwick contained such a group, he might hear something about it during his visit to the Hart and Hare.

As he walked into the taproom, deserted at this early hour before the end of the workday and the arrival of the evening mail coach, he was greeted by the savoury smell of roast and a broad, red-faced man with a shock of sandy hair. Taking the latter to be the proprietor, Ned held out his hand. 'Mr Kirkbride? I'm Ned Greaves, the new estate agent at Blenhem Hill.'

'Jonathan Kirkbride,' the man replied, giving Ned's hand a firm shake. 'Welcome to the Hart and Hare, Mr Greaves! Old Martin told us Lord Englemere had sent out a new manager. The whole business happened so quick, didn't know until two days ago that the former agent had left. Took his foreman with him, too, I understand.'

The girl behind the bar sniffed. 'Good riddance to bad rubbish, that one.'

'Mr Barksdale wasn't much liked hereabouts, I'm hearing,' Ned said.

'Very true,' the innkeeper agreed. 'But Martin is already singing *your* praises, sir. And not just Martin! Tanner said you've engaged him to repair the stonework on several of the cottages at Blenhem—for a very fine wage. Employing carpenters and blacksmiths, too, I hear. Good for the workers hereabout and even better for my business!' Kirkbride declared with a laugh.

'Good for everyone, I would hope,' Ned said, smiling back.

'Sit yourself down, sir,' Kirkbride urged. 'Mary, bring Mr Greaves a mug! Won't you stay and sample my wife Peg's roast? 'Tis not a better cook to be found in the county!'

'Thank you, I should like that,' Ned said. 'Before I take my ease, though, I have an errand to discharge. Mary, isn't it?' he asked, walking over to the barmaid.

Giving him a frankly appraising glance, the girl curtsied. 'Aye, sir, I'm Mary.'

Ned flipped a gold coin on to the bar. 'This is from Mrs Merrill—the new mistress for the school we are establishing. She told me how helpful you were to her the night she came to Hazelwick. To my great regret, there was some confusion about the date of her arrival, else I would have had a gig waiting to meet her. I appreciate your directing her to Blenhem Hill.'

For a moment the girl goggled at the shiny coin before snatching it up and tucking it into her ample cleavage. 'Glad to help. Unlike some—' the barmaid looked over to the innkeeper, whose face reddened '—I knew right away she was a lady.'

'Just heard from Martin you meant to start a school for the tenants. Very sorry I am about the misunderstanding with the mistress!' Kirkbride added quickly. 'Being as I didn't know Mr Anders were gone, and seeing how he had, ah, ladies sent out regular, naturally I thought she was another one of his women. 'Twas an honest mistake.'

'Oh, naturally,' the barmaid muttered. 'Travelling alone, she must be a doxy.'

Giving Mary a sharp glance, the innkeeper said, 'Please

offer the lady—Mrs Merrill, is it?—my apologies and tell her I'll be happy to stand her a mug of ale and a good dinner, next time she comes to the village. Wouldn't want any hard feelings between the Hart and Hare and the household at Blenhem Hill,' he added, obviously impressed by Ned's gold and anxious not to give offence to one capable of such largesse.

'An unfortunate mistake,' Ned agreed.

'Ah, here's my Peg with your dinner. Hope you enjoy it, Mr Greaves.'

'Nice to have your custom, sir,' the innkeeper's wife said, setting a steaming plate of roast and potatoes before him, her face red from the heat of the kitchen. 'There, now, tuck into it.'

'Thank you, ma'am. It smells delicious.'

'You be new to the county, ain't you?' she asked. 'Where d'you hail from?'

'Kent, ma'am.'

'Very good eye for the land, my brother tells me. Tim Johnston, he is. Farms a hundred acres of wheat for Lord Englemere, out past the Redman place. He says you're looking to hire more men to repair cottages and build some new barns.'

'That's right, ma'am. Mr Kirkbride,' Ned said, turning to address the innkeeper, 'I'd be much obliged if you'd let your patrons know that any man who's looking for work can apply at Blenhem Hill. There are a number of farms vacant and I'd like to get more fields under cultivation as soon as possible.'

'Aye, many men left their farms to look for work in the mills in Manchester,' Mrs Kirkbride said. 'Who could blame 'em, what with enclosures gobbling up the common lands and rents going up and up like they was? Don't know as they've fared any better in the city, though.'

'Times are hard,' Ned agreed, choosing his words carefully. 'Makes a man angry, working all day and still being hard put to feed his children.'

'Some be more 'n angry,' she said.

'Now, Peg, leave the man be to eat his dinner,' the innkeeper inserted hastily. 'That's my Peg, talk the ear off a donkey, she would. Just like some of them men. All talk, but we don't want no trouble here like they had at Loughborough.'

Loughborough, outside Manchester, where last summer, Ned recalled, a group of Luddites had attacked Boden's mill, smashing the knitting machines. Troops had been called out, a number of men apprehended and tried. Six had been hanged and three more transported.

'Any likelihood of trouble like that here?' he asked.

The innkeeper gave his wife a sharp glance before saying, 'Men talk, that's all. Ah, there be the squire come in. Peg, best get you back to your kitchen. Excuse me, sir.' With a nod to Ned, the innkeeper hurried off to greet his new customer.

So there was something afoot here, Ned mused, reading between the lines of what the couple had said. At least a group of malcontents meeting to talk. Although, if those who attacked his carriage had been local men, obviously some of them were ready to do more than exchange words.

Several more patrons entered, working men and farmers by their dress, keeping the innkeeper and the barmaid busy with their orders. Ned finished his meal in silence, then took his dishes up to the bar.

'Another mug, Mr Greaves?' Mary asked as she loaded up a tray full of ale.

'Thank you, no. Best be getting back to Blenhem Hill.'

She threw a glance across the room to the innkeeper, who was still waiting on the squire. 'A group meets most every evening,' she said in a murmur almost inaudible under the hubbub of chatter. 'Forbes, Harris, Matthews are the leaders. Don't hire anyone with those names. Hotheads they are, more ready to find a grievance than do an honest day's work.'

'Forbes, Harris and Matthews,' Ned repeated. No mention

of Sergeant Jesse Russell, he noted. 'I'll remember the names. Thank you, Mary.'

'You seem like a decent sort. Generous, too,' she added with a flirtatious look. 'You get lonely some night out at Blenhem Hill, I'd be agreeable to offering you a bit of companionship.' She gave him a wink.

Ah, that it were Mrs Merrill leaning towards him with that come-and-get-me look! Attractive as she was, Mary didn't tempt him at all…unlike a certain auburn-haired, green-eyed school mistress. Stifling a smile, Ned said, 'That's…neighbourly of you, Mary.'

She grinned. 'Be happy to be "neighbourly" to a fine-looking gentleman like you, Mr Greaves. Tell Mrs Merrill I'm glad she made it safely to Blenhem Hill.'

'I'll tell her,' Ned promised. 'For the ale and my dinner,' he said, laying some coins on the bar.

The innkeeper bustled over. 'Nay, Mr Greaves, none of that! Tonight is our welcome to you. By the way, I should introduce you to the squire. Second only to Lord Englemere at Blenhem Hill, he farms more acres than any other property owner in the county.'

'I'd be honoured,' Ned said, always glad to meet a fellow agriculturalist.

He followed Kirkbride to a table at which sat a portly man stylishly appointed in a tight-fitting bottle-green coat over fawn Inexpressibles, his beefy hand curled around a pint of ale as he chatted with a party of friends. Shooting coats tossed negligently over the backs of their chairs and rifles stacked by the entry proclaimed the group must have spent the day hunting.

'Excuse me, Squire Abernathy,' the innkeeper said. 'May I present to you a newcomer in the county? Mr Greaves is Lord Englemere's new agent at Blenhem Hill.'

The squire tossed Ned an indifferent look. 'Greaves.' He acknowledged Ned with a nod before shifting his attention back to the innkeeper. 'Kirkbride, where is that extra mug? Here I've been boasting all day about the excellence of your home-brewed and my friend Haslitt here is about to expire of thirst. And my roast?'

'Indeed, I feel I shall perish,' his friend exclaimed, looking past Ned as if he were a piece of the furniture.

'Right away, sir,' the innkeeper said, bowing low. 'Mary! Where are those mugs?' he called as he hurried off to the kitchen.

'Coming!' The barmaid slipped around Ned, brushing her arm against his as she passed, then bending low over the table as she unloaded her cargo of mugs, giving Ned a wink as she offered him an excellent view of her impressive cleavage.

Ignoring his mug, Haslitt stared bug-eyed at the display, practically salivating. 'If you'd told me there was such a pretty wench here, Abernathy, we'd have put up our guns hours ago.'

'Know just where you want to put up that gun,' another of the friends said, setting all three off into a guffaws of laughter.

'Come, my lovely, have a seat and entertain us,' Haslitt said, trying to pat the barmaid on her bottom.

Evading his hand, she said brightly, 'Sorry, gentlemen, but the room is full. Old Kirkbride will send me packing if I don't keep all the tables served.'

Brushing past Ned again, she murmured, 'Come back again, Mr Greaves. Soon.'

As she trotted off, the squire and his friends resumed their conversation, leaving Ned standing in the middle of the floor. Shock at first held him immobile; never had he been treated so slightingly.

Welcome to the status of farm agent, he told himself, amusement tinged with an edge of dislike replacing his initial surprise. An estate owner who tended his land as he ought, Ned reflected, his opinion of the squire plummeting, cultivated a close working relationship with the managers of all the surrounding properties, regardless of their rank.

'Nice to meet you, too, Squire Abernathy,' he murmured under his breath.

But as he turned to exit the room, he noticed the tall, slim figure of a man standing just inside the entrance to the Hart and Hare. Simply garbed in the frieze coat, breeches and boots of a farmer, his upright stance and squared shoulders announced his former profession as eloquently as the empty sleeve pinned to his breast.

This had to be the sergeant Mrs Merrill had told him about, Ned thought, wondering if he should confront the man directly and introduce himself.

But as he was poised to walk towards the newcomer, he realised Sergeant Russell's gaze wasn't scanning the patrons, searching for a convivial group to join, or observing with curiosity the squire's boisterous table. Instead, his whole attention was riveted on the swaying figure of the barmaid as she wove her way back to the bar.

Of course, Ned thought, suppressing a smile, the amply endowed and friendly Mary was well worth a man's scrutiny. His amusement faded, though, as a look of longing, regret and some darker emotion Ned couldn't identify passed across the Sergeant's unguarded face. With a grimace, he clenched his one thumbless hand into a fist.

Something more than casual lust was at work, Ned felt certain. Was it significant that Mary had not mentioned Russell when she had warned him about the group that met here?

Uncomfortable as he felt about blatantly observing the man, nonetheless Ned made himself sidle behind the squire's table next to the wall where he could unobtrusively watch the Sergeant.

He probably needn't have worried about remaining inconspicuous. Totally oblivious to Ned's scrutiny, Jesse Russell blew out a breath, set his jaw and stomped past the squire's table towards the barmaid.

Mary reached the bar and set down her tray. As she looked back and saw the man approaching, she started, her lips opening in a gasp. For an instant she darted a hand forwards as if in supplication, almost knocking over one of the mugs on her tray, then quickly thrust the hand back at her side. Pain came and went in her eyes before she lifted her chin, a defiant, almost mocking look on her face as she waited for Sergeant Russell.

So the two were definitely acquainted—more than acquainted, by the fierceness of the Sergeant's gaze, though apparently they'd had some sort of lovers' quarrel.

Despite that, was she still involved with the soldier? Was she trying to protect him by not revealing his name as one of the disaffected group who met at the Hart and Hare?

Or was Ned merely making a great nothing out of a simple tiff between a man more enamoured than he should be of a light-virtued lady who did not appreciate his possessiveness?

Nonetheless, still feeling the voyeur, he continued to watch them, though the babble of voices in the public house made it impossible for him to overhear their conversation.

Resting his hand on the bar, the soldier leaned towards her and spoke urgently, his whole body radiating tension. Mary drew back and tossed her head, as if dismissing his words—or warning—then glanced purposefully in Ned's direction.

The look was so unexpected Ned barely had time to swivel his gaze towards the squire's table, as if he were following the ongoing discussion there. Relieved she hadn't caught him spying on them, he continued to watch obliquely, his face angled slightly away from them. Still, he had no trouble reading the anger in the gesture the Sergeant made towards *him* before the man turned back to the barmaid, who seemed to be merely hearing him out, her face impassive.

Had the Sergeant been standing at the doorway long enough to overhear Mary's invitation to him? If so, tonight might not be the best time to introduce himself to a young man who was clearly jealous.

A moment later, Jesse Russell whirled around and stalked away from the bar. With eyes gone suddenly bleak, Mary watched him until he'd thrown himself into a chair.

Trying to ascertain if the Sergeant were also irate over other, more political, matters was a question Ned would be prudent to leave until another occasion. Along with the query about what Mary might—or might not—be concealing about the Sergeant's activities at the Hart and Hare.

And maybe on the road to Blenhem Hill.

That sobering thought in mind, Ned slipped quietly out of the room.

Chapter Eight

⌒⌒⌒⌒⌒⌒⌒

The next morning, Joanna dressed carefully in her best gown, her nerves humming with anticipation. Today she would meet the children who would be her pupils—and even better, Mr Greaves would be her escort for the whole of the morning as he took her about the estate introducing her to the tenants and their offspring.

She wanted to look presentable when she met the people of Blenhem Hill, she told herself as she sat before the glass. But a devilish twinkle in the eye of the woman staring back at her countered that it wasn't the tenants she wished to impress with her intricate crown of braids and form-flattering gown.

With a sigh, she stared sightlessly at the mirror, recalling her interlude with Mr Greaves at the school yesterday. Had she really swayed towards him, mouth lifted, practically begging for his kiss? Heat flushed her cheeks. What had come over her?

Fortunately, after a fraught moment in which he leaned imperceptibly closer, making her heart hammer and her body tremble, greedy with need, he'd abruptly pulled back. Behaviour much more prudent than hers and honourable, too, as it underscored with action rather than just words his contention that he did not trifle with female dependants in his household.

Prudent and honourable he certainly was, but a little glow of purely feminine satisfaction burned within her at the conviction that, refrain from kissing her or not, he had been tempted. She'd read it in the desire that turned his tawny eyes molten, in the rasp of his breath and the abrupt clench of his fingers, in the sudden heat that wafted his scent to her, a compelling mix of shaving soap and virile male.

Which had elicited a matching response from everything female within her. Would it be so awful if they were to dally?

The doctor who had attended her after she had lost Thomas's child predicted sadly that she would probably never conceive another. But it would not be wise to put so much trust in those words that she recklessly embarked upon a potentially scandalous tryst with Mr Greaves.

Goodness, she could scarcely believe she was actually contemplating committing in truth the sin for which, all innocent, she'd recently been ejected into an uncaring world! She should remember the horror and sense of impending disaster that had filled her heart and mind as the driver from Selbourne Abbey deposited her at the dark and silent coaching inn, leaving her without a backward glance like rubbish by the roadside.

The good folk of Blenhem Hill would likely be as adamant as Lady Masters in calling for the immediate dismissal of a schoolmistress whose morals were not what they should be. Should she lose this situation, she was in an even worse position than she'd been two weeks ago, for she had no money at all with which to travel to London—or care for a child, were she to leave with a bastard babe in her belly.

Unless Mr Greaves offered to marry her. That sudden notion for settling her future had a startling appeal. Not only would she be able to indulge the sensual yearnings that afflicted her whenever they were together, she'd already found working with Mr Greaves on his many projects about the estate highly satisfying. She liked learning the intricacies involved in successfully farming a plot of ground. For the first time, she appreciated how great a benefit it was to the tenants to have the skilful direction and concerned assistance of an estate agent of Mr Greaves's expertise.

She'd always enjoyed the sense of being useful she'd felt in running Papa's household and tending her younger sisters; 'twas that feeling of fulfilment as much as necessity that had led her to accept the governess position with Lady Masters. She'd been content caring for the little Masters girls too, before her ignominious exit.

Now that she'd been forced to abandon her hopes of sharing her life with the man she adored, pledging her hand and her loyalty to a man as honourable and attractive as Mr Greaves seemed a sensible and attractive alternative. As schoolmistress, she'd be able to aid him in his work and assist in his many efforts to better the life of the tenants of Blenhem Hill. Be of use not just to a single family, but to the entire community.

She'd forfeit her status as a gentleman's widow, of course, but that position had brought her little but loneliness and the humiliation of being repudiated by the Merrill family, who thought her connections too lowly to be associated with their exalted lineage. Far better, in this parson's daughter's opinion, to be the wife of an honourable man of less exalted birth who performed a more useful service for his fellow man than owning several households, spending summers and autumns on his estate or at his hunting box and indulging himself during the Season in London's clubs, shops and entertainments.

She was sure that given just a little more encouragement, she could entice Mr Greaves to kiss her…and more. But it was a very long leap for a man between the pleasures of a tryst and an eager embrace of the parson's mousetrap.

Honourable as Mr Greaves was, with his firm personal code forbidding the seduction of women in his household, should she tempt him into dalliance, he might well feel compelled to marry her afterwards. Liking and respecting him as she did, she could not deal him so monstrous an injustice as to compel him into matrimony, nor had she the least desire to wed an unwilling partner.

With a sigh she rose from her dressing table. Better instead to tame her unruly desires, discipline her mind and resist Mr Greaves's appeal as effectively as he seemed able to resist hers. Firmly squelching the insistent little voice pleading with her to ponder further how she might seduce Mr Greaves without forcing them both into wedlock, she vowed henceforth to concentrate her thoughts and energy only on the successful establishment of the school.

Goodness knows, having never instructed more than three children at once and then all from the same family, she should devote some serious contemplation to that matter. How was she to teach half a dozen or more active youngsters, all accustomed to spending most of their time outdoors, some probably none too eager to trade the freedom of the fields and kitchen gardens for a hard bench in her schoolroom?

She'd have time enough later, after she mastered that complexity and had refilled her now-empty purse, to decide whether to remain at Blenhem Hill or try to return to her family. Leaving behind both the sense of satisfaction—and the constant temptation—of working for the all-too-alluring Mr Greaves.

Four hours later, Mr Greaves pulled up the gig at the last tumbledown cottage on their tour. They had already called upon some dozen or so families, meeting everything from open resistance to grudging agreement for the children of the household to attend school.

Mr Greaves, Joanna noted, had exhibited a deft touch even with the most reluctant. Rather than arguing with or trying to bully the sceptics, he had first acknowledged their concern at taking children from their chores, then had gone on to explain how schooling would allow them to make even more important contributions. Whether it be totalling the sums due at harvest, keeping household accounts, or reading local journals to discover which towns were paying the best prices at market, off-spring skilled at letters and sums would not learn to think themselves above their stations, but to harness their natural talents to render the whole family more prosperous and successful.

She could only shake her head admiringly at his persua-sive rhetoric as they left each farmhouse having extracted en-thusiastic, or at least grudging, approval for the children within to begin their school careers.

'One last stop,' he told her now, smiling over the reins.

He'd smiled at her often as the day progressed. Every time, a little thrill sparked through her. Despite her stern advice to herself earlier this morning, she couldn't seem to help staring at the dimples a smile created at the corners of his mouth—imagining what it would be like to taste them. Which led to imagining what it would be like for him to taste her...and not just her lips, but all those parts that seemed to have suddenly awakened, whispering of need.

Battling those inappropriate desires once again so dis-tracted her from attending to the rest of his speech that she was surprised when the door to which he led her was opened by a solitary, elderly crone who appeared well past the age of being able to add any pupils to her venture.

'Excuse me,' she murmured. 'What is the name of the lady we are calling on?'

'Dame Cuthbert,' he replied, giving her a concerned look before turning back to greet the old woman. 'Good to see you, too, ma'am. I've stopped by today to introduce Mrs Merrill, the mistress for our new school.'

'Why, Mr Greaves, what a surprise! How kind you be, taking the time to brighten an old lady's afternoon.' She hesitated a moment, throwing a nervous glance over her shoulder before turning back with a tentative smile. 'Well then, come in, the both of ye, and welcome, Mrs Merrill! I've heard tell of the school. What a boon for the neighbourhood, Mr Greaves, letting the children get some learning! If I weren't so old and half-blind, I'd be tempted to go myself. Come to the table and let me pour you some cider,' she said, ushering them to a bench. 'I've bread fresh from the oven, thanks to ye for the flour, Mr Greaves, and some fine butter too.'

'Thank you, ma'am, we'd be delighted to sit for a minute. I fear I've fatigued poor Mrs Merrill, dragging her around to all the farms this morning. I knew you would offer her a welcome that would bring the roses back into her cheeks.'

He must have noticed her inattention as they walked from the gig, when she'd been preoccupied with her fantasies of lovemaking. Feeling her cheeks redden in earnest, Joanna protested, 'Indeed, I am not at all fatigued, but I do appreciate your kind hospitality.'

Thank heavens the burn of her cheeks couldn't reveal the reason for her chagrin!

After halting in the centre of the cottage, staring past them while she gave her head an odd little shake, the old woman continued on to the larder to fetch the cider. 'What Mr Greaves means is, jawing as I do worse 'n a Methodist preacher on Sunday, I'll prob'ly keep ye at table so long, ye'll be frisky as a newborn lamb by the time ye kin get away!' she told Joanna.

''Tis all yer own fault, though, Mr Greaves,' she continued in mock-severe tones, directing a look to Blenhem's manager. 'Encourages me to chatter on whenever he visits, as if he didn't have a thousand other things to be doing! By the way, sir, I thank ye kindly for the ham and jugs of cider you left day afore yesterday. Treats me fine as if I were his own kin!' Biddy Cuthbert pronounced as she sliced bread and set it with a crock of butter before them on the rough wooden table.

By now, Joanna noted with interest, Mr Greaves's face exhibited a blush that extended to his ears. Embarrassed to hear himself praised, was he?

Seizing a chance to try to glean from the talkative old lady more about the manager's activities on behalf of his tenants than that reticent gentleman would probably volunteer on his own, Joanna said, 'So I've been hearing. Sergeant Jesse Russell stopped by the school yesterday to have a letter written and also brought a good report.'

Before Mr Greaves, his flush darkening, could insert a word—and turn the subject, Joanna suspected—true to her claims of loquaciousness, Biddy Cuthbert cut him off. 'Aye, there's much to report!' she exclaimed. 'Now that the thatch is on the schoolhouse, the workmen are coming here tomorrow to do my roof. All the farmers hereabouts has told me the same, how Mr Greaves promised 'em new tools for the fields and carpenters and stonemasons to repair their homes. Not just promised, neither, but already hired the masons.

'Dame Johnston stopped by after he called at their farm yesterday,' she ran on enthusiastically. 'Brought me some of her chicken stew—which you set her on to, I know, Mr Greaves, so don't you try and deny it!—and told me her man was going to Manchester to fetch back her brother to work at the new mill. Mr Greave's promised wages, real money wages, to all that be willing to work there and on the land. He's nothing less than the saviour of Blenhem, and God's truth, how it needed saving!'

Joanna's delight in hearing praise of Mr Greaves diminished as a distressing realisation filtered through Dame Cuthbert's paean. It must have been Greville who'd allowed the situation here to deteriorate. Though the manor house ran smoothly enough, she was admittedly no judge of land management. Just how badly had her brother handled the estate?

Something in her face must have given away her dismay.

After glancing at her, while Biddy Cuthbert paused for breath, Mr Greaves said quickly, 'Blenhem Hill is blessed with good land and industrious tenants. All the property requires is attentive oversight by a man of broad agricultural experience to bring it back to prosperity. Mrs Merrill's efforts at educating the children will be an important part of that effort. With cities and manufactures expanding, they need to be ready to fill a place either on the farm or in industry. Now, Mrs Cuthbert, with a mind as shrewd as yours, perhaps you ought to reconsider your decision not to claim a seat at the school— eh, Mrs Merrill?'

Before replying, Joanna had to swallow a trembling breath, moved as she was by his attempt to excuse the brother she remembered so fondly. Giving him a tremulous smile, she said, 'Indeed! One is never too old to learn. Such joy it brings! I can't tell you, when I was far away in India, how many times a book or poem would trigger fond memories of the parsonage of my youth. Or how I've been enthralled by the glimpses into a foreign world obtained in the pages of a travel journal.'

'Granny, I want to go to school too!' called an eager voice from the dimness behind them at the corner of Biddy Cuthbert's cottage.

Startled, Joanna looked over her shoulder to see a young boy pushing aside a homespun curtain that divided a sleeping space off from the rest of the room. 'I know you warned me to stay hidden,' he addressed the old woman as he walked towards them, 'in case the master come after me, but he won't never stir this far outta Manchester. Old Barksdale's gone, so he can't send me back. I kin do all the work I promised when ye took me in and go to school, too. Can I please come, ma'am?'

Halting before Joanna, fervour shining in his eyes, he continued, 'I wanna be able to read. I wanna know if the preacher be right when he quotes from the Bible of a Sunday. I wanna know all about them foreign lands. Gonna sail to 'em some day and make my fortune, like Mr Jones at the cotton mill,' he pronounced as the old woman hurried towards him.

Grabbing his thin wrists, she pulled him behind her and placed her frail body in front of his. 'Davie, I told ye to stay back there and hold yer tongue,' she scolded before turning appealing eyes to Mr Greaves. 'You won't send him back, will you, sir? He's hardly more'n child hisself! And a useful lad. I'd swear on the preacher's good book he never done nobody wrong, no matter what Mr Barksdale claimed!'

She gestured urgently towards the table and larder. 'You kin take back all ye brung me and never bring no more, but please don't send the boy back!'

After moving protectively towards Joanna the moment the boy emerged, having apparently decided the child posed no threat, Greaves halted a pace away. 'Please, Mrs Cuthbert, you mustn't be upset,' he said in soothing tones. 'I'd never send away any kin of yours.'

The old woman swayed on her feet, looking as if she might collapse. 'Oh, bless you, Mr Greaves, bless you!' she cried before dissolving into tears.

Instantly interpreting the frantic glance Mr Greaves sent her, Joanna stepped over to support the lady, curious to note that the otherwise supremely competent Mr Greaves seemed undone at the prospect of handling a weeping women.

'There now, calm yourself, Mrs Cuthbert,' she said soothingly, patting the old woman's narrow back. 'Come back to the table and take a sip of this good cider. Of course Mr Greaves would not harm a child!'

In the meantime, the lad about whom this little tempest had broken stood his ground, hands on his narrow hips as he regarded Mr Greaves defiantly. More child than young man, but so thin it was difficult to judge his age, Joanna guessed he might be anywhere from ten to fifteen years old. Despite his dearth of years, he had a strength about him, along with a fine-boned, determined face that might turn out to be handsome with a bit more growth and some flesh on it. Some indefinable something in his stalwart stance—the angle of chin, the line of his shoulder—suddenly reminded her so forcibly of her Thomas, she ached to draw the boy into her arms.

'Don't you worry, Granny,' he told the old lady. 'I ain't goin' back, and he can't make me.' Turning to the manager, he said flatly, 'I mean to stay and help Granny like I promised, and go to that lady's school if she'll let me. Lessen ye call the magistrates to haul me away, I'm stayin' right here.'

Apparently more comfortable addressing a hostile youth than a sobbing old woman, Mr Greaves simply nodded at lad. 'Davie, isn't it? Why don't we sit down and discuss it?'

Warily, as if he expected that any moment Greaves might jump him and try to drag him away, Davie pulled a stool towards the table. After waving off Joanna's offer of cider, he sat, his eyes never leaving the older man's.

While Biddy Cuthbert's sobs dwindled to sniffles, Mr Greaves said, 'Please tell me from the beginning, Davie. Under what circumstances did you leave Blenhem and how did you come to return?'

The boy made a derisive noise. 'Didn't exactly "leave", mister. Old Barksdale knocked me over the head and carried me off. Next thing I knowed, I woke up in the middle of this blinding noise of a cotton mill in Manchester, Jeffreys standin' over me with a whip. Told me Barksdale had sold me and now I belonged to him.'

'Barksdale…sold you?' Mr Greaves repeated incredulously.

'Mr Barksdale told us he caught Davie stealing his watch, that he brung him afore the magistrate, who sent him to Manchester,' Biddy Cuthbert inserted. 'But we none of us believed it. Davie were always a feisty lad,' she allowed, giving the boy a fond smile, 'but he weren't no thief. Once he growed bigger, he stopped payin' much attention to Barksdale. Stood up to 'im, mocked 'im, even. But I didn't know 'til he snuck back here last night what really happened.'

'Didn't your family protest when you were taken away?' Joanna asked, appalled by the narrative.

The boy shrugged. 'Ain't got no family. After Pa died, we couldn't pay the rent on the farm, so Barksdale turned us out. Ma went to Lunnon to find my sister, who run off with a soldier a few years back. I didn't want to go to the city, so I stayed, doin' odd jobs in town and hereabouts.'

'Did you steal Barksdale's watch?' Mr Greaves asked.

'If'n I'd stole his ticker, would I be fool enough to wait around and let him catch me?' Davie said scornfully. 'I'd a scarpered off to sell it, fast as a hare with a garden carrot. But I didn't steal nothin'. I just got big enough that I didn't let his threats worry me no more and, coward as he was, he couldn't abide it. So he ambushed me one night and took me to the mills. I vowed soon's I come to, even afore I tasted Master Jeffrey's lash, that I'd get outta there and come back to Blenhem.'

'Your master beat you with a whip?' Joanna asked, more horrified still.

Davie gave her a grin that in a few more years promised heartbreak to susceptible female hearts. 'Oh, the beatings weren't so bad, nothing much more than I'd got from old Barksdale and my da, too, afore he passed on. It were the mills theyselfs.'

His face sobered abruptly. 'You can't imagine the noise, ma'am, a clanging and a clatter like to drive a body mad. Workin' from the barest glimmer of daylight 'til 'tis so dark you can't see yer fingers afore yer face. Breathin' dust and fluff and the stench of bleach instead of clean country air. Though 'twas the littlest had it the worst.'

He shook his head, his eyes taking on a faraway look. 'They was made to climb under the big power looms, gathering up thread bits or lost spindles. Saw a boy get his fingers caught once. Smashed his whole hand thin as a flat-iron afore he could hardly scream. Then his ma got two weeks' pay docked for him getting his blood on the cloth they was weaving.'

For a moment the boy's lips trembled and tears glazed his eyes. 'I couldn't do nothin' but watch,' he continued, his voice still rough. 'Not for him nor for any of the other lads. But I promised right then 'n there while he bled to death under that loom that I'd get outta of that mill, get some schooling and go make myself a fortune. Some day, when I'm rich enough, I'll go to Lunnon and tell the toffs in Parliament itself that it ain't right. And I'll make 'em change it.'

For a moment after the boy's impassioned voice faded away, none of them said a word. Beside her, Biddy Cuthbert wept quietly and Joanna had to hold back tears of outrage and sympathy herself.

First the soldier tossed aside, and now this! Truly, what was England coming to, that children could be abducted, made to work in vile, dangerous places, and no one made a move to stop it?

Shaken, touched, appalled, Joanna wanted to gather the boy in her arms—but a look at that proud young face, so old and determined for its years, told her the boy wouldn't welcome an embrace. How she wished she could bring him back to the manor and care for him!

'So you returned here, to the only place you knew,' Mr Greaves said quietly.

The boy nodded. 'Heard in the village that old Barksdale be gone, so thought I'd see if I could help out Granny for a while. Much better here in the countryside—kin always find a squirrel or a rabbit—' he gave the old lady a wink '—for Granny's stew pot.'

'Can't you leave him stay with me, Mr Greaves?' Biddy Cuthbert asked. 'Like he told ye, he's got no kin and times being like they is, not many be willing to take in an extra mouth. I haven't much to offer, but with a snug new roof on the place, 'twill be better for him to sleep here than in them ruined cottages, like he's been doing.'

'I kin help 'er, too, chopping wood for the stove and finding vittles. I'm right handy with a slingshot,' Davie added.

To Joanna's and doubtless the old lady's relief, the manager nodded. 'You mustn't worry, Mrs Cuthbert. Barksdale had no right to send the boy away and 'tis certainly illegal to "sell" him to a mill foreman. However, young man, if you wish to achieve those lofty ambitions, you'd best not let the gamekeeper catch you snaring something larger than a rabbit or a squirrel out of these woods, for poaching is an offence for which you could be transported. Though you should help Mrs Cuthbert, a lad of your years needs more than that to keep him out of mischief. But what?' Tapping his chin, Mr Greaves gazed at Davie thoughtfully.

'Sometimes the groom at the Hart and Hare lets me muck out the stables.' Turning to Joanna, he said, 'That's where I seen the letter you writ for Jesse Russell. I wanna write like that, making all them pretty curvy lines and dots that somebody miles away kin understand. You think I could?'

Even if he hadn't reminded her of Thomas, loving learning as she did, how could she resist the appeal of a child with such a hunger for knowledge? 'Without doubt. Mr Greaves, Davie's occupations must surely include his attending the school.'

The manager nodded. 'Yes, Davie, for you must master writing and sums as well as reading, if you hope to become a man knowledgeable enough to influence others. You should also help Mrs Cuthbert as you promised, since a man intending to lead must demonstrate he can discharge his own responsibilities. Mr Martin has been a great help to me, but he's getting on in years. Having an assistant who possesses his intimate knowledge of the farms and the people here could be a great use. If you can demonstrate over the next month that you are such a man, I'll pay you two shillings a week.'

Mr Greaves stood and held out his hand. 'Do we have a bargain, Mr…?'

The boy leapt to his feet, almost knocking over the stool. 'David Smith, sir!' he cried, seizing the agent's hand and shaking it enthusiastically. 'A bargain, indeed, sir.'

Dame Cuthbert's eyes threatened to overflow again. 'Ye'll ne'er regret taking a chance on Davie, sir!'

Hastily Mr Greaves waved a hand. 'No more tears or I shall have to withdraw my offer! Mrs Merrill, have you finished your cider? We must be on our way if I'm to drop you by the manor and get planting started at the Radnor place before dark.'

'Yes, I'm ready,' Joanna said, surreptitiously wiping a tear from her own eye as she started to gather up the mugs. The solution Mr Greaves had devised for Davie was as fitting as the one he'd devised for her—and far more than she'd dared hope to obtain for an orphaned boy with neither wealth nor kin. How compassionate and perceptive Mr Greaves was!

Which, alas, only increased her desire to kiss him.

Chapter Nine

While Joanna reflected upon that intriguing but complicating reaction, Dame Cuthbert and Davie walked them to the cottage door.

'Should I meet you at the manor tomorrow morning?' he asked Mr Greaves.

The manager nodded. 'Right after you've built up Dame Cuthbert's fire and helped her break her fast.'

'Mr Greaves, I'd be honoured if ye'd call me "Granny", like everyone hereabouts. For sure, though ye be from Kent, no kin coulda treated us kinder!'

Once again a blush coloured Mr Greaves's cheeks. 'The honour is mine…Granny. Davie, I'll see you in the morning. Mrs Merrill?' He gestured towards the door.

After expressing her thanks for the old woman's hospitality and exchanging goodbyes, Joanna accepted Mr Greaves's hand up into the gig. Savouring the feel of his strong fingers linked with hers, she held on, she had to admit, a few seconds longer than absolutely necessary.

Not that he seemed to object. In fact, he stood motionless beside the gig, clutching her hand and looking up into her eyes so intently, her breath caught.

Before she could succumb to the urging of her treacherous body and lean her mouth towards his, the horses stirred, recalling him to his task.

Just as well, she thought as he climbed into the gig, for driven as she was for a physical taste of him, taking that first step would irreversibly change the relationship between them. It might well lead to the intimacy she craved. But there was also a strong possibility that, by tempting him to abandon the high principles he'd avowed, her forwardness might make him retreat, spoiling the closeness and camaraderie that had developed between them. She wasn't yet ready to risk losing the morning and evening chats that had become the most enjoyable parts of her day.

Contenting herself with relishing the warmth of him as he settled beside her on the narrow bench, determinedly she fixed her thoughts back on the activities of the day. A glow filled her heart as she recalled all the eager young children she'd met and their hard-working, plain-spoken parents.

How much she and Mr Greaves had accomplished together! With the school building nearly complete, she'd soon be able to lead those bright young faces into the world of learning. And the unusual, exceptional Davie Smith.

'Your offer to employ Davie was as kind as it was generous,' she said, turning to look up at him.

'He seems to have a quick mind and a strong sense of purpose, just requiring someone with a firm hand to send him in the proper direction. I'm betting he will excel at assisting me.'

'Granny Cuthbert believes so,' she replied. 'Could the master at the mill in Manchester really track him down and force him to return?'

'With the hardships in the countryside, so many poor families have crowded into the cities that replacing him will probably be too easy, as Davie said, for the foreman to trouble himself looking for one runaway. Certainly Barksdale couldn't "sell" him—that claim was probably meant to scare Davie out of running off—but if Barksdale did in fact contact the local authorities about Davie's alleged misconduct, the boy might have been turned over to the parish. Those in charge of the poor rolls might have sent him out to the mills to earn his keep.'

'But that's dreadful!' Joanna cried, distressed as she recalled the vivid scene Davie had painted of the mill. 'You heard him describe the conditions!'

Mr Greaves nodded soberly. 'True. But farm work isn't without its risks, either, the parish officer would tell you. While men of influence in Parliament would probably allege that workers, by voluntarily accepting employment at the mills, also accept the risks, and that it isn't the business of government to intervene in what is a private matter between employer and employee.'

'"Voluntarily" accept the risks?' she replied scornfully. ''Tis work begun no more "voluntarily" than Davie's if someone with an empty belly and no other prospects of filling it takes such a position. Have, as Davie called them, the "toffs" in Parliament never considered that fact? Do the Lord Masters of the world not recognise they derive their power from the land—land that could be seized from them, if they push people beyond what they can bear?'

A shudder passed through her as she recalled her midnight walk through the rain to Blenhem Hill. Truly, she would have taken whatever honest employment was available to escape the fate Lady Masters predicted for her, had she not found sanctuary within. Despite her horror of bloodshed, even she might have come to the point of supporting a cause that proposed to strip power from those who abused it as Lord Masters had.

Mr Greaves gave her a quiet, penetrating look, as if he could guess the tenor of her thoughts. 'I don't know if the Lords have considered it, but if they haven't, at some point they must.' He smiled again, obviously trying to reassure her. 'Hopefully, they will do so well before Davie has grown old enough to confront them.'

As always, his smile distracted her. More—worse—than that, his ready understanding of her concerns and his prompt, efficacious response to the plight of that orphaned child made her want to throw her arms around him and thank him with all her heart for his sterling example of Christian charity.

Of course, if she were to embrace him, after an instant of feeling his warm breath on her neck, his body pressed to hers, the gratitude of her heart would swiftly be swamped by the desires of her body. She smothered a sigh of mingled longing and regret.

His smile broadened. 'Disappointed that I did not carry the boy off with us? I half-expected you would insist that I clothe and house him at Blenhem Hill.'

Had her compulsion to care for the child been that evident? 'Not at all,' she replied mendaciously, feeling heat warm her face. 'I haven't the right to demand such a thing, even if I wanted to. Although I would surely have violently opposed it had you suggested the boy be sent back to Manchester! But your plan for his future seems as fitting as it is benevolent.'

'He was certainly intelligent enough to immediately demand that schooling with you be a part of that future! Not that I was surprised. You possess a special rapport with children, from the littlest begging for a hug to the older ones who initially seemed to think they were too knowledgeable and experienced to be going to school.'

Though she shrugged, knowing he was probably only trying to encourage her for the formidable task ahead, she could not help feeling a rush of gratification. Perhaps, as she fervently hoped, she would be able to meet everyone's daunting expectations and make a success of the school. 'You are too kind,' she murmured.

'Not at all—merely reporting what I observed this morning. Once the doors are open, I'd wager every youngster you met would sneak away from their chores and find their way to the schoolhouse, had their elders not approved their attendance. Since such rampant disobedience would have earned them quick punishment, 'tis lucky I was able to induce the parents to permit it.'

'You've quite a persuasive tongue yourself, sir! I believe you could have talked the parents into letting their children follow you wherever you led, the Pied Piper of Blenhem Hill. You've already demonstrated so much expertise on behalf of and concern for the people of the county, perhaps you ought to petition Lord Englemere to let you stand for Parliament. Certainly, from my observation, the peerage desperately needs a lesson in the proper use of the privileges they acquired at birth—from your friend the Marquess on down the ranks!'

An odd expression passed over his face before he said, 'I've no political ambitions. Like you, my concerns lie closer at hand. I can see why your father turned over to you the management of his house and the training of your sisters, for you've excelled both at preparing the school—and charming its future pupils. It must have been a sorrow that your late husband didn't leave you any children of your own.'

A stab of pain lanced through her heart, so unexpectedly sharp it robbed her of breath. Damnation, she thought she'd made good progress in banishing the anguish and regret! Yet his casual remark recalled it as fiercely as if the double loss had occurred a month instead of nearly two years ago.

In the silence while she tried to master her emotions, he turned his attention from the horses to cast her a glance. Consternation in his voice, he said quickly, 'Excuse me for broaching so private a matter! But you've spoken about your family and the Masters children with such warmth that—I'm sorry, I never meant to upset you.'

She made herself summon up a smile. 'I shall be all right in a moment. It's just…Davie reminded me of my late husband and the…the babe I lost, born three months before his time. 'Twas to help me recover my health afterwards that Thomas insisted I leave India and return home.'

Her smile turned wry. 'Capricious aristocrats again! I might have recovered faster, I believe, had my family rejoined me in England as expected when Thomas persuaded me to go. But the Earl who'd long promised Papa a living after the incumbent retired chose at the last moment to appoint someone else. So all my close kin remained in India and I was left to grieve alone in London.'

Embarrassed as she suddenly realised how self-pitying her explanation might seem, she exclaimed, 'Heavens, what a poor helpless soul I make myself appear!' Thrusting away the bitter memories, she said briskly, 'I've done well enough, everything considered. I do love children, which is why I accepted the governess's post. Perhaps 'tis also why I was so quick to agree to launch a school, a project on a scale beyond anything I've ever yet attempted.'

The compassion he'd shown for Davie gleamed now in his eyes. 'You are a lovely, accomplished young woman, Mrs Merrill, and you will be a brilliant schoolmistress. But unless the gentlemen from Blenhem Hill to London are blind and dumb, surely you can look forward to marrying again and having children of your own to delight you.'

A wicked little thrill licked at her nerves at the thought of how those children would be created. She recalled the times, lying wakeful in her solitary bed, she had thought about him lying in his own just down the hall. She burned anew with the vision of how he might respond, were she to tiptoe to his room late some night…

Did his eyes glow with ardour now, or was it merely her own desire that made her think so?

And in predicting marriage in her future, did he include himself among the discerning gentlemen who might appreciate her? Or was he only resorting to gallantry to distract her from the distressing memories he'd inadvertently roused?

Probably the latter, she thought, her excitement dimming. Ruthlessly reigning in her imagination, even as she appreciated his efforts, she replied at last, 'Prettily said, and I thank you for the compliment. But for the moment, I shall concentrate on getting the school established and doing what I can to assist the pupils—especially Davie.'

Talk then turned to the supplies she needed to gather for the school's opening and all too soon, they arrived back at Blenhem Hill manor. After helping her down from the gig— ah, how the mere touch of his hand on her arm sparked the fantasies again!—he tipped his hat and drove off.

Thoughtfully she watched the gig until it disappeared down the drive. The glow of their morning together—and the heat of her agitated senses—warmed her still.

Already his suggestions, comments and assistance had been enormous. Conferring with him as they established the school was going to be as much of a joy as the previous evenings had been, when they'd sat late before the fire while she spun tales of India and they discussed every topic under the sun.

Despite her efforts to suppress it, his remark about her eventual remarriage wriggled to the forefront of her memory. Dare she hope he might indeed some day see her as more than just a companionable colleague and fellow employee of the estate?

View her instead as a passionate woman with whom he wanted to share his future—and his bed?

How wonderful that would be! Restraining the sudden urge to whoop with glee, she lifted her skirts and danced up the steps to the manor.

She paused before entering the building, breathing deeply of clean country air—and the faint scent of shaving soap that still lingered on the shoulder of her gown where Mr Greaves's coat had rubbed against it during their drive. Truly, on such a glorious day it was hard to keep her imagination from soaring as high and bright as the clouds in the beautiful blue Blenhem Hill sky.

After setting Mrs Merrill down at the front door, Ned drove off, his thoughts in a turmoil. What demon had possessed his mind and tongue during that episode at Granny Cuthbert's and again during the drive to the manor?

He should have stayed silent and let her register the full import of her brother's responsibility for the dire state of Blenhem Hill as revealed by Biddy Cuthbert's impassioned remark. Such a realisation would move her closer to acquitting Nicky—and all gentlemen of rank, he hoped, still feeling guilty about listening without protest to her condemnation of the peerage—of the venality engendered by her own experiences and her resentment over her brother's supposedly unfair treatment. It might also, he hoped fervently, make her more forgiving of his deception when he was at last able to reveal his true identity.

But unable to bear the wounded look in her eyes as her quick intellect swiftly discerned the indictment of her brother implicit in the old woman's statement, he'd felt compelled to soften it. It was true that though service in Wellington's commissary department must have given Greville Anders experience at handling goods, Ned's observation and the testimony of the tenants revealed the man knew nothing about farming. That did not, however, excuse the man's negligence or compliance in tolerating the abuses and neglect inflicted upon the estate and its tenants by his Army associate Barksdale, whose venality had apparently been equalled only by his greed.

Then again during their drive, from where had those comments about marriage come tumbling out? Tumbling her, he certainly wanted to do, and had from the first. For a moment, a swell of longing escaped his rigid attempt to control it.

Admittedly worthless at handling agitated women, he should just have kept his mouth shut after blurting that ill-judged remark about her late husband. Except…he was honoured that, though he'd obviously upset her, rather than chastise him, she'd taken him into her confidence about the extent of her loss.

He thought of Nicky's son Aubrey and how devastated both his friend and Sarah would be if anything were to happen to their precious child. Indeed, loving the lad as he did, a pang of alarm and anguish squeezed his own heart at the possibility, and he was only a fond uncle. He couldn't imagine the heartache of burying a babe lost just on the verge of viability. Small wonder her husband had insisted she leave a place renowned for its dangerous fevers and recover elsewhere. Though it turned out to have left her in London alone, the man's intention had been to look after his wife's welfare, as a husband should.

Husband…a role he had contemplated twice in the last few years. Was it time to cast off the caution he'd been trying to maintain and risk his heart again? Certainly he was eager to bed the beauteous Mrs Merrill, but his feelings for her were far deeper than simple lust. With her stories, her inquiries, her amusing commentary, she'd made his evenings come alive. He rose energised every morning at the thought of seeing her at breakfast, spending part of each day working with her, knowing that she seemed to appreciate and support his dream of a Blenhem revived.

Why not marry her? He liked her tremendously. Though she'd initially known nothing about farming, she was a quick learner, having made several astute observations just this morning about the fields and farms past which they'd travelled. She'd be an excellent partner, skilled at running a house, a school, a nursery.

A vivid image flashed into his mind: the small stone Romanesque church in Hazelwick decked in late-summer blooms… Children from the Blenhem school tossing the petals of mums and late damask roses along the pathway as Mrs Merrill walked beside him to meet the parson at the altar… Repeating the ancient vows, sharing a joyous bridal feast with the villagers and tenants… Nicky, Sarah, Hal and his other friends and family raising toasts to them before he took his lovely bride away…

Why not marry her and carry her to bed, as he ached to do every night he tossed and turned against his pillow, his needy body afire for the lady who slumbered unknowing in her chamber just a few rooms from his?

She was no innocent, but a widow who'd shared love and borne a child. Who recognised the heat between them for what it was—and several times, had almost acted upon it. He pictured her again at the school, her bow of a mouth lifted towards his, the fingers resting on his sparking sensual fire to every nerve.

He saw *her*: that lush mouth set in a pouting smile, her green eyes smouldering, slowly pulling a silk night rail over her head. Leaning back against the pillows, arms extended, body displayed, her unbound hair spilling over the pillows in a ripple of flame. Igniting to a conflagration the desire always simmering within him, beckoning him to plunder, please and enjoy…

He caught his breath, almost dizzy with need.

A shout jolted him from his heated imagining. Looking about in befuddlement, he realised he'd reached the Radnor Farm. Banishing the vivid images with difficulty, he dragged his thoughts back to the present and returned Jake Radnor's wave of greeting.

But before he set his mind back to the affairs of the moment, one conclusion emerged. He'd never thought himself a coward and he didn't intend to play one now. Regardless of the risk to his heart, once he solved the mystery of the attack on his carriage and resolved the matter of the Spencean group meeting at the Hart and Hare, he would declare his intentions and energetically pursue the entrancing Mrs Merrill.

Chapter Ten

⁓⁓⁓

As the sun slanted to afternoon ten days later, Joanna surveyed with satisfaction the inside of a building that had almost completed the transformation from ruined stone cottage to schoolhouse. The carpenters had completed several rows of student desks and benches and a tall stand for her at the head of the room. To one side, a wooden partition screened off a small alcove behind which she could store supplies and personal items.

The masons had built upon the stone foundation to create new walls over the original wattle-and-daub, adding two windows on the entry side that flooded the room with light. Before he had left this afternoon, Mr Tanner had told her that, save for a small portion of wall behind the screen, for which he needed rock of a different size to fill in over the original foundation, the dwelling was finished and ready for her to welcome students.

Ready to begin! A little quiver of anticipation and trepidation rippled down her spine. Soon she would discover if her preparations had been sufficient and the community's confidence in her justified. How ardently she wished for the school to be a success!

She yearned to open the eyes of these children to the world beyond their fields and farms, to continue devoting her talent and energy to so deserving an enterprise. And, she had to admit, she wanted just as ardently to earn the approval of Mr Greaves.

She wanted to justify his decision to hire her, as unexpected as it was compassionate. She wanted this tireless worker and an expert in his field to consider her a dedicated and skilled practitioner in hers.

Most important, she wanted Ned Greaves to believe her worthy of his time, his admiration—and his affection.

Edward, his name was, the butler had told her. A noble name, one handed down through lines of kings.

Would it ever be linked with hers?

The way she longed, every time they drove about the estate together, to link her fingers with his? The way she yearned, in the secret reaches of night, to mingle and join their arms, limbs and hearts?

A shadow fell over her, startling her out of the rising flood of imagining. A man stood in the doorway, tipping his hat. 'Good afternoon, ma'am.'

'Good afternoon to you to, sir,' she said, offering a curtsy. 'May I help you?'

'I certainly hope so,' the stranger said, smiling as he walked into the room.

Of medium height, with a face that was pleasant but not remarkable, he wore the jacket, breeches, boots and modest cravat of a country gentleman. Joanna didn't recognise him from her Sunday attendance at church, the only time she mixed with neighbours not residents at Blenhem Hill, but perhaps not all the gentry attended regularly. Or perhaps he wasn't from this county at all.

Though he'd given her no reason to feel uneasy, suddenly she was very conscious of the fact that the workmen had departed and she was alone with him, far from the nearest farmhand or cottage dweller. Unconsciously she took a step backwards.

'What can I do for you, sir?' she asked guardedly.

'I heard you were establishing a school. I hope your good efforts come to fruition, though I'm afraid the tenants hereabouts aren't a very ambitious or industrious group. Set in their ways and resistant to change, even when it's good for them! But I didn't stop by to discuss that. You are Mrs Joanna Merrill, aren't you?'

When she nodded agreement, he continued, 'George Hampton here, ma'am. Pleased to meet you! I happen also to have the pleasure of knowing your brother. An excellent, hospitable, upstanding young gentleman!'

Her heart lit at this glimmer of a link with family. 'You know Greville?'

'Indeed, I can claim that honour. Your brother was my convivial host for several gatherings at Blenhem Hill. 'Twas a terrible injustice, what happened to him, by the way. I imagine you were quite distressed when you arrived to find him gone.'

Though she was no longer so sure that her brother's firing had been an injustice, to the latter part of his statement she could agree with perfect truth. 'Indeed, I was most distraught. You're a friend of his, you say? Would you happen to know his current direction?'

She flushed, embarrassed to admit that his own sister had no idea where her brother was. 'In the…agitation of the moment, we lost touch.'

Mr Hampton shook his head regretfully. 'I'm sorry, I do not. Indeed, I stopped by hoping that you might know, that I might contact him myself. He departed in such haste, I hadn't the opportunity to see him before he left and discover whether he had yet obtained a new situation. If not, I had some possibilities to suggest. Gentleman should help friends in need, don't you think?'

She could only applaud that sentiment. 'How very good of you! I'm sure my brother appreciates having such a loyal friend.'

'You might do something for him, too, you know. If you wished.'

'I might?' she asked, instantly anxious to make a difference. 'What could that be, pray? Of course I'm eager to help Greville in any way I can!'

'What happened to your brother is only a symptom of what's wrong in this county—and every other. Men like Lord Englemere holding all the power, free to trample over others who ought to be considered as worthy as they are, just because they work with their hands in the fields and factories. Men who actually produce the goods that enrich their landlords, yet have no say in the running of their own government! Well, the time is coming very soon when such aristocrats will pay for their arrogance.'

Alarmed at Mr Hampton's increasingly strident tone, Joanna opened her mouth to protest. Mr Hampton waved her to silence.

'I know you'll say there's not much a mere woman can do, even one as intelligent and resourceful as you, Mrs Merrill. But you're wrong. Women in several counties have stood beside their men in opposing injustice. You could avenge the humiliation of your brother's discharge—and help the common folk of the county at the same time.'

Abruptly abandoning his speaker's-platform tone, he focused his piercing gaze on her, raking her with a blatantly appraising glance from bonnet to boots. 'A lady of your skill and beauty could do far better than wasting her talents on a crude country school…allied with a gentleman who knows how to appreciate her.'

Her uneasy feeling intensified into the same sense of threat she'd felt when confronted by Lord Masters. Taking another step backwards, she said, 'If you mean to subvert the law, I fear the result would only be greater harm to common folk. Powerful men would not yield their power easily, choosing instead to bring down the full and severest penalties obtainable from the government—and fearsome they are!—upon those who oppose them.'

Mr Hampton laughed. 'Only if the reformers are stupid enough to get caught.' He gave her another of those appraising looks. 'A man clever enough to merit a woman like you would take care to avoid…unpleasant repercussions. But if breaking a few arbitrary and unjust statues goes against the grain, you could serve in…other ways.'

The same type of hot, leering look she had received all too often from Lord Masters settled over Mr Hampton's countenance as he gazed at her. Pulses flashing an alarm, Joanna resisted an instinctive desire to rush past him out of the room.

Striving to keep her expression neutral and her voice even, she said, 'I appreciate your…fervour on behalf of the common folk, but I really don't think I can help your cause.'

To her huge relief, he halted the sensual appraisal as abruptly as he'd begun it. 'No?' he asked, raising a sceptical eyebrow. 'There will be big doings afoot soon, I guarantee you. Why don't you recall what happened to Greville, and think on it?'

Praise heaven, he then put his hat back on and bowed. 'Good day to you, then, Mrs Merrill. Perhaps I'll call again later.'

'Good day, Mr Hampton,' she replied, wrapping her hands around her chest in an unconsciously protective gesture as, thankfully, he strolled out of the door—as nonchalantly as if he'd not just tried to incite her to law-breaking and perhaps more!

She heard the wicker of his horse, then the clop of hooves as he set off down the lane. A violent shudder shook her frame and she found her knees suddenly too weak to support her.

She staggered to one of the student benches and sat down heavily, her pulse still racing.

Was this man involved in the Spencean group Mr Greaves had warned her about? He certainly talked the part of a radical reformer. And he was a friend of Greville's? Had Greville been involved in this dangerous thinking as well? Had he neglected his tasks and espoused an uncertain ideology of reform?

Frowning, she recalled her brother had sometimes in their youth remarked how unfair it was that their distant cousin Nicky was to become a Marquess, while Papa was just a minor son of gentry who had to work at a living, as his son would after him.

Mr Hampton had spoken with the fervour and eloquence of a committed advocate—perhaps even a leader of a local group. Mr Greaves would doubtless want to know everything she could recall about him. Not until after the sounds of the horse faded into the distance did she realise she probably should have walked to the doorway and watched him ride away, so she might have also been able to provide a description of his mount.

Another shiver passed through her. He'd had such an unsettling effect on her, she wasn't sure she could have made herself go and stand in the doorway, where he might have been able to glance back and subject her to another blatantly sensual scrutiny. Nor had she any desire for him to catch her watching him, as if she were interested in his proposal—or in him.

Trying to shake off a lingering unease, she rose and walked there now, berating herself for cowardice when she had to peep out of the doorway to be certain Mr Hampton had really ridden out of sight before she could make herself cross the threshold into the afternoon sunshine.

She might as well return to the manor for the day. She'd done all she could here; slates, chalk and counters were stored in the alcove, primers she'd ordered from London set up on the shelves in easy reach. Her school now needed only pupils.

From her place in the nearby meadow where Joanna had

tethered her, the mare Mr Greaves had provided for her use nickered a greeting. Apparently the mare was eager to get home to her barn as well.

Joanna gave a wistful sigh. 'Twas too early for Mr Greaves to have finished his day's work and come riding by on his own way back to the manor. She'd have to content herself to returning home without his escort. After all, she couldn't expect him to rearrange his duties every day so he might be available to accompany her to and from the schoolhouse.

Even if they eventually married.

A little thrill rippled through her as she fell back into the pleasant daydreams Mr Hampton's visit had interrupted. How eager she'd be for the day's work to end and the night to begin, should they marry! Knowing what was to come, she'd hold herself in delicious anticipation all through the afternoon, bide her time during the evening meal by watching his mouth, the movement of his throat as he swallowed, the play of his tongue as he ate. Contemplating other ways in which he might use that tongue and those lips, while she plied her own to taste his mouth and nuzzle the pulse at the base of that throat, thrilling to feel it gallop with need as fiercely as her own…

She was sighing at that image when her newly reactivated sense of danger warned her someone else was approaching.

The momentary jolt of panic eased when she recognised the man's limping gait. Returning Sergeant Jesse Russell's wave of greeting, she waited for him to reach the schoolhouse step.

The soldier smiled as he made her a bow. 'Good afternoon, ma'am. I didn't expect to have to beg your good services again so soon, but here I am. If it would be convenient?' He angled his head, looking around. 'I see the workmen have left. If you are ready to head home, I can return—'

'No, it's all right, Sergeant,' she interrupted. 'You've brought your supplies—' she indicated the saddlebag over his good shoulder '—which is fortunate, since as of yet I have only slates and chalk here. But the benches and tables are complete, and there's light aplenty to illumine them. Won't you come take a look? The carpenters and stonemasons have outdone themselves.' With justifiable pride, she led him inside.

Sergeant Russell gazed around the room, his eyes widening before he nodded an approval. 'A fine job indeed! Looks far more hospitable than the schoolroom where I was educated in Nottingham. Hard benches, a few oil candles as smoky as they were dim, cold, windowless stone walls—and a stack of switches in the corner, which the master used regularly!'

Joanna felt a momentary qualm. 'I certainly hope I shan't need any of those!'

'I don't expect you will,' Sergeant Russell replied. 'All the children I've encountered hereabouts are excited to begin— though their enthusiasm at escaping their chores may wane when they discover that school means work, too. Except for Davie Smith. There's a lad of drive and ambition who seems mad for learning. I hear Mr Greaves has taken him on as an assistant.'

'Yes, but he shall be released from some of his duties to attend school. He does seem particularly eager, and he's certainly apt.'

The soldier nodded. 'With his youth, a sound body and spirit, and the assistance of a man with such exalted connections as Ned Greaves, he should make something of himself.' He gave a wry grimace. 'He'll probably never need the sort of assistance to which those less able must resort.'

In Davie Smith he probably saw himself, Joanna thought, before the war and circumstances had mangled his body and stunted his dreams. Oh, that the Sergeant might once again believe that he was so much more! 'One of the benefits of learning, as you must know, is realising a man's true worth lies not in strength of body, but in the breadth of his mind and the fullness of his heart.'

He gave her a sad little smile that made her chest ache. 'Would that the world saw it that way, ma'am. But I do thank you for the encouragement.'

Hoping she'd cheered him at least a little, Joanna accepted the saddlebag he offered. 'With what can I help you today?'

The smile faded altogether. 'Lord Evers declined my request for a loan. I don't much like the prospect, but I've an army friend, wounded like me, who told me while we recovered that if I encountered problems in the future, to contact him. He claimed his father had extensive holdings and might offer me a leasehold.'

The soldier sighed. 'I don't want to farm, but I might convince the father to extend me a loan instead of the lease. After my sojourn in Hazelwick, I'm more than ever determined to emigrate. There's nothing left here. I might as well cease fighting the fact—and tormenting myself with what can never be.' He gave her a lopsided grin. 'Not really fair to blame a girl for not wanting a crippled, useless old soldier, no matter what promises she made him before the war.'

So the Sergeant had come back to some local sweetheart, only to be rejected because of his injuries? With outrage and the empathy of one who knew what it was to be heart-wounded, she cried, 'Nonsense! You may be at a standstill for the moment, but with your education and intelligence, you will find another position, perhaps even a better one!'

'Oh, I shall come about, one way or another,' he declared. 'Forgive me for sounding so down-hearted. It's just…when a man loves a girl, he wants to be able to offer her everything— the strength of a sound body as well as a full heart, and all the bright future he promised when she pledged him her faith. Whether or not she honoured that pledge,' he added bitterly, staring into the distance.

A moment later, he snapped his attention back to Joanna. 'She made her choice, and it wasn't me. Hard as that is to accept, it's time I settled that into my head and moved on.' His bitter tone abruptly lightening, he gave her a rueful smile. 'Though a lady does have a way of invading a man's mind and heart such that it's awfully difficult to pry her out and feel whole again.'

Her thoughts went immediately to Thomas—and her heart twisted. 'I protest, Sergeant! My sex is not alone in the ability to invade and bruise hearts—or cause a grief from which it is very difficult to recover.'

A ready sympathy sprang into his eyes. 'Forgive me for prosing on about my disappointment when your loss of a loyal husband must cut far deeper than my regret over a faithless jade. Well, distasteful as I find it, shall we do that letter?'

Nodding, she set out the supplies on the table, then scribed carefully as he narrated, though her attention kept straying to the sad business of the lady who had disappointed him. After he'd packed up his supplies, thanked her and they'd exchanged goodbyes, she couldn't help adding, 'The love of a wise, loyal, honest man is a priceless thing, Sergeant. Whoever the young lady was, she was a very great fool to let you go. I pray you will find another more worthy of you.'

He gave her another sad smile. 'Thank you, ma'am. I hope someday you'll find another good man, too.'

I already have, a little voice in her heart said—if he wants me.

After a wave goodbye, she stood in the doorway and watched as Sergeant Russell walked back in the direction of the village. Her lingering sadness veered abruptly to a sense of joy when, coming from the opposite direction, she spotted the approach of a familiar gig.

Perhaps Mr Greaves was driving by after all!

Chapter Eleven

Ned's heart lightened as, his new assistant Davie at his side, he directed the gig down the lane towards the schoolhouse, returning a wave of greeting from Sergeant Russell as they passed. He really should have put in a few more hours at Miller Farm, but when Tanner the stonemason told him as he drove his cart by Miller's field that all the workmen at the school had finished for the day, he hadn't been able to resist the temptation to halt long enough to escort Mrs Merrill home.

The gig rounded the bend and he saw her, framed in the doorway of the school. The copper glow of her hair and the brilliance of her smile seemed to capture the warmth of the sun itself, stealing his breath and making his body ache with need and gladness.

'I hadn't expected to see you,' she said as she walked over to greet them. 'Are you travelling towards the manor?'

'Yes, I thought we would swing by and accompany you home before I drive Davie back to Granny Cuthbert's.'

'Mr Tanner said the school be nearly done,' David said.

'Yes, it is.' No doubt noting the excited look on the boy's face, she said, 'Would you like to take a look?'

He nodded eagerly. 'If'n I might, ma'am.' After a nod of approval from Ned, he scrambled from the gig.

She gestured to the door. 'Please, go in. Select a seat, if you wish.' After waving the boy past, she glanced back to Ned. 'Have a look yourself, Mr Greaves.'

He smiled back. 'Perhaps I will.'

She followed Davie back towards the entrance while Ned alighted and secured the gig. His spirits quickened as he went to join her, every sense springing to the alert at the prospect of being near her.

Struggling to keep his thoughts focused on the boy, Ned stopped beside her on the threshold. 'He can't wait to begin,' Ned said, watching Davie wander about, wonderment on his face as he traced a reverent hand over the smooth surfaces of the benches and desks.

'So Sergeant Russell said,' she replied. 'Instructing him will be a joy.'

Abruptly recalling they had just passed the soldier on the road, Ned felt a sharp stab of what felt uncomfortably like jealousy. Had the Sergeant tarried here, alone with Mrs Merrill?

'You've spoken to Russell recently?' he asked, trying to keep an unwonted irritation from his tone.

'A few minutes ago. He wished me to write another letter for him.' Her bright look dimmed to a frown. 'Unfortunately, it appears the gentleman who was to employ him has declined to offer any other assistance, so he is forced to look for another source of funds. He is still set on emigrating…' She paused, then shook her head with a little sigh. 'Though his family resides in Nottingham, apparently he returned to Hazelwick seeking his former sweetheart, who either decided not to wait for him, or rejected him after he returned wounded. Oh, to add that emotional pain on top of his physical losses! How badly I feel for him!'

Ned recalled the scene at the Hart and Hare. Could the barmaid Mary have been Russell's former love?

Admittedly Ned understood women about as well as a tailor knows ploughing, but he would have guessed a girl would prefer marriage to an educated man with good prospects like the Sergeant—regardless of his political views— to the questionable security of the path Mary now trod.

But perhaps he was mistaken, and the Sergeant's faithless love was another girl entirely.

He emerged from his contemplation to find Mrs Merrill studying him hopefully. 'You've been able to do so much for the rest of Blenhem Hill's people. Might there be among your acquaintance, or that of your employer, someone who could find a position for a soldier who has served his country as faithfully, and paid for that service as dearly, as Sergeant Russell?'

Ned supposed it was a positive sign that she'd even considered having him solicit his 'employer' on the soldier's behalf. Still, if the Sergeant were deeply involved in Spencean planning, he might well be counting on emigration as a possible escape, should a plot gone awry throw him into the hands of the authorities.

Nicky wouldn't thank him for embroiling him in the affairs of such a man, though Ned had as yet nothing but a handful of words to indicate the Sergeant might in fact be a radical. Besides, if the soldier were a potential agitator, better to export him to the Americas and let him work his mischief there.

All rational reasoning aside, when the lovely Mrs Merrill stared at him with that look of appeal in her moss-green eyes, seeming to exude confidence in his ability to successfully resolve the situation, how could he refuse?

'I'll see what I can do,' he said at last.

With a radiant smile, she clasped his elbow, sending little shivers of delight up his arm and down his body to settle in his loins. 'Thank you. I knew you couldn't simply stand by and watch such an injustice.'

Ned wasn't sure about that, but he did know he could stand *here* forever, breathing in her exotic spicy scent, eyelids fluttering shut in rapture at the feel of her fingers against his arm, while the sweet torture of her nearness set his loins aflame. He swallowed hard, his pulse pounding at the effort necessary to curb the nearly overwhelming need to draw her into his arms.

Just then Davie bounded towards them. To Ned's mingled relief and regret, Mrs Merrill released his arm and stepped away.

'It's wonderful, ma'am! A whole sight better'n a big dark room full of clacking, clanking looms! Kin I sit right here?' He pointed to the desk in the front row beside the window.

'Of course. If Mr Greaves agrees, we shall open the school the first day of next week.'

'So soon?' Ned replied, a bit surprised the workman had progressed that far. 'I can see the carpenters have finished, but I understood from Tanner that the stonework wasn't yet complete.'

'There's just a bit left, for which Mr Tanner is obtaining the rock. Truly, there is so little still to do that they all abandoned me early this afternoon.'

A slight shadow passed over her face. 'Though I did have one…unusual caller, whom I felt sure you would want to know about.'

The troubled look cleared the last vestiges of sensual fog from his brain. 'Tell me, then,' he urged, now completely on the alert.

'A Mr George Hampton stopped by, saying he was a friend of my brother. Are either of you acquainted with him?'

Ned shook his head, while Davie said, 'Ain't never been anyone hereabouts by that name.'

'He said he'd often been a guest at Blenhem Hill when Greville was the manager, and expressed his concern over what he thought was the…shabby way my brother had been treated.

He said he'd sought me out hoping I might know Greville's current direction, as he had some situations in mind for him.'

'Often had parties of gents from Lunnon at the manor,' Davie confirmed. 'Females, too, though they weren't—' At a sharp look from Ned, the boy halted abruptly, his face flushing.

'Quite gentlemanly of Mr Hampton to enquire about your brother's welfare,' Ned inserted smoothly. 'But, forgive me if I'm misreading this—' he cast another look at her still-troubled face '—you seem somewhat distressed after his visit.'

Her eyes widening in surprise, she replied, 'How perspicacious, Mr Greaves! Indeed, I am. You see, after expressing his solicitude for my brother, Mr Hampton went on to espouse quite radical sentiments about the inequity of the aristocracy holding land and power, then professed a scornful disregard for the consequences visited upon those who break the law. You mentioned earlier that there might be a group of Spenceans in the area. I haven't any experience with the sort, but from my observation of military men, combining as he did the look of a gentleman with a decided eloquence of speech, Mr Hampton appeared more likely to be the leader of such a group than a follower.'

She gave a nervous laugh. 'Trying to play on my sympathies for my brother, he even tried to recruit me.'

Excitement and urgency stirred Ned's hunter's instincts to full cry. Might this mysterious stranger be the man who had orchestrated the attack on his carriage, who directed—or at least encouraged—the meetings of the disaffected local workers at the Hart and Hare?

'Did Mr Hampton say where he was from?' he asked.

'No, though from his words and accent he didn't appear to be local. More London-bred, I would think.'

'Can you describe him?'

'Not in a way that would be of much assistance. Medium height and build, nothing notable about his face, clothing such as any country gentleman might wear. And forgive me, I neglected to get a look at his horse, so…unsettled did he make me.'

Something in her tone and expression penetrated his urgency to discover more about Hampton's political connections, arousing his deepest protective instincts. 'Did he *threaten* you about joining his cause?'

'Not…exactly.' She cast a look at Davie, her face flushing. 'He just made me…uncomfortable.'

He'd made advances, Ned realised at once, his desire to find and confront Hampton intensifying to a rage. Mrs Merrill obviously didn't want to provide any further details in front of young Davie, but if this miscreant had laid so much as a single rabble-rousing finger on her slender arm, Ned was ready to tear his throat out.

When the sudden haze of anger in his brain settled, he found Davie frowning. 'Not right for a gentleman to threaten a female. 'Specially not a lady like you, ma'am. Don't you worry none, though. Blenhem Hill don't get many strangers. If he lingers hereabouts, someone will notice, and we'll take care of him.'

By querying the group that met at the Hart and Hare? Davie, who sometimes mucked out stables there, might know more about such a group. After giving the boy a look that implied they would discuss the matter further out of Mrs Merrill's hearing, Ned said, 'We will indeed. Until the matter is settled, however, if you are planning to work again at the building before the pupils arrive, I should feel better having Davie accompany you.'

For an instant, she frowned and made as if to reply, then halted, her eyes darkening with a look that might be disappointment. Would she prefer it to be him, rather than Davie, who stayed near to safeguard her, though she'd not wound the boy's feelings by saying so? he wondered hopefully. Or had lust and longing made him read into her expression a meaning that wasn't there?

She gave them a rueful smile. 'It's hen-hearted of me, I know, but I must admit, I would feel easier about completing my work here if I had an escort. At least until the mysterious Mr Hampton is run to ground.'

As if to verify his suspicions, she turned her attention to Davie. 'Accompanied by a young gentleman who stood up to a villain like Mr Barksdale, I shall feel quite safe.'

Davie stood a little straighter, puffing out his chest. 'Mean snake of a man, Barksdale. More'n chousin' folks out of their rents, he liked for 'em to be afraid of him.' He grinned. 'Which was why he had no use for me.'

'And why he had to ambush you at night,' she replied.

'But I'm on my guard now. Seen folks just like Barksdale in the mills. Bully always backs down if a body stands up to him.'

As Davie pronounced that truth, Ned's attention was caught by the sound of hoofbeats. Turning towards the road, he saw one of the mill workers riding up at a gallop.

'Mr Greaves, come quick,' the man shouted as he slowed his mount to a trot. 'There be a fire at the stocking mill!'

Chapter Twelve

Dread curdled in Ned's gut, banishing all other worries. Though the mill walls were stone, in a wooden-beamed, thatch-roofed building whose floors under the looms would, by this time on a work day, be covered by a fine snow of cotton fluff, a fire could spread swiftly. If that were not bad enough, stored all around were spools of cotton thread, boxes of finished goods ready to be sent to market and the looms themselves, skeletons of wood bound in a spider's web of warp and woof, all fuel to feed, fan and spread the flames.

'Get the fire wagon from the village!' Ned commanded the rider, who'd slowed rather than pulled up his horse.

'On my way, sir!' the man replied and spurred his mount.

While the horseman galloped off, Ned turned to Davie and Mrs Merrill. Before he could utter a word, with a look she curtailed the instructions he'd been about to issue Davie to take her back to the safety of the manor. 'Give me but a moment to fetch the medicine chest,' she said as she hastened into the schoolhouse. 'How glad I am now that I made one for the school, rather than relying on borrowing Mrs Winston's from the manor!'

He was left with nothing to add but a superfluous 'Hurry'

before heading over to ready the gig. An instant later, she returned with the wooden box and handed it to Davie while Ned helped her up, then jumped in beside her to spring the horse.

'I know you were working to refurbish the mill,' she said as they jolted down the road at a breakneck pace. 'Were there any workers within?'

Grimly he pictured the eight looms on each floor—fully manned for the first time only this week. 'If all the operators were at their stations, there might have been as many as sixteen.' Those on the ground floor should have been able to exit quickly, but if the fire had been sudden, those on the first…

Images flamed through his mind, so horrific he decided to try again to spare her. 'After years of farming, I'm a dab hand at tending the sick. I'd feel much better, Mrs Merrill, if you'd let Davie drop me off and drive you to the manor.'

'And abandon the workmen in such a desperate moment?' she asked. 'Unthinkable!' Hands gripping the rails to maintain her balance in the lurching gig, she threw him a sideways glance. 'Mr Greaves, though I appreciate your concern, I've been a soldier's wife in an often hostile land. I've witnessed— and treated—wounds I'd rather not describe and probably have more experience than you at dealing with the injured…fervently as I am praying that such skill will not be necessary.'

'Amen,' Davie muttered.

'Very well,' Ned capitulated, knowing she was correct, despite his desire to save her sensibilities. 'I shall be very grateful for your help.'

After that brief exchange, they fell silent, all preoccupied, Ned assumed, by the same urgent questions that assailed him: Had all the workers got out? Were any seriously burned? Would there be anything salvageable left of the mill?

Recalling accounts of factory fires he'd read about—and the aftermaths he'd witnessed—Ned tightened his jaw and applied the whip.

Even the grim imaginings crowding his thoughts during that frantic transit couldn't completely him distract from appreciating the sparks of a different sort produced each time Mrs Merrill's body bumped and rubbed against his in the necessarily close quarters of the gig. All too soon, however, the acrid smell of smoke dislodged from his nostrils the spicy scent of her perfume. And as they neared the mill, they could see flames licking the sky above the tree line, while the sound of the fire increased to a greedy roar that drowned out the pounding of hoofs.

The scene when they arrived was as bad as he'd envisioned. The lower level of the mill was engulfed in a conflagration that totally obscured the first storey. Wooden floors, frames and roofs succumbed to the flames in an explosion of cracks and hisses that provided a macabre accompaniment to the fire's roar.

He pulled up the gig and jumped out, then helped Mrs Merrill, who collected her medicine chest. Even here, more than a hundred feet away, the fire's heat was staggering.

Mill workers and men from the nearby farms had already formed a bucket brigade, drawing water from the well in the courtyard and handing it forwards to try to douse the flames, though the heat of the fire made it impossible to approach close enough for their efforts to have much effect. With the billowing smoke obscuring vision and the confused mass of people running about, as neighbours summoned by the passing rider continued to arrive, Ned couldn't tell whether there was anyone injured.

He recognised the man at the well, hauling up full buckets to pass down the line, as the farmer whose fields he'd just tended. 'Mr Miller,' he called, hurrying towards him, 'did all the workmen get out?'

'Don't know for sure, sir,' the farmer said. 'The fire come up so quick, Perkins, who works the loom by the front door, told me the whole top storey was alight before those below knew what had happened. Young Tanner be working the loom upstairs at the far back. When we couldn't account for him after his da got here a few minutes ago, weren't nobody could keep Tanner from going in to try to find him.'

Glancing back at the building aflame, Ned's breath seized in his lungs. Praise the Lord in heaven, if the two men didn't get out of there within seconds, they'd be doomed. But even as that realisation formed, in a gap between the flames near the front door flickered the image of a man stooped low, dragging someone behind him.

If they could just get out before the wooden frame collapsed...

In a single swift movement, Ned grabbed the bucket from Miller's hands and dumped it over himself, then stripped off his soaked jacket and threw it over his head and shoulders as a shield. Setting off at a run, he headed for a stone shed beside the entrance where he'd stored one of the new fire-extinguishing machines his contraption-mad friend Hal had sent him.

George Manby's invention might provide him enough water to douse down the entryway so the men could escape— if the compressed air that made it work held its pressure. Sending another prayer to the Almighty that it would and that he could buy the men within enough time to get out, Ned activated the device and headed towards the door.

After wetting down the flaming doorframe, he sprayed the last of his water over Tanner's face and shoulders, then threw the device down and helped the coughing stonemason drag his inert son out of the building. Several of the bucket-handlers, having doused themselves like Ned, ran to help, while over the noise of the fire Ned heard the distant sound of church bells, announcing the departure of the fire wagon and summoning the villagers to come and assist.

He was coughing himself by the time they deposited their

burden near the safety of the well. Ned staggered upright to find Mrs Merrill at his side.

'Are you uninjured?' she asked, sounding as calm and composed as if they were sitting to dinner at the manor rather than standing near a raging conflagration. When, still unable to speak, he nodded, she immediately turned to Tanner and his son.

'Sit, please, Mr Tanner,' she said, indicating a spot beside the young man. 'Your hands and face are heat-blistered. Have you any other injuries? If not, after I tend your son, I will cleanse them and apply a salve.'

Attempting to reply, the older man produced only another fit of coughing before pointing to his offspring. Nodding, Mrs Merrill knelt in the dirt beside the young man and made a swift inspection. 'I don't find any burns more serious than your own,' she told his father. 'His heartbeat is strong and steady and his breathing not overly laboured. Once the fresh air clears his lungs, I believe he will come back to himself.'

Having offered the father as much reassurance as she could, Mrs Merrill began washing away the soot and grit covering the young man's face and hands.

Throwing another glance at the burning building, Ned shook his head. 'With the flames and heat so intense, I cannot imagine how you managed it,' he croaked to Tanner, finally finding his voice, 'Praise the good Lord that you were able to get him out.'

'Praise…heaven indeed,' the stonemason replied between coughs, his own voice smoke-roughened. 'Praise too…that the walls…be good stone…and the stairs…some distance from the flames.'

Clapping the man on the shoulder, Ned turned to Perkins, the millworker who'd provided the first account of the blaze, who had trotted over to see about young Tanner.

'Is everyone out now?' Ned asked.

'Aye, sir, all accounted for.'

Looking back at the burning structure and realising there was little that he or the bucket brigade could do before the arrival of the fire wagon—and probably not much even then, he thought grimly, surveying the flames now soaring twenty feet beyond the rooftop—Ned turned his attention to the one useful task he could do.

Discover as much as possible about the fire.

'Mr Perkins, can you tell me how the fire started?'

'Don't really know, Mr Greaves. Those of us downstairs was attending to our weaving when Fuller and Bixby come pelting down the stairs, shouting about fire. Seemed like the roof above our heads went ablaze nearly as they spoke. Thought Tanner was right behind them…but by the time anyone realised he weren't out, 'twas near impossible to go back in.'

Perkins looked over at the grime-besmirched father. 'Sorry, sir. We'd a gone right back up for him, if'n we'd known he were still there. But…'twas so confused, smoke everywhere and everyone shouting—'

Tanner reached out a grimy hand to pat Perkins's arm. 'Understand,' he croaked.

'Powerful brave of you to go in after him,' Perkins said. 'Powerful brave of you, too, Mr Greaves,' he added.

Ned felt his already-reddened face warm with a heat that had nothing to do with the fire. Anxious to continue his enquiries, he waved off their praise and continued, 'The flames came on suddenly, you said? What do you think started it?'

Perkins shrugged. 'Don't rightly know, but Fuller might.' He beckoned to a tall man Ned recognised as the most experienced of the weavers.

Fuller left the group of bucket-wielders who, recognising as Ned had that their efforts were futile for the moment, now stood simply watching the flames. 'Wish I could tell you how,' he said, responding to Ned's repeated query, 'but it seemed I just looked up and it were everywhere.'

'Might a spark have exploded out of the fireplace and set the dust under a loom afire?' Ned asked.

'Not under mine, nor any near me. We be careful about sweeping beneath them looms and putting the screen back every time the fire's stoked. It seemed to come through the roof beams, though I admit, I didn't stop to wonder on it, just lit out fast as I could with the flames chasing at our heels.' Fuller frowned and shook his head. 'Not 'til just now, talking with Bixby, did we think it odd that it come up so sudden, and from above.'

At that moment, the unconscious young man whose burns Mrs Merrill was tending jerked to alertness and began coughing. His father leaping to assist her, Mrs Merrill helped him to a sitting position, while Bixby hurried to fetch him a drink of water.

After thirstily downing the water between bouts of coughing, the boy waved away the cup. 'Fire started…right in front of me… Roof just fell…already aburning…like flames come…out of the sky. Trapped me…behind the loom.'

Before Ned had time to mull over the implications of young Tanner's description, in a clanging of bells and thunder of hoofs, the fire wagon arrived.

Abandoning the Tanners to Mrs Merrill's competent care, Ned raced over, the other workers following him. Before the vehicle had come to a halt, they had the pumping machine unloaded, while others began rapidly filling buckets to dump into the holding container. Ned helped the men wheel the device as close as he dared to the burning building, then grabbed one of the pump handles while a second man took the one opposite and others manned the pedals.

Frantically he forced the lever up and down, doing his part to spray gushes of water upwards on to the burning building. Though the water covered the front wall and a part of the roof, Ned feared the stream wouldn't reach far enough to extinguish the flames on the back wall.

Determined to save whatever he could, however, he renewed his efforts, waving away a worker who would have relieved him. Soon sweat soaked his body, his muscles burned and all he could taste or smell was smoke.

As he continued the dogged but, he knew in his bones, ultimately doomed quest to salvage the building, anger and despair warred in his mind.

Fire did not fall out of the sky. Had the mill been set ablaze deliberately?

Suddenly he remembered the man who had harangued Mrs Merrill just before he and Davie had arrived. Was it only a coincidence that a stranger mouthing radical rhetoric had accosted her just a short time before the mill went up in flames?

Had 'Mr Hampton' been responsible? But how could anyone be devious and uncaring enough to deliberately spark a blaze that had injured—and might well have killed—innocent workers?

Fuller interrupted his thoughts with an offer to take his place. When Ned, compelled to continue doing as much as he could to combat the blaze, refused him, Fuller said quietly, 'A real shame, Mr Greaves. You just got all the equipment in place and the men back to work—and now this. Blazing like it is, be lucky to save anything.'

That comment needing no answer, Ned kept to his work.

Finally, a timeless agony of aching muscles and frenzied effort later, with the well nearly dry and the flames reduced to an occasional crackle amid a steaming, smoking ruin, Ned and the other grimy, exhausted bucket handlers abandoned their efforts. Stoically Ned strolled over to survey the wreckage.

The stone walls still stood and through the smoky haze, he could see charred hunks of framing from the floor and roof that had collapsed into the first storey. But even though it was still too hot to approach close enough for a thorough assessment, he knew that the weaving frames themselves, along with all the supplies and the finished goods awaiting transit, were a total loss.

Five weeks of hard labour and a sizeable capital investment, lost in an hour.

Too numb and weary to ponder the repercussions now, Ned turned his back and went to check on the injured. The only blessing in this catastrophe, he reflected, was that thanks to the bravery of the elder John Tanner, no precious life had been lost.

The first thing he saw as he made his way through the crowd of people to the makeshift aid station was Mrs Merrill, kneeling beside a man on an improvised stretcher. Speaking in a low, soothing voice, she gently washed soot and blood from a wound over the man's ear. Several other fire fighters who'd sustained burns, scrapes or bruises sat next to the Tanners, sipping water with bandaged hands.

Mrs Merrill's gown was muddy at the hem and liberally besmirched with dirt and soot, the straw of her bonnet had disappeared beneath a coating of fallen ash, and several strands of copper hair had escaped her braids to curl like feathers of flame across her soot-streaked cheek. But to Ned, she had never looked lovelier.

People responded to her calming touch. Already she'd made herself valuable within the Blenhem Hill community, her efforts on their behalf accepted with respect and gratitude. A glow of affection and pride in her, in himself for his part in having the wisdom to keep her here, lightened the gloomy depths of his fatigue.

She could be just as useful and valuable as chatelaine of his other properties, applying that competent, soothing touch to quell his ache of need and quench the flames of desire as skilfully as she was succouring the injured.

Hanging on to that bright thought to counter the bleakness struggling to swamp his spirits, he went to kneel beside her.

'How can I help?'

She turned to smile at him and a jolt of connection zinged between them. As he had at the schoolhouse, he was suddenly overwhelmed by the compulsion to pull her into his arms—this time out of a need for comfort as well as from desire.

She returned some answer about having enough assistants to fetch water, his frazzled wits barely registering her words as he struggled to submerge his craving. How long could his steadily crumbling control resist that ever-more-powerful need?

He shook his head, trying to refocus on the present. 'How do all your patients?'

'No severe burns, thank goodness. A few cuts from falling timbers and one of the weavers turned his ankle while escaping the blaze. The Tanners' injuries are more serious, but if they do not develop a contagion of the lungs from the smoke, I believe they will both recover. This salve will do for their burns now, but if Mrs Winston doesn't have carron oil in her medicine box, I must make some up, and obtain some silver nitrate from the apothecary in the village to continue their treatment.'

She glanced over at the father and son, both reclining exhausted and pinch-faced against the side of a wagon. 'Some laudanum for pain wouldn't come amiss, either.'

'I'll send to town and make sure you have all the supplies you need.'

'Are you all right?' she asked, angling her head to inspect him. 'You've a cut over your eye.'

Ned didn't remember sustaining the injury. Now that she had called his attention to it, though, he realised his forehead did sting, a minor discomfort compared to battling the heat of the inferno.

''Tis nothing,' he assured her.

'Nonetheless, it should be tended. Let me cleanse it for you.'

Ned barely restrained a gasp as she leaned forwards to touch his face. Even through the smoke stench that clung to all of them, he still caught just a hint of her perfume. After a slight detour to make his heart lurch, the scent went straight to his loins, intensifying once again the longing he'd been trying to subdue.

Despite his soggy, filthy garments, their position kneeling on muddy ground and the crowd all around them, Ned ached to place a kiss on the sweet curve of a mouth hovering so close to his own.

Fortunately for his sanity and her reputation, a farmer emerged from the milling crowd and dropped to a crouch beside them, forcing Ned's attention away from the intoxication of Mrs Merrill.

'Mr Greaves, you know yet how the fire started?' Miller asked.

Before he could frame a cautious answer, Jim Meadows, who worked the first-floor loom nearest the stairs, joined them. 'I was going to the well when it started. Went out of a building that had not a puff of smoke nor the scent of a spark anywhere, and when I looked over after pulling up a bucketful of water, the whole roof were ablaze.'

A weaver's wife, engaged in offering water to the wounded, halted her task to say, 'I was walking up to bring Fred his dinner. Out of nothing, the roof just went covered with flame, like Meadows said.'

Fire didn't fall from the sky—nor did roofs on buildings suddenly burst into flame. Ned's conviction that someone had deliberately set the mill fire strengthened, along with his determination to ferret out the truth and punish whoever was responsible.

By now, a small knot of people had gathered around them. 'I was driving Da's gig to the village,' one of the farm boys piped up. 'Passed a man on horseback, riding hard in the other direction, just before Bixby run out shouting about fire.'

The crowd stirred and rustled, the mutterings growing in

volume as the news spread. Exclamations of surprise and outrage began to punctuate the rumble, while Miller exclaimed, anger in his tone, 'Begins to sound like this weren't no accident!'

Davie appeared beside Ned, his dark eyes anxious. 'Why would a body try to hurt people like that?'

'Maybe someone didn't want the mill here to succeed,' Fuller, the head weaver answered. 'Someone who didn't want us getting a chance to earn a living here instead of having to go off to some big factory in Manchester.'

'Someone, perhaps, who didn't want the folks of Blenhem Hill to believe in a better future—so he might more easily persuade them to abandon their principles and break the law,' Ned added. Probably among the crowd here, which now included most of the villagers and nearby farmers, would be some of the disaffected men who'd been meeting at the Hart and Hare. Hopefully they would carry his words back to their fellows—and their leader.

'That "someone" be a very bad man,' Davie pronounced.

While nodding at Davie, Ned happened to look straight into the eyes of Jesse Russell, who held his gaze for a brief moment before turning away.

The soldier had left the school building right before the mysterious Mr Hampton. Yet despite his suspicions about Russell, Ned just couldn't believe a man who had offered his life in defence of his country would stoop to putting the lives of innocent people in danger, regardless of his political aims.

Still, he thought, his heart made heavy by the realisation, though Jesse Russell had obviously been on hand to help fight the fire, Ned would have to investigate the soldier's possible involvement in starting it as well.

Ned's first instinct, though, was to get his hands on the ersatz 'gentleman' Mr Hampton and question him about his whereabouts before the fire—among other things, he added silently, recalling his certainty that the man had made unwanted advances towards Mrs Merrill.

But for the moment, he and the rest of Blenhem Hill had done all they could here.

'Friends and neighbours,' Ned said, raising his voice to reach to the outskirts of the crowd, 'thank you for your efforts today. I'll want to talk to many of you later as I try to determine the cause of the fire. Rest assured, if it was deliberately set, the perpetrators will be found, tried and punished. No one in this country will be allowed to destroy property and endanger lives without suffering the severest consequences of the law.'

Pausing, Ned scanned the crowd until his gaze locked with that of Jesse Russell. The soldier, his expression hard, returned a barely perceptible nod.

His hopes bolstered that perhaps the Sergeant wasn't involved after all, Ned continued, 'It will take a day or so for the ashes to cool before we can assess the damage, so those of you who work here, take an extra day's rest. But keep your eyes and ears open. If any of you hear or see anything you think might be connected to this tragedy, please come and see me.'

Amid nods and murmurs of agreement, the crowd began to disperse. Wearily Ned helped the men load the water pumper back on its wagon and then set about arranging transport home for the wounded.

Chapter Thirteen

⚬⚬⚬⚬⚬

An hour later, the courtyard was nearly deserted. In the last of the fading daylight, Ned paced around the perimeter of the smoking building, halting in the back.

A stand of trees guarding the rear of the structure would have made it easy for a man to approach unseen from that direction. With a little advance preparation the night before—sifting gunpowder into the thatch or dousing it with lamp oil—someone might have been able to set the roof alight by the simple means of climbing a tree and tossing a flaming brand onto it.

If someone *had* set the fire, the heat of the blaze, intense enough to have scorched the limbs nearest the building, would have burned away any trace of gunpowder or oil the perpetrator might have spilled during his preparations. Despite Ned's bold words to the crowd, without eyewitness testimony, it would be almost impossible to prove someone had committed arson.

Even so, he'd ask young Tanner if he remembered smelling the scent of lamp oil.

Sighing in frustration, Ned returned to the gig. After giving the smouldering ruin one final glance, he helped Mrs Merrill up beside Davie, took his own seat and directed the horse towards Biddy Cuthbert's cottage.

They dropped the boy off, remaining a short while to give the anxious old lady an account of the day's events, then resumed the drive back to Blenhem Hill.

With the boy safely home, for the first time since he'd raced the gig to the burning mill, Ned had nothing to do but contemplate those events. Perhaps Mrs Merrill was thinking about them as well, for she too remained silent, the only sound during their drive the rhythmic clop of the horse's hoofs. Not even her beguiling presence beside him could distract Ned from dwelling on the catastrophic results of the fire's devastation.

Deciding, after inspecting Nicky's half-finished mill soon after his arrival, to complete the project, Ned had written to Hal asking about the latest safety devices available. Along with Manby's fire extinguisher, Hal had recommended he purchase a firefighting machine for the building, or at least have the village fire wagon fitted with a coupling that would permit the attachment of leather-covered hoses. The hoses would allow firefighters to precisely direct pumped water into and around the building, rather than just spraying it from the machine towards the roof. But with his supply of ready coin running low, he'd not yet ordered either an additional machine or the hoses.

Had a firefighting pump been available to the weavers as soon as the blaze broke out, might they have been able to prevent young Tanner's injuries, extinguish the flames—or at least prevent the building from becoming the total loss he feared it was?

He'd already spent just about all the ready cash he possessed to buy seed, farm tools and supplies, finish the stocking mill and provide wages for the workers. Where was he to obtain the capital to begin over again? What were the weavers and their families to do until the mill could be reopened?

Maybe he could apply to Nicky for a loan.

Ned smiled grimly. He'd been so confident when he offered to buy Blenhem that he could perform miracles here. Trust the good Lord to humble a man who got too sure of himself.

Well, miracles might be beyond him, but there was still much good he could do. Ned was damned if he'd let an evil man bent on destruction deter him from his twin goals of providing hope and employment for the people of Blenhem and restoring its land to prosperity.

Whatever the cost.

Darkness had fallen by the time they reached the manor. Handing off the gig's reins to the groom who trotted up, Ned assisted Mrs Merrill to alight.

The sensual pull between them that his sombre thoughts had suppressed immediately intensified, jolting him with a sizzle of sensation when he clasped her hand.

Drawing a sharp breath, he marvelled anew at the power of her effect on him. Though he was discouraged and bone-weary, he needed only the briefest of touches to spark his simmering desire to a boil.

But after kneeling from afternoon into evening in the dirt, Mrs Merrill was nearly as filthy and probably just as exhausted as Ned. 'You must be longing for a hot bath and some rest,' he said as they walked up the steps into the manor. 'Shall I tell Mrs Winston to hold dinner until you've changed and then bring you a tray in your chamber?'

'I could certainly use the bath. But unless you prefer to be alone, I would rather dine with you.'

A surge of gladness filled his heart. After the shocks and disappointments of this day, he wanted her company too— more desperately than was good for him, he reflected, little ripples of anticipation already sparking along his nerves. Given how low he felt and how shaky his grip on his self-control was, he ought to send her to dine alone. But after a brief inner struggle, he simply couldn't make himself forego the pleasure of her company. 'Shall I tell Myles to have dinner ready in an hour?'

They met in the dining room to share a subdued meal, both seeming content simply to be in each other's presence without need for much conversation. In addition to his general weariness, Ned's throat was raw, making speech uncomfortable, while his face, back and hands smouldered from burns probably sustained during his foray into the building to bring out the Tanners, though fortunately none of the reddened places had blistered.

When the meal concluded, by mutual unspoken agreement, Ned walked Mrs Merrill to the study. For a time they both sat quietly, sipping wine as they watched the low flame dancing on the hearth. What a strange and marvellous world, Ned thought, where a substance which cooked his food and warmed his house could, in a few brief moments, turn into a raging beast capable of devouring men, homes and livelihoods.

Like desire, he mused, which could intensify and deepen affection—or, unrestrained by will and moral principle, could wound, exploit and destroy.

'It must be difficult,' Mrs Merrill spoke at last, pulling him out of his reverie. 'Seeing all your hard work and a sizeable investment literally go up in smoke.'

'Difficult indeed,' he acknowledged.

'Do you worry you will be held responsible for the loss of the mill?'

Ned smiled ruefully. 'I am responsible.'

'But no one could have done more to fight the fire than you! Manning your post at the pump far longer than anyone else, inspiring all who observed you to further effort, to say nothing of the daring intervention that allowed the Tanners to escape with their lives! Nor could you have done anything to prevent it.'

Despite her work among the injured, she must have been watching him closely, Ned thought with surprise—and a glow of satisfaction. Though he was not nearly as sanguine about his conduct as she was.

Briefly he explained the benefit of having installed a pumping machine at the mill and the usefulness of hoses. 'Trying to stretch my limited funds, I delayed ordering both. If a firefighting pump had been available, perhaps the weavers might have been able to extinguish, or at least minimise, the blaze and prevent the injuries.'

'Perhaps,' she acknowledged. 'But would even a hose device have helped if, as some are saying, the fire was deliberately set?'

'There's no way to know,' he acknowledged. 'Rather than agonise over decisions that cannot be undone, I must now ponder how best to proceed.'

'I'm sure you will work out something. Will you consult with your employer?' Her eyes widened. 'Do you fear Lord Englemere will discharge you because of it? That would be wholly unjust!'

Ned smothered the first glimmer of amusement he'd felt in hours. 'I think I can assure you that he will not.'

She breathed a small sigh, as if relieved. 'Your connection is close, then?'

As he had once before, Ned hesitated, teetering on the edge of revealing the true nature of his relationship to Nicky—which would also mean revealing his identity. But convinced as he was that the mill fire had been set and recognising that the two men most likely to have been responsible—the stranger Mr Hampton and the soldier Jesse Russell—both of whom seemed to have singled out Mrs Merrill for attention, Ned refrained from telling her the truth.

They had sought her out before and might again. Better that she not be privy to information that, if inadvertently—or forcibly—revealed, might put her in additional danger.

In the meantime, he'd make sure Davie accompanied her whenever she set foot out of Blenhem Hill manor.

Choosing his words with care, Ned replied at last, 'I've worked with Lord Englemere for many years and always found him to be fair and just.'

To Ned's relief, she nodded, apparently satisfied with that explanation. 'Do you intend to rebuild the mill? From what I overheard today as I tended the injured, the people here are most anxious for the enterprise to continue.'

'I would certainly like to rebuild it, though I fear I would have to obtain additional funds. I'll not know for sure until we are able to make a detailed inspection of the building. But one way or another, I will make sure the workmen do not suffer.'

'I know you will. And so do they. You are quite a figure of inspiration to them, Mr Greaves! Not just your conduct at the fire, though I heard many admiring voices raised there. They already respected you for the hard work you've done and the genuine concern you've expressed for the well-being of everyone at Blenhem, be they farmers, weavers, cottagers— or indigent old ladies.'

Embarrassed as he was by her praise, Ned also felt a guilty delight, so greedily did his thirsty soul drink in the admiration and respect in her voice.

'We are a community here,' he said. 'We must all work together if change and improvement are to come.'

'Indeed,' she said, giving him the soft smile that turned his heart to mush. 'Now, speaking of improvement, it appears that your face has sustained a mild burn. Your hands, too, I'll wager. Let me fetch the medicine box and apply some salve to them.'

She rose quickly and walked out. He felt the loss of her presence like the chill on one's skin when the sun retreats behind a cloud, his heart's leap of gladness when she returned like sudden warmth and brightness when clouds dissipate and the sun reigns again in a clear blue sky.

'You learned about healing in India?' he asked as she set down the mahogany case.

'Yes,' she replied as she pulled out several jars and vials. 'With so many dangerous maladies and fevers peculiar to that country, it was important for each household to have someone skilled at treating illness and injuries. Papa employed an *ayah*—a native nurse—to help with my younger sisters, and she taught me. Along with a variety of ailments among the staff, I tended Papa through a serious bout of fever and my sisters through various childhood complaints. Now, if you would angle your head down, please?'

Stifling a sigh, he closed his eyes and allowed himself to revel in her touch, intoxicating despite the soreness of his burned skin. Gently she smoothed on a substance with the texture of soft butter and a strong fragrance of lavender, working her fingers over his cheeks and forehead to his ears, his chin, his neck.

'Is that…better?' she asked, her voice strangely rough.

Intending to tell her gratefully how cool and soothing the lotion was, he opened his eyes—to find her face just inches from his own, her green eyes so close he could see the amber highlights sparkling at their centre. His sharp inhalation of breath brought with it a heady noseful of her special scent.

Fatigue and the discomfort of his burns were instantly swamped by a tidal surge of desire.

After the anxiety, anguish and anger of the day, more than ever before he craved the comfort and limitless pleasure he knew he would find in her arms, her bed.

He could almost taste the berry-sweetness of her lips and mouth, feel the velvet weight of her breasts in his hands, the tight embrace and smooth satin glide of his aching member as he drove himself deep within her willing warmth.

He burned to use his lips and tongue and body to turn her sighs of pleasure into moans of delight, to make her breathing accelerate from a pant to a sob until she fisted her hands in his hair and her whole body convulsed as he lifted her over the edge and sent her soaring, her cries of ecstasy echoing in his ears as he followed her into the abyss.

Staring into her widened eyes, he realised she wanted that, too. Smiling in unmistakable invitation, she leaned closer until her breasts brushed his shirt, igniting a bolt of sensation that hardened him in an instant.

He would make it so good for her, for them both. Succumbing to the desire that had intensified day by day between them since that first night when he had caught and carried her in his arms, they could in physical union reinforce the strong connection they already shared, an intimacy more intense than any he'd ever experienced.

Who knew better than his lovely Joanna how hard he'd worked to make Blenhem Hill a success, how much he cared about the land and its people? She'd already captured him heart and soul—why should he not also offer his body to the woman who was a part of Blenhem and cared as deeply about it as he did?

One inch. Ned need incline his head only one tiny inch to claim the lips she offered and set them both on a path to heaven.

But taking her now wouldn't be right. She was offering herself not to Sir Edward, but to Ned Greaves, the man she believed to be simply an estate agent. He could not take advantage of her trusting faith to irrevocably bind her to him until she knew exactly who it was that she drew into her body and clasped to her heart.

Moving away from those slightly pursed lips and the soft weight of those breasts against his chest—while every nerve in his body screamed for him to seize the delights she offered—was the hardest thing he'd ever done.

He was soaked with sweat and trembling with effort when he finally managed it. 'I m-must be more t-tired than I thought,' he stuttered as he backed away from her, knowing if he did not take himself out of her presence immediately his resolve would crumble and he would leave the room with her in his arms, to spend the night in his bed. 'Until tomorrow.'

Ned hastened towards the door, pain and regret lancing through him as he watched the desire in her eyes turn to confusion, then hurt. Gritting his teeth and clenching his fists, he made himself turn his back on her and walk out.

The following morning, a listless Joanna sat beside Davie as he drove her to the schoolhouse, bubbling over with enthusiasm after telling her proudly how, for the first time yesterday morning, Mr Greaves had entrusted him with the reins for a short while.

This would probably be the last day she needed to work at the building. Mr Tanner was coming by with the final load of stone; the carpenter had given Davie wooden pegs to attach by the door for the children to hang their cloaks and jackets, and while they toiled, she would review her books and primers one final time to be ready for the beginning of school next week.

She ought to be excited and full of anticipation. But after a sleepless night followed by a solitary breakfast—for Mr Greaves had been called away early, Myles told her—she now felt dull, confused and frustrated.

Perhaps it was best that she hadn't seen him this morning. She'd lain awake all night with every nerve afire, desperate with need, bereft after hovering a touch away from having him set off the spark that would ignite the long-building conflagration between them. With every particle of her being, she'd longed to immerse herself in a fire that would consume them as fiercely as the one that had engulfed the stocking mill.

In the keenness of his gaze, the sheen of moisture on his skin and the tension radiating throughout his body, she read that Ned Greaves craved her as much as she wanted him. Responding giddily to that knowledge, she'd done everything short of stripping him from his garments to let him know how eager she was to comply. So why, at the end, had he repulsed her?

After incredulity, her first response had been indignation. How dare he turn his back and walk away with some feeble excuse about needing rest, when what *she* needed was the imprint of his hands on her body, the taste of his tongue on her mouth and her skin, the feel of his manhood sheathed within her?

After the several shocked moments of immobility required for her to accept that he *had* walked away, she'd slipped from the room to her chamber, still burning with a lust overlaid by remorse and embarrassment. Why, when he so clearly wanted her, had he chosen not to take her?

Perhaps the burns were paining him more than he'd revealed. Perhaps, having declared he would not trifle with a woman under his protection, he thought it dishonourable to go back on his word.

Through the long hours of the night as she tossed and turned, she'd decided the first possibility might have some merit. But she'd dismissed the second. How could she have made it any plainer that she considered him honourable—and wanted him anyway?

Or did he merely desire her as a man desires an attractive street trollop, tempted by her sensuality but not interested in coupling with a woman who showed herself to be blatantly available?

Had her forward behaviour repelled him? A wash of humiliation heated her skin as she recalled the final and most distasteful explanation she'd entertained before falling at last into a fitful sleep early this morning.

Now she wondered if there might not be another more

compelling reason. Could it be that, though he might desire her, as a manager of some standing within their community, an experienced man with close ties to a highly placed aristocrat, he did not wish to entangle himself with the widow of a gentleman whose family had repudiated her? A woman with few connections that might be turned to his advantage; indeed, as the sister of a man his employer had recently discharged, one whose ties might be used to his *disadvantage*.

With his expertise and capability for hard work, a man like Mr Greaves might well earn a chance to manage a much more extensive and important property for his noble patron—especially if he allied himself to a female who had well-placed relations.

Whereas she could do nothing to advance his career.

Suddenly Davie pulled up the horse, startling her out of this latest of her gloomy reflections. With a second shock, she realised they had already reached the schoolhouse.

'Got you here all right and tight, ma'am,' he said as he came around the gig to hand her down. 'Just like I promised! See, 'tweren't no need for you to stare straight ahead and clutch the rail like you feared any minute I was about to run us into a ditch!'

How fortunate Davie could have no notion of the true cause of her abstraction. 'Not at all,' she replied, flushing a bit at having spent the transit indulging in morose contemplation of what was looking more and more like not a mutual passion, but an unrequited affection for her employer. 'Just…pondering.'

'Don't need to worry none about the school,' Davie assured her. 'Children hereabouts are most of 'em as eager to start as me. If'n they give you any trouble, I'll be here to deal with 'em. Anything else I kin help with after I put up them pegs? Mr Greaves charged me strict that I weren't to leave you alone, so I'll be hanging about until the workmen come. Might as well make use of me.'

Seeking a task he might enjoy, she said, 'Perhaps you can help me sort the books and slates.'

At the mention of books, his eyes lit. 'I'll be done with these pegs in a trice, then.'

True to his word, Davie had the pegs aligned and tapped into place before Joanna had organised the first armload of supplies. 'You're a dab hand with a hammer,' she observed. 'Did you ever think of training as a carpenter?'

'Ma thought I might, but Da wanted me to take over the farm. Never wanted that myself—don't like the feel or smell of dirt on my hands. Used to scamper off from the fields to the village and hang about at the carpenter's and the smith's.' He grinned. 'Da soon learned where to fetch me. Got a beating for it, but didn't discourage me none.'

Joanna shook her head and laughed. 'Apply that determination to your studies and you will go far! Now, would you fetch the rest of the books from the shelf in the alcove and bring them to the table, please?'

With a nod, he loped to the storage area. 'Whoa, now, what's this?' he asked with a laugh from behind the enclosure. 'This hole here under the thatch screen be what Mr Tanner's going to finish today? Best he does, else some young one might sneak back here, wriggle through and be off to the fishing creek afore you know he was gone!'

'Truly?' Joanna asked as the grinning Davie emerged with the books. 'Then until after the mortar hardens on Mr Tanner's repair work, I must remember to ask only the largest of my pupils to fetch supplies.'

Carefully Davie set the books on to the table. 'What be all these for, ma'am?'

One by one she showed him the primers, one with sums for math, another with the alphabet and simple sentences. Davie lingered over a larger, longer illustrated book. 'And this one, ma'am?'

'That's a book about India, full of legends and mysteries. I plan to read some of the stories aloud to the children.'

Reverently Davie paged through the book, pausing to admire the copperplate illustrations. 'Looks powerful interesting. Some day soon, I'll be able to read it all for myself.'

'You will indeed,' she replied, her heart touched anew by the intensity of his hunger for learning. 'And when you can read it, Davie, it shall be yours.'

He looked up, startled. 'You mean—to keep?'

'To keep,' she promised.

He shook his head. 'You couldn't, ma'am. Such a beautiful book, it must cost a powerful lot.'

'A costly book should be owned by someone who fully appreciates its value. I can't think of anyone who would make it a better owner than you.'

His face beaming, Davie was stuttering an incoherent thanks when the sound of a galloping horse interrupted them.

Recalling the disaster to which the sound of pounding hoofs had called them yesterday, dread seized Joanna's throat. Without a word, both she and Davie sprang up and hurried outside to greet the rider.

'Mr Elliot,' Davie called to the man who pulled up before them. 'What be amiss?'

'One of the men what's always hanging about the Hart and Hare, a drifter from Nottingham who's done some farm work hereabouts, come to Mr Greaves this morning and told him the man behind the mill fire was hiding in the area. They done traced him to one of the abandoned farmhouses out beyond the Miller place. Heard he mighta taken a hostage and the word is, 'tis Granny Cuthbert. I'm riding to fetch my brother so we can go help.'

Davie ran over and grabbed at the horse's reins, preventing Elliot from riding off. 'Granny's in danger?' he cried. 'Are you sure?'

'No, but Mr Greaves said we should act as if the threat was real. If you're ready to spring that pony trap, lad, you can come along.'

'Sure would like to.' His pale face strained with apprehension, Davie looked back at Joanna. 'But…but I promised Mr Greaves I'd stay with Mrs Merrill until Tanner and the stone-masons arrive.'

'Just passed Tanner's wagon heading this way,' Elliot said. 'Should be here any minute.'

Davie nodded. 'Soon's he arrives, I'll come on after you. A cottage out past the Miller place, you said? Expect I can find it.'

Though Joanna was uneasy at the idea of being alone, if the arrival of the stonemasons was imminent, the urgency the boy must be feeling to see to the safety of the kind old woman who'd taken him in was far greater than the comfort she'd derive by compelling him to remain. 'No, go on now, Davie. Granny may need you. I'll be all right until Tanner and the men arrive.'

Davie's anxious eyes searched her face. 'You're sure, ma'am?'

'I'm sure,' she assured him. Almost before the words had left her lips, Davie released the bridle of Elliott's horse and raced to the gig. 'Lead on!' he cried as he untied the reins and scrambled up to the bench.

Smiling after the boy as he whipped the horse and drove off, Joanna turned to peer down the road. Would the man they tracked turn out to be the one who'd set the mill fire? Might it be the disturbing Mr Hampton?

A little shiver of unease slithered down her spine. Something about the man convinced her that despite his appearance as a gentleman, he was capable of single-minded zeal in fur-thering his cause—and would not be daunted by the prospect of taking innocent lives.

Whoever it was they chased, she hoped by mid-day he would be safely in the hands of the sheriff.

The rider and gig having disappeared down the lane, it seemed overly quiet. Though in truth, she had to admit that in full mid-morning light, with birds chirping in trees that swayed and danced in the breeze, throwing a kaleidoscope of changing patterns of sun and shade across the grass, the scene was no different than it had been on any of the other days she had worked here. Still, Joanna admitted, she would feel better once Tanner arrived.

Telling herself she was being a nodcock to let the memories of the unsavoury Mr Hampton unsettle her, she went back inside the schoolhouse. With the stonemasons soon to arrive and cover the alcove with dust while they mortared in the last of the stone, she'd better move the rest of her supplies over to her desk.

Keeping her ears pricked for the sounds of a heavily laden wagon coming down the lane, she set about her task.

Some half an hour later, she'd moved all her books and supplies out of the work area, but the masons had still not arrived.

Perhaps they'd stopped to water the horses. To distract herself from a lingering unease, she opened the book about India and flipped through the pages, pausing over the illustrations that had so fascinated Davie. Would he one day journey there to make his fortune, as he'd predicted? She was smiling at the image of him as a young India nabob when a soft, sibilant scraping caught her ear.

The tiny hairs on the back of her neck bristling, she turned towards the door. Where, to her dismay, Mr George Hampton, a saddlebag slung over one shoulder, slipped through the door and halted just inside the threshold.

Chapter Fourteen

Hampton started, as if surprised to see her even as she leapt to her feet. Fumbling to doff his hat, he offered her a patently false smile.

'Hello there, ma'am. Didn't see your gig outside so didn't think you were here yet,' he said, confirming her impression. 'A good day to you, though.' Seeming to regather his confidence, he advanced into the room. 'Have you thought any more about what I told you yesterday?'

Despite his jocular tone, behind his conventional greetings she sensed a fervid, almost desperate air that set all her protective instincts on full alert. Eyeing the distance between her desk and the door, she gave him a reluctant curtsy.

'Twas impossible; she could never get past him and out of the only exit without him catching her—if he indeed wished to prevent her leaving. And what would she do if she made it outside? Davie had driven away in her gig, and, hampered by her skirts, she could surely not outrun him.

What in the world was keeping Tanner and his stonemasons?

Telling herself she was being ridiculous, for the man had done nothing as yet to warrant her alarm, she willed herself to reply calmly, 'Yes, but I'm afraid I must return you the same answer.'

Despite her resolve, a cold sliver of dread knifed into her belly as he walked closer, smiling. 'Are you sure? My obligations now take me to London. I might have good use there for an attractive lady like you, while you could disport yourself at the shops and the theatre. You'll find me a generous man, my dear—and I do promise to keep you well…entertained.'

Last night she had nearly expired with desperation for the sort of 'entertainment' he was implying. The thought of Mr Hampton touching her, however, sent a shiver of revulsion through her.

'A kind offer, sir, but I lived for some years in London. While the metropolis does have its charms, I prefer the country. I don't wish to be impolite, but you mentioned having a journey to begin, and I must complete some work. Perhaps you can stop by when you are next in Hazelwick?' Pasting on a smile, she motioned to the door.

And then froze, her attention seized by the sound of someone approaching—not the clop of hoofs and the creak and squeal of a heavily laden wagon, but a rumble of voices and the tromp of many footsteps.

This was not, she suspected, Tanner and his wagon.

'Excuse me,' she said, walking towards the door. 'I'll just see who—'

She gasped as he seized her arm and pulled her back. 'Sorry, but you're not going anywhere, schoolmistress.' Slamming the front door shut, he threw the bolt.

'What do you mean by this?' she demanded, as incensed as she was alarmed.

'Remember you mentioned retribution to those who cross the authorities and I told you a clever fellow don't get caught? Well, you're about to witness that. Sit down on that bench and keep silent unless I give you leave to speak. Do what you're told and I won't have to hurt you.'

'I have no intention of remaining here—!' she began hotly, only to have him grab her by the arms and slam her against the door. Her head jerked back to hit the sturdy wooden panel so violently, lights and stars danced before her eyes.

'Sit and be silent,' he growled, 'or I'll give you another taste of that.' Roughly he thrust her towards the bench.

Still dizzy, Joanna nearly fell into the seat. Queasy as little dots of light continued to swim before her eyes, for a few moments she had to concentrate all her energy on taking deep, slow breaths, until her stomach settled and the pounding in her head eased.

Meanwhile, Hampton dragged two more wooden benches over and placed them behind the door as a makeshift barricade. As the noise of the approaching group grew louder, he closed and locked the window shutters, then took two pistols from his saddlebag and primed them.

She could hear the group right outside the building now. A moment later came the sound of a fist pounding on the door.

'Mrs Merrill, are you there?'

Hampton levelled one of the pistols at her and motioned her to silence.

A few long minutes ticked by. 'Don't seem like nobody's inside,' man's voice said.

'I know she's there,' Davie's voice answered. 'Hardly been half an hour since I left her—besides, she don't never close the shutters when she leaves. Mrs Merrill!' he called. 'Are you all right?'

'Answer him and I'll shoot you,' Hampton warned softly.

'Probably she went home,' another voice said. 'Let's get going! That varmint must still be in the area somewhere! Mr Greaves is counting on us to check the cottages here to the west while he makes a sweep towards the village.'

Her hopes, soaring at the sound of Ned Greave's name,

plummeted. Ned was a mile away in town, too far distant to help her. She would have to deal with Mr Hampton alone.

'No,' Davie's insistent voice recaptured her attention. 'She's in there, I'm telling you! She knew I'd be back for her; she wouldn't a left alone. If she ain't answering the door, 'tis cause someone's not letting her. Hold on, Mrs Merrill, we'll get you out! Johnston, grab the axe by the woodpile. I say we break down the door.'

With a curse, Hampton turned to her. 'Tell him if they try to break in, I'll shoot you. And I will.'

Logically she knew that committing cold-blooded murder before a crowd of witnesses wasn't a very rational action—but Hampton didn't look rational. Fear choked her as the sounds of scuffling outside were followed by the bang of something slamming into the door.

Desperation flashing in his eyes, Hampton hissed, 'Now, or by God, I'll put a ball into you!'

'D-Davie!' she called, her voice shaky. 'It's Mrs Merrill. I am here, being held against my will. Mr Hampton has a loaded pistol and threatens to shoot me if you try to break in.'

Mutters and outcries from the crowd followed her speech. A moment later, Davie's voice called, 'What do you want to release her, Hampton?'

Joanna looked over at Hampton.

'Tell them to leave, all of 'em,' he replied, still keeping his voice low. 'Once they are out of sight, I'll come out—and you with me. If anyone tries to stop us, I'll shoot you.'

He gave her a smile that chilled her to her marrow. 'Once we're safely away, I'll release you…or maybe I'll keep you, if you bring me good luck. A red-haired wench is always hot for pleasuring. Greaves had his fill of you yet?'

Despite her resolve to stay calm, tears of fury and frustration at her helplessness trickled down her cheeks. 'You are despicable,' she whispered.

He laughed at her. 'And you're as gullible as your lazy brother. Long as I got the manor fixed up and made sure he had doxies to service him regular, he was happy as a pig in muck.'

Shock momentarily suppressed the fear. 'Mr Barksdale?' she whispered.

'Aye, Barksdale—the man who saw to it your idiot brother made it through the war. Would have got his worthless posterior shot off in the first engagement if it hadn't been for me. Owed me for that, he did! I was making a fine living, squeezing coin from this hogswill of a farm, until he decided to verify the accounts. Threatened to turn me off, after all I done for him! Well, I made sure Martin whined to your fancy cousin Lord Englemere and got him turned off first—afore I took care of him. Englemere owes me, too, but he'll get his later. Right now, 'twill be sweet to have Greville's pretty sister part her legs and work off some of the honeyfall he made me lose. Now—' he waved the pistol at her again '—tell that crowd of bumpkins what they need to do. Fast.'

Just how had Barksdale 'taken care of' Greville? she wondered. 'Why must I answer—?' she began.

'Just tell them,' he snarled, the leer leaving his face as his expression hardened.

Quivering between terror and outrage, she called out, 'He wants everyone to disperse. After you leave, he will come out, taking me with him. If you don't let us go away unmolested, he says he will shoot me.'

'What, Hampton can't speak for hisself?' Davie's voice answered. 'What kind of man is he, hiding behind a woman's skirts? Must not be the crafty rascal we're looking for. That one be smart, a real leader. This here must be a common hooligan—or maybe 'tis no man at all.

'Maybe it's just Crazy Peg from Hazelwick,' Davie continued, his tone becoming taunting. 'Heard about the mill fire and thinks she's a Spencean, like some of them no-goods been hanging out at the Hart and Hare. Listen now, Peggie girl, you put down that pistol and come on out.'

Davie must have urged on the other men, for several more voices echoed, 'That's right, Peg' and 'Come on out, girlie.'

Hampton–Barksdale's jaw tightened as the mocking calls continued, and for a moment, Joanna thought he might fire at her. Then, with a roar, he yelled, 'Enough! I'll show you a leader at the end of my pistol, you gutter rat, if you don't quit your yapping and move off with your friends. Or do you want the Merrill woman's death on your heads?'

For a moment Barksdale's threat echoed in the sudden silence. Then Davie's voice came again. 'Hear that, Tanner? I was right! Ain't no clever man we got trapped here. Just that great bully and coward Barksdale.'

'Barksdale?' Various voices disputed before a moment later Tanner replied, 'Davie's right. That is his voice!'

'Sure nuff is,' Davie said. ''Tis just like him, too, threatening women, beating on children. Had to knock me over the head and drag me away in the middle of the night, so brave he was about facing a boy half his age. Afraid if you tussled with me in the daylight, I might slip away like a youngin through a hole, Barksdale?'

'The mill boss should have whipped you to death,' Barksdale roared back. 'But never you worry, guttersnipe. One day soon I'll be back to finish the job.'

'Threats and bluster, just like always,' Davie called back. 'If you're so much a man, come after me now! You got a pistol and all's I got's this little slingshot. Open one of them windows and we'll see who's the better shot.'

'Davie, no!' Joanna cried, echoing the warnings of a number of the men outside the building.

'Or are you too much a coward to shoot, even from behind that big stone wall? Better face me now, 'cause I ain't gonna sneak away out some hole, scared of the likes of you!'

With a growl of fury, Barksdale charged to the window, un-latched and threw open the shutter. Crouching behind the wall, so as to make it difficult for anyone in the crowd who might possess a pistol to get a shot at him, he peered over the frame at the schoolyard. 'Show yourself, whoreson, and we'll see who can shoot!'

As Barksdale focused his attention out of the window, Joanna's muzzy head suddenly cleared.

'Slip out like a youngin through a hole…' Davie was trying to infuriate Barksdale enough to distract him so she might try to escape!

To her horror, Davie must have come out into the open, for a chorus of voices shouted, 'Davie, get down!' 'Don't go out there!' 'Fool, you'll get yourself killed!'

Chuckling darkly, Barksdale levelled his weapon out the window and fired, then ducked back as a flurry of stones whizzed through the frame to clatter on to the tables inside.

'Told ya he couldn't hit nothing,' Davie's voice taunted. 'Did I part your hair with them rocks, Barksdale? I'll bruise your pretty cheek with the next round! Or is you out of shot and too scared to show your face?'

With a growl, the furious man threw down the empty pistol and seized the other, then peeked once again around the window frame. 'Won't talk so big with a load of shot in your belly, whore-bait!'

Saying a prayer of thanks for Davie's audacious bravery, along with a fervent plea that Barksdale's second shot would be no more effective than the first, Joanna took a deep breath and waited for him to squeeze the trigger. During the noise of the report, while both Barksdale's weapons were unloaded and he was preoccupied ducking Davie's second volley of rocks, she would have to take the chance his cleverness offered and try to get out.

Would she be able to wriggle through the small gap? Better

to try and fail than do nothing and sit there meekly for Barksdale to use as a hostage—and then his trollop.

As the blast for which she'd been waiting assaulted her ears, she darted to the alcove, though her stealth hadn't been necessary. His full attention focused on Davie, Barksdale never looked in her direction.

Her heart sank as she fell to her knees by the opening and ripped apart the temporary thatch cover that protected the unfinished section of wall. A mischievous child might be able to scramble out through the narrow space remaining, but she was never going to make it.

Despite that conviction, desperately she set to work with palms and fingers, pushing and tugging to dislodge more rock.

The sound of her sobbing breath roared in her ears. Knowing she had at best seconds before Barksdale turned from the window to reload his pistols—and notice she'd gone missing—she threw herself on to the dirt floor, jammed her head through the hole and pushed with all her strength.

It was no use—turn and twist as she might, she couldn't get both shoulders to slip through. And then she heard what she'd been dreading.

'What the…?' Barksdale exclaimed. In the small cottage, there wouldn't be much doubt where she'd gone. Tears dripping down her face anew, she slammed her shoulders against the rock.

Seconds later, the trotting of footsteps was followed by the sound of Barksdale's malicious laughter. 'Why, Mrs Merrill, with your bum in the air and your skirts around your knees, what a tempting morsel you are. Alas, that I must wait until later to enjoy you.'

While she scrabbled for something outside the stone foundation to cling to, Barksdale seized her ankles.

Chapter Fifteen

Anxious and frustrated, Ned rode his horse into the stable-yard at the Hart and Hare, where he was to rendezvous with the others of his party after they finished conducting a house-to-house search through the town. Ever since Miller had brought the Nottingham journeyman to him early this morning, claiming to know the whereabouts of the leader who'd set the mill fire, he'd been in a fever of anticipation and fury to apprehend the man who had cindered his investment and seriously injured his workers.

But it seemed they had missed the man they sought at every turn. In the hot ashes of a cooking fire and scatter of provisions within the first cottage, they had found evidence of recent habitation, but not the inhabitant. Proceeding east, they had searched several other abandoned cottages, each of which also showed signs of occupancy, though none as fresh, seeming to indicate the man who'd left those traces had moved around. Or that several men had quietly taken up residence on Blenhem land.

Thankfully, a quick stop at Granny Cuthbert's cottage found the old lady safe inside, proving at least one of the reports he'd been given by men who'd joined the search—that she had been carried off by the 'mystery man' they sought—was false.

At that point, after several fruitless hours, he was considering giving up the search entirely when one of the trackers sighted a man threading his horse along the edge of the woods bordering the road to Hazelwick. Sending half the group to continue searching in the opposite direction to the west, Ned had set off with his group into the woods. Thus far, however, he had discovered the stranger neither among the trees nor in any of the dwellings at Hazelwick.

Did the informer truly know who had set the fire? Was the occupant of the abandoned cottage in fact responsible, or was he simply a common workman, one of the several displaced men who'd recently left Manchester to come to Blenhem to claim the jobs Ned was offering?

What if the information was correct, but instead of making for town, the miscreant had doubled back somewhere in the woods and gone in the opposite direction?

West…towards the schoolhouse. Uneasy foreboding sat like a plough-breaking bolder in his gut. Surely Myles would have told Mrs Merrill the reason behind his early-morning departure today? Surely knowing that, she wouldn't have ventured out of the manor to the school?

Even as he thought that, he had to smile. This was the Mrs Merrill he hadn't managed to dissuade from accompanying him to the fire. If she felt there was work to be done, she was unlikely to cool her heels meekly at the manor while search parties chased around Blenhem in hopes of capturing someone who, thus far, he could not even say for sure was a villain.

Besides, if she did go, Davie would go with her. The lad wasn't yet a man full grown, but he was clever and resourceful beyond his years. Ned knew he'd utilise every trick he possessed to keep Mrs Merrill safe.

Still, Ned would feel much better if they could run this stranger to ground so he could return to check on the schoolmistress.

While he waited, he might as well go into the taproom and ask anyone who chanced to be there if he'd seen a stranger. Mary, standing by a table occupied by a young man goggling in admiration up at her, smiled at him as he walked in.

'A mug of ale, Mr Greaves?' she asked.

'Not now, thanks. I'm looking for a newcomer who's been staying in one of Blenhem's abandoned cottages. Might be an unemployed mill hand come over from Manchester. Have you had any new customers of that description?'

She shook her head. 'Nay, nor have we had much custom at all today, save Mr Abernathy here, the squire's son just down from school.' While the two men nodded a greeting, Mary continued, 'Mr Kirkbride lit out early, after Miller's brother came by saying you were chasing the man who set the mill fire. You've not found him then, yet?'

'No,' Ned said regretfully. 'I've got men searching all the houses and barns at Blenhem and in the village. If we don't find him there, we'll scour the woods. One way or another, we'll flush him out today.'

Just then, the innkeeper, Mr Kirkbride, came running into the taproom.

'Mr Greaves, come quick! A man be holed up in the schoolhouse, holding the schoolteacher! They're saying it's that villain, the old agent you replaced, Barksdale!'

Before Ned could make it out the door, Mary's face blanched linen-white. 'No!' she screamed, taking two running steps towards him before pitching forwards, as if falling into a faint.

Desperate to leave, Ned nonetheless halted long enough to catch the girl. Immediately after he steadied her, though, she thrust herself unassisted back to her feet. 'Nay, I'm fine. Go! Go at once!' she urged, motioning Ned towards the door. 'Oh, you must get to Mrs Merrill before Barksdale…hurts her, like he did me!' she cried, her voice ending on a sob.

Kirkbride, who like Ned had rushed over to assist her, stopped short. 'Barksdale hurt you? When?'

'You think I was born a doxy?' she fired back. ''Twas Barksdale attacked me, coming home from the village one night. Barksdale who fathered the babe I lost. Threatened to turn my folks off the land if I ever told anyone the truth.' Tears streaming down her cheeks, she cried, 'If Mrs Merrill is hurt, 'tis all my fault! Thought I'd seen him sneaking through town yesterday…but then I thought 'twas only my old nightmare, that for years had me seeing him everywhere. I should have warned Jesse—oh, but 'tis nothing for it now! Go, Mr Greaves!' she said, giving Ned an urgent shove.

'Tommy,' she called over her shoulder to the squire's son as she followed Ned out, 'let Mr Greaves borrow your gelding. The horse is fast, sir, and fresher than your mount.'

'Aye, take him,' the young man seconded.

Nodding his thanks, Ned leapt into the saddle. As he rode off, Mary, weeping openly, called after him, 'Save her, sir! You must save her!'

Mary's desperate words echoed in his head as Ned pushed the unfamiliar mount to full speed. Discovering thankfully that the animal was as fast as Mary had claimed, Ned urged him in a ground-eating gallop towards the school.

Could he get there in time? How would he induce Barksdale to give her up, if he was indeed holding her hostage?

Ned refused to even consider the possibility that he might not. He would free her, whatever it took, and afterwards pound Barksdale into the ground like a fence post if he'd harmed her in any way.

Forcing his mind from contemplating the awful image Mary had planted, Ned made himself focus instead on the jumble of facts he'd just learned. Barksdale—the detested former estate agent—was in the area? Ned doubted he could be the leader behind the group at the Hart and Hare; the man was far too infamous in the county to induce even otherwise disaffected men, related as they doubtless were to some of the tenants at Blenhem, to follow him. If he did have some connections with the group, he would have to work through intermediaries.

Like a Nottingham workman…or refugees from the mills in Manchester—perhaps from the same factory where he'd 'sold' Davie?

But as he drew closer to the school, he could no longer distract himself from the fear and worry battering aside all other thoughts. All that mattered was getting Joanna free and unharmed.

Was it his fault she'd fallen into danger, for not delaying his departure this morning long enough to deliver a personal warning that she stay at the manor? For being so obsessed with capturing the villain that he'd trailed the man towards town, rather than riding west to see to her safety? For not re-vealing his identity and his reasons for concealing it long ago, so she might be forewarned?

Mary's testimony had removed any doubt about how black was the character of the man holding her. But if Barksdale were trapped, surrounded by an angry, threatening crowd, surely his first thought would be to use her to bargain for escape—not to harm her. Not with a throng of witnesses who'd be happy to testify against him. That road led as straight and direct to a hanging as a tightened noose.

No, keeping her safe was the only rational course—if rational he still was.

Time suspended, minutes stretching into hours, punctuated by pounding hoofs and his frantic heartbeat. At last, far too many of those minutes later, he urged the horse down the final stretch towards the schoolhouse that, he could see as he peered into the distance, was surrounded by a crowd of men.

Urging the spent and lathered horse to one final effort, he

was pulling up, about to vault from the saddle, when he heard an urgent voice shriek his name.

Joanna's voice. Swivelling in the direction of the sound, he searched for her as she screamed again, 'Ned! Here!'

Then he saw her, her head and one shoulder crammed through the small space in the rock foundation Tanner had yet to seal on the side of the schoolhouse. She was struggling to get out, clinging to the exterior stones with the fingernails of one hand as someone—doubtless Barksdale—tried to drag her back inside.

He leapt from the saddle and set off. Branches tore at his clothes and one raked across his face as he raced over, threw himself to his knees and seized her.

'Let her go, Barksdale,' he yelled, trying to brace her against him and minimise the scrape of her body against the rocks. 'It's over. You can't win. Give yourself up and it will go more leniently for you.'

While clutching Joanna as tightly as he dared and calling to the man inside, Ned kicked at the stone foundation with his boot. After a moment's frantic effort, he dislodged one stone, then another, until the old, weakened mortar crumbled and, with an enormous heave, he broke her trapped shoulder free.

With the ferocity of a rat cornered in a barn, Barksdale refused to release her. 'Think you got the winning hand, Ned Greaves? Well, I know a thing or two, and she'll be mine in the end! Let her loose, or I swear I'll break her ankles!'

Before Ned could decide how to counter that threat without causing Joanna any further injury, a huge crashing sound emanated from the front of the building. 'That's it, men!' Davie's voice shouted. 'Another blow, and we'll have the door open!'

The surprise of the men's attack distracted Barksdale for the instant Ned needed. Feeling the resistance to his pull on her lessen, Ned yanked with all his strength. Suddenly Joanna broke free and tumbled out, knocking them both to the ground.

From the other side of the schoolhouse came a roar that indicated the men had succeeded in breaching the door. Doubtless realising capture was imminent, Barksdale thrust his face and shoulders into the opening, trying to scramble out through the hole Ned had created. With a growl, Ned slammed his boot into the man's face. Even as Barksdale cried out and brought an arm up to protect himself, to the shouts and cries of the men in the schoolhouse, he was seized from behind and pulled back into the building.

Ned scrambled up to help Joanna as she staggered to her feet. She'd lost her bonnet, damp earth covered her gown and wisps of hair escaped from her braids straggled on to her dirt-smeared face. 'Dear Lord in Heaven, tell me you are all right!' he begged, his anxious eyes scanning her.

'I am now,' she cried, and threw herself into his arms.

His heart pounding so hard his head felt dizzy, Ned clung to her fiercely. 'You are truly all right?' he asked, resting his cheek against the silken flame of her hair. 'He didn't…?'

'No. I'm all right, truly,' she murmured against his chest.

Just then Davie came pelting around the building, Tanner and others from the crowd at his heels.

'Mrs Merrill, are you all right?' he asked.

'Yes, Davie,' she said, stepping out of Ned's embrace.

Every nerve and all his roiling emotions protested against losing her. Despite the audience, he had to grit his teeth to resist the urgent need to pull her back, to burn into his soul the feel of her in his arms and reassure his frantic heart that she was truly free and relatively unharmed.

'Your nails is all broke and your hands bruised,' Davie said, inspecting her. 'And look—' he pointed, his eyes widening '—the back of your head is bleeding!'

While Ned took a pace behind her to inspect the wound, Davie fell to his knees. 'It's all my fault, Mr Greaves!' he cried as he looked up at her, tears tracking down his dirty cheeks. 'You told me never to leave her! I thought Tanner would be here in a twink. When I got back and saw them shutters closed up and the door locked, I was scareder than I'd ever been in my life!'

'Calm yourself,' Joanna soothed him. 'You couldn't have known Tanner would turn back to join the searchers. Nor would Mr Greaves have been able to free me if you hadn't managed—with incredible, foolish bravery—to trick Barksdale into giving me time to escape. But for you I might even now still be his hostage, held at gunpoint, all of you helpless to secure my safety without meeting his demands.'

'You done a powerful brave thing, lad,' Tanner said. 'Mr Greaves, sir, you shoulda seen him, dancing around them shots!'

'I'd a taken one to get her free,' Davie told Ned. 'I know what he's like, the snake! I'd rather be dead than alive knowing he'd hurt you, ma'am.' He looked her up and down. 'Even so, you is all scraped up 'n bleeding! I'm powerful sorry!' His youth showing through now that the crisis had ended, he put his head into his hands and wept.

'Hush, now,' Joanna said, stroking the bent head of the boy he still was. 'All I have are small hurts that will heal quickly. Without your help, it would have gone much worse for me!'

While she reassured Davie, the villain himself was marched forwards, his cheek bleeding from the kick by Ned's boot and his hands bound behind him.

'Mr Tanner, I shall want a full account later—and from you other gentlemen as well—but for now, we must take this man to the magistrate,' Ned said. 'Mrs Merrill, you should return to the manor and let Mrs Winston tend your head. Will you drive her, Davie?'

The boy whipped his face up to stare at Ned. 'You'd trust me now?'

'From what I've heard, Mrs Merrill would still be a captive, had it not been for your cleverness. Of course I trust you.'

Dashing the tears from his eyes, Davie leapt to his feet.

'Thank you, Mr Greaves. I'll never let you down again, I promise!'

'I'll probably need you to testify later,' Ned added.

Davie gave Barksdale a look of loathing. 'Be glad to.'

Barksdale, who had been standing impassively through these exchanges, suddenly leaned forwards and spat at Davie. 'That's for your "bravery", halfling! As for testifying, we'll see about that. I'm not done yet, Greaves.'

That, from a man who had abducted and brutalised an unarmed, innocent lady! Filled with a visceral loathing so strong he had to jam his fisted hands behind his back to keep from taking a swing at Barksdale, Ned barked, 'Enough! You'll have your say before the judge. Now, as anything you utter can be used against you in a court of law, I suggest you keep silent. Before one of the gentlemen here decides to silence you for me.'

Amid mutterings, jeers and offers from the assembled crowd to do just that, Ned turned back to Joanna.

He didn't want to send her off with Davie. Not because he didn't trust the lad, but because he still ached to draw her into his arms and hug her for at least a decade or so, until his heart-beat finally steadied and a soul that had been more paralyzed by fear than ever before in his life finally accepted the fact that she was safe.

Somehow she'd suffered a head wound, so the sooner she was returned to Mrs Winston's competent care, the better. Though he wanted nothing more urgently than to drive her slowly, carefully back to the manor himself, to personally inspect, bathe and tend all her wounds and then see her put to bed with a healing compress on her head, he knew his first duty was to ensure that the slippery villain Barksdale made it to gaol in Hazelwick.

After the events of this morning, fear and anxiety had sup-pressed his normally simmering lust to the point that he would be fully satisfied—at least for the moment—to return and sit quietly beside her bed, keeping vigil.

A sense of anguish so acute he felt almost physically ill swept through him once again at the realisation of how close he'd come to losing her before he'd even had a chance to try to win her.

He'd deal with that later, he told himself, mastering the nausea in his gut. Now to finish the task with Barksdale so he could return to her.

Given the ugly mood of the crowd, he'd better accomplish the transit quickly. On many of the angry faces, he read a strong desire to carry the captive not to gaol, but to a nearby hedgerow, where they might utilise a convenient rope to terminate the life of the man who had made their lot at Blenhem miserable for years.

Though he agreed with them that the man was as loathsome as black smut on a fine ear of corn, whatever punishment the villain received must be meted out at the hands of the law. Reluctantly, Ned turned to Davie.

'Make sure you drive slowly, Davie, so that Mrs Merrill is not jostled too much.' Waving aside Joanna's protest that her injuries were minor, he continued, 'Summon Mrs Winston the moment you arrive and turn Mrs Merrill over to her care before you deal with the gig. I'll be back as soon as this matter—' he jerked his chin in Barksdale's direction '—is settled.'

'Might I say something?' Joanna interjected, amused exasperation in her tone. 'I've lost a little blood, not my wits nor my tongue.'

Though he wanted badly to embrace her again, he limited himself to a simple clasp of her hand. 'Please, indulge me in this and let them both tend you, ma'am,' he said softly. 'I shall not feel easy again until I know you are completely recovered.'

He gazed intently into her eyes, hoping in his she could read all the emotion he dare not express before this interested crowd.

After gazing back at him for a long moment, she nodded. 'As you wish.'

'Then I shall see you later. Take her home, Davie,' he said, giving her hand over to the boy, who took her arm and escorted her away as slowly and carefully as if she were a blown-glass goblet that might shatter at too rough a touch. Once she was seated in the gig, Ned gave them a wave goodbye and turned to the men who held Barksdale.

'Gentlemen, let's get the prisoner into Tanner's wagon and into town.'

It was several hours later before Ned was finally able to begin his journey back to Blenhem Hill. He'd had to send a man to hunt down the constable, who'd been away from town with another group of searchers, then wait upon the official's return before he could turn Barksdale over to that representative of the law.

Since lashing out at him and Davie at the school, during the transit to town and while they tarried at the gaol, the prisoner had taken his advice and remained silent, ignoring both the taunts of some of the farmers and the angry jeers of the villagers.

Despite his loathing of the man, Ned had to grudgingly admire the coolness of his exterior. 'Twas apparent he'd been a soldier who'd handled himself well under fire—which made it all the more unfortunate that the man was an out-and-out rogue.

Impassive though he'd been, Ned suspected that after witnessing the level of hostility directed towards him by the crowd, Barksdale was glad the village gaol had stout stone walls and the constable was an honourable man who'd never stand for lynching.

Finally the search party had returned, the constable at its head. Tanner related to both him and Ned the story of what had transpired at the school.

So Barksdale had been posing as the mysterious Hampton! No wonder he'd wanted to have Mrs Merrill speak for him to the crowd. He had to know that, to safeguard the life of a woman highly regarded by the community, his pursuers would probably have agreed to a Mr Hampton's demands—and taken themselves out of sight while he rode away with her. It would have been much more difficult for him to persuade them to let the hated overseer Barksdale escape.

Any admiration for Barksdale's defiant courage before the crowd, however, evaporated in a revival of his anger at the thought of what the man had intended to do to Joanna, what Mary warned him Barksdale would have done, had Davie's audacious intervention not succeeded.

Hearing the tale of the lad's courage and ingenuity made him doubly appreciative of his potential. The boy should be more than just a land agent's assistant; he should be provided with an education, sponsorship and the opportunity to serve at the highest level.

After leaving Barksdale safely incarcerated, as Ned crossed the stable yard at the Hart and Hare, a distraught Mary ran out to confront him. Though he quickly assured her that Barksdale had been captured and Mrs Merrill freed unharmed, she fell to her knees, weeping and castigating herself anew for not telling anyone she'd seen the former agent back in the area.

When the group of men who'd accompanied Ned to the gaol gathered around, questioning her, she rose proudly to her feet. Facing them squarely, she repeated in more detail what she'd revealed to Ned earlier: that several years ago, Barksdale had attacked her in the woods as she walked home from the village. That he'd got her with child, the babe everyone believed had been sired by her soldier sweetheart Jesse Russell. That even after her parents turned her out as a doxy and a kind Peg Kirkbride had taken her in, after she lost the babe and began working in the taproom, she'd kept her secret, for Barksdale continued to threaten that he would evict her family from their farm and sell her little brothers to a factory boss, like he had Davie, if she ever revealed what he'd done.

Looking up at Ned in the stunned silence after her testimony, she said quietly, 'I'll tell it all again to the constable, sir, if you think it might help.'

'Thank you, Mary. I'll call on you if it's needful,' he replied, outraged anew at Barksdale's depravity and determined if he could to spare Mary the anguish of describing again to that official what had happened to her.

While his mind skipped to contemplating what else he might do to address the grievous wrongs she had suffered, Jesse Russell, who had been standing unnoticed among the crowd behind Mary, limped over and halted beside her.

'Barksdale was already gone when I came back,' he said softly. 'Why did you never tell *me* the truth?'

She looked up at him, tears beaded on her lashes. 'I was too ashamed.'

'Ah, Mary, love.' He sighed and with his one good arm, pulled her against him. After an instant's resistance, she threw her arms around his neck and buried her face against his chest.

While the rest of the crowd quietly dispersed, Ned mounted his horse and rode off, the sight of the couple's tentative reconciliation leaving a glow in his heart. Perhaps the estranged lovers could resolve their differences after all.

He certainly hoped so. He knew exactly how it felt to fear that you'd lost the love of your life forever.

Now, all he wanted to do was gaze upon his so he might reassure his still-anxious nerves that she was safe.

As he directed his tired mount on to the road to Blenhem Hill, though, a new thought occurred, energising him with a surge of hope and excitement.

If it turned out that Barksdale—whether out of hatred for the landed classes or a simple desire to revenge himself upon the Marquess who'd sacked him—was in fact the secret leader of the Spenceans, the man responsible for the mill fire and the attack on his carriage, Ned might soon be able to resolve all the problems that had required him to assume an alias.

He could confess his identity to Joanna and come out into the open to court her. And if heaven smiled upon him, he might at last be able to claim her as his wife, to love and keep for the rest of his days.

Joy flooding his soul at the thought, he spurred his mount to greater speed.

A short time later he turned his horse on to the drive leading to the manor. Grimy and sweaty from a long day in the saddle, he hadn't eaten since sunrise, but all that could wait. Proper or not, before he did anything else, he intended to slip into Joanna's bedchamber and reassure himself that she was bathed, bandaged and safely asleep in her bed.

After he'd eaten and cleaned up himself, if residual fear still held desire in check, he might even follow through on his first impulse and return to keep vigil beside her through the night.

On that happy thought, Ned rode to the stables, turned his horse over to a groom and loped to the house.

Chapter Sixteen

An hour later, a glass of brandy in hand, by the light of a single candle Ned sat reading by Joanna's bed. Though she had clucked at him and shaken her head when he had first told Mrs Winston he meant to usurp her role and assume watch over her patient, before he needed to remonstrate further, she had hopped up and ceded her place.

''Tis not proper, I expect, but I know she'll come to no harm under your care,' she'd whispered, patting his arm before gathering her knitting and tiptoeing out.

As he had eaten a hasty dinner earlier, Mrs Winston had related how she had treated a number of minor cuts and bruises for Mrs Merrill. Except for a knot on the back of her head—sustained when the villain Barksdale had slammed her against the door, that lady related with indignation—the housekeeper thought the hurts insignificant. After keeping her patient awake long enough to determine the head injury wasn't severe, she'd put Joanna to bed with a soothing compress and a warm draught to help her sleep.

Abandoning the book, Ned indulged himself in this rare opportunity to unabashedly stare at her. Unbound hair, free of any restraining caps, fell loose over the pillows, the compress Mrs Winston had applied visible at the back of her head. With one hand at her temple, long sooty lashes brushing her cheeks and her face in repose, she appeared to be the girl he'd first thought her the night she'd arrived at Blenhem, dripping, scared and lost.

She lay now on her side, probably to avoid putting pressure on what must be a very tender head. Ned felt another surge of outrage at the injury Barksdale had done her.

Maybe lynching wasn't so bad an idea after all.

The childlike image was belied, however, by the swell of her breasts outlined by a draping of bedlinen. Visible above the coverlet was the neck and collar of her cotton night rail, an unadorned, business-like affair devoid of ribbons or lace that covered her up to her chin. But as desire gradually broke free of the restraint fear for her welfare had imposed over it, Ned was having increasing difficulty keeping himself from envisioning how her figure might look draped instead in a whisper of silk, fine and thin enough to be almost transparent.

As if co-operating in his fantasy, she turned to her back and sighed, inhaling a deep breath that made her breasts strain against the concealing cotton. In a surge of sensation, Ned felt himself harden, his own member straining uncomfortably against the confines of his breeches.

Sweat breaking out on his brow, he shifted position. Perhaps, after he remained a bit longer to make sure she'd fallen, not into the deep stupor of the brain-injured, but simply a normal healing slumber, he'd take himself off to his room.

Before the temptation to rouse her overwhelmed him.

But as he reached that decision, she stirred again and awoke. After a dazed moment, her eyes focused on him—and she smiled.

His heart swelling with gladness, Ned felt himself smiling back. 'How are you feeling?'

'Better. Much better, now that you are here.'

Savouring her words, without conscious thought, Ned took her hand. A mingling of grief, anger and pain shook him as he looked at the cuts and bruises on her knuckles.

'I'm so sorry you were hurt,' he murmured, placing a gentle kiss on her fingers. 'Barksdale will pay for it, the blackguard.'

'He's in gaol, then?'

'Safely locked away—and glad to be there, I think. I believe he realises that without its protection, some of the tenants might try to make off with him—and that would be the last anyone ever saw of one Nate Barksdale.'

'Better to let the law he abused punish him. And speaking of punishment, how are you? You must have nearly as many bruises as I do—and I fear I scratched you when—' she halted suddenly, swallowing hard, tears trembling on her lashes '—wh-when you pulled me free.'

She squeezed the fingers that held hers. 'Thank you for coming to rescue me. If you hadn't arrived just at the moment you did, he would have pulled me back inside. I might even at this minute be with him on the road to London, forced at knife or pistol point to…to do his bidding.'

The image of her in Barksdale's power made him so crazy, Ned had to push it away. 'The intrepid Mrs Merrill, who'd almost succeeded in digging herself out of that cottage like the craftiest of hares that ever waltzed out of a kitchen garden after stripping it clean? I think not! Brave as you are, you would have worked out some way to escape him.'

She shuddered. 'I'm not brave. I was terrified.'

'Indeed, you are brave,' he argued. 'You didn't sit there wringing your hands and cowering, you crept away. That's the essence of bravery—acting despite your fear.'

'I was terrified until I saw you riding up. Then I knew I would be all right. One way or another, eventually you would have got me away from him.'

'I would have ridden without food or sleep like a madman

until I freed you,' Ned agreed flatly, shuddering inwardly at the awful image of her entrapped by Barksdale. Shaking his head to expel it, he said, 'But let us talk no more of that. I cannot bear even the thought of you in Barksdale's thrall.'

'Let us speak instead of Davie's courage and ingenuity, then! You saved me from Barksdale, but I would never have had a chance to break away, had it not been for Davie's cleverness. You should have heard him!'

She chuckled. 'One could almost sympathise with the extreme measures Barksdale took to rid himself of the boy, for Davie certainly had studied to perfection how to mock and goad the man! He distracted him so completely, if that breach in the wall had been any larger I would have been able to scamper away as swiftly as that hare you mentioned. By the way,' she continued, her mirth fading, 'you're not angry with Davie, I hope. He had no way of knowing that Tanner would turn around to join the searchers instead of continuing on to the school, as Mr Elliot had assured us.'

'No. Even if I were, remorse has punished him more severely than any chastisement I could devise. He's already shown himself an exemplary assistant. Once he's learnt the rudiments of reading and sums at your school, I believe he should be sent to university. A young man of his ingenuity and daring should go far.'

'So you will speak to your patron about sponsoring him?' she exclaimed, her face lighting. 'That would be wonderful!'

'Of course I shall,' he recovered, his face heating at his near-blunder. Thank heavens the need for subterfuge would soon be over, allowing him to speak his thoughts freely without having to guard his heart and tongue.

How he longed to share with her all the details of his life he'd thus far had to withhold! Not just his hopes and aspirations for Blenhem, but the whole of his life.

His childhood and growing up with a doting mother and a

fond, absentminded father who'd preferred scholarship to the vicissitudes of farming. How from earliest memory he'd loved the land, the smell of it freshly ploughed in spring, its damp mustiness after a gentle rain, its baked-dry tang in the heat of midsummer. How he'd eagerly assumed responsibility for the family properties when his father had offered to transfer its management over to him at an early age. How he'd yearned for a kindred spirit to share his passion for tending it and improving the lives of the people who worked on it.

He couldn't wait to win her hand and take her to Oxford where, once Ned assumed the reins of the family properties, his parents had retired so his bookish papa might pursue his studies in medieval history. Meet his mother, a perfect scholar's wife who'd never seemed to regret exchanging the vast halls and drawing rooms of Wellspring Manor in Kent for a handful of rooms in the city with only a tiny staff to manage. Content to arrange the dinners and soirées at which her husband and his scholarly cronies argued over the policies of King John and the Hundreds Rents while she chatted with the other wives.

They would both love her—and be delighted that their only son had found a lady to love at long last.

Ned emerged from this happy vision to find Joanna staring at him. Alas, candour and the dreams they might set free would have to wait until the business of Barksdale, the mill fire and the carriage attack was settled. And now that he was assured that her injuries were not serious, propriety dictated that he leave her.

No matter how fiercely both heart and his aroused senses protested against that conclusion.

After another tender kiss to her abused knuckles, reluctantly Ned relinquished her hand. 'I'd best go and let you return to your rest.'

Her fingers tightened on his. 'Don't go,' she murmured.

A bolt of desire, hot, demanding, shot through him, turning his blood to steam and his quiescent member to rock.

She was scraped and bruised and her head ached. This couldn't be the invitation his greedy body wanted it to be, he told himself, desperately swimming against a strong sensual tide. She wanted reassurance after the terrors of the day, that was all.

'I ought to go,' he said, as much to himself as to her. 'Now that you are awake, it's not proper that I stay.'

But he couldn't make himself pull his hand free.

A slow, wicked smile that promised mischief and delight lit her face. Ned stared, not quite able to believe what that smile promised, while his mouth dried and the bottom dropped out of his stomach.

'I don't want "proper",' she said, her husky voice brushing like velvet against his over-sensitised skin. 'I was so frightened today, while Barksdale held me captive. But after I tried to escape, my only thought when he grabbed my ankles, trying to pull me back, was how much I've wanted to be in your arms. My only regret was that I might live out the rest of my probably short life without ever experiencing that rapture. Now that a merciful heaven has given me another chance, I don't want to go another night without it. Please, Ned…stay with me.'

How could he deny her, when he had known the same fear—and was filled to overflowing by the same desire? While his heart thrilled to the sound of his name on her lips, he nonetheless struggled to find the words to return a more prudent answer.

Then she pulled his face close and kissed him.

He tasted the sweetness of honeyed herbal tea on her mouth, while his head filled with the scent of a minted compress and the spicy, exotic perfume that never failed to arouse him. Confronted with the reality of the kiss he'd imagined countless times, he simply couldn't do the honourable thing and pull away.

Just one kiss, he told himself. He'd allow only that before obeying the stern order of honour and duty that he take himself off. And if he had only one kiss, he would infuse it with all the tenderness, love and yearning that flooded his heart at the thought of having her in his arms.

Placing his hands gently, mindful of her bruised shoulders, he drew her closer. Slowly he deepened the kiss and when, with a thrill that sent another bolt of lust through him, she opened her mouth, he couldn't help sliding his tongue within to gently caress hers. With a little sigh that reverberated through his body, she joined in the game, mingling her tongue with his, stroking, teasing, caressing.

The sweetness of it made his heart swell in his chest, while further south, other parts of him that had no need of additional stimulation throbbed and burned. Breathing and heartbeat accelerated, while time seemed to slow to the rhythmic pulse of blood through his veins.

With a moan he felt straight to his loins, she brought her hands up to clasp his head. Without conscious thought he found himself lowering her back against the pillows and deepening the kiss. Just a little more, he promised the stern voice that, over the increasing conflagration in his senses, continued to reprove him. He'd give her just a taste of the desire that drove him mad every time she was near, a hint of the fulfilment to come.

She met the bold strokes of his tongue with her own, angling her head to give him fuller access, while she tangled her fingers in his hair, brushed her fingertips over his ears and down his neck, setting off shivering waves of sensation.

He must, he would, stop…but not quite yet. For a few more precious seconds he would savour her lushness, just long enough to store up memories to carry him through the raging emptiness that assaulted him every night in his lonely bed while he dreamed of claiming her, licking up every drop of her sweetness, from the russet tendrils at her temples to the dimpled recesses of her ankles.

He moved his mouth to nuzzle her lips, then traced his tongue over her jaw line and upwards, into the shell of her ear. Her stroking fingers stilled, clutched in his hair, while a deep moan issued from her throat.

Triumph flooded him at this evidence that his effect on her was as heady and immediate as hers on him. He couldn't stop now, not without first rewarding her for that admission with nibbles to her earlobe and across her cheek, soft wet kisses trailed from her chin down her neck to the pulse beating wildly at her throat.

While he played with his tongue in the hollow there, she seized one of his hands and cupped it to her breast. The breath stopped in his throat as he felt the nipple peak beneath his thumb, while with her other hand, she pulled at the knot of his cravat.

Using the unwinding neckcloth to pull his face back level with hers, gazing at him intently with passion-dark eyes, she said, 'Now.'

'Are you—?'

'Now,' she repeated, cutting off his query with a hard, demanding kiss that left no room for doubt.

In that instant, resistance crumbled and he was lost.

Willingly he submitted as she undressed him, jerking free the buttons of his waistcoat, tugging off that garment and then pulling the shirt over his head. He intended to return the favour, teasing her out of her night rail, but before he could grasp it, she urged him on to the bed beside her, then leaned over to circle his bared nipples with her tongue. Rational thought departed for good when she began to suck and nip him, while one hand smoothed its way down his belly and beneath the waistband of his trousers.

He raised his hips, his torso straining upwards as he sought to move his throbbing member nearer her lazily descending fingers. But still suckling him, each pull on that sensitive flesh sending darts of sensation downwards, she teased her fingers over his hipbones, his abdomen, around the curve of his waist towards his buttocks. He groaned in frustration and frenzy.

Murmuring soothingly, she removed the hand from beneath the garment. Before he could utter a panicked protest, she set about unbuttoning his trouser flap. An instant later, cool air flooded over that most overheated part of him as his erection sprang free.

She bent over him, her unbound hair sweeping across his naked skin with the silken caress of a thousand tiny fingers. Then he felt the hot wetness of her mouth at his belly, stroking and licking in a slow descent to the place he most wanted her to be.

His only rational thought was the realisation that, once she reached there, he would last about as long as a child's sweet ice on a hot day.

Even so, it took him several seconds to be able to utter a strangled 'No!' and move a hand to stay her.

She looked up to smile at him, her eyes heavy lidded. 'I want this,' she said softly, reaching down and tracing a finger up his member, which leapt under her hand. 'I've wanted it practically since the night we met,' she continued, cupping her hand around the tip. 'Let me, please?'

Words were scrambling in circles to the rhythm of her slow massaging strokes. It took several seconds before he could capture enough to nod his assent and reply, 'My... pleasure.'

A mischievous glint lit her eyes. 'I certainly hope so,' she replied, and bent to take him in her mouth.

All that remained then was sensation, exquisite flooding waves of it pushing him rapidly to the pinnacle and beyond. With a cry he tried to stifle, he felt himself shatter in a burst of ecstasy.

When the world righted and the stars settled back in their places, he opened his eyes to blink up at her smiling face. 'Was it?' she asked.

'Was it…?' he repeated stupidly before catching her reference, then shaking his head in wonder. 'Words cannot express,' he said simply, reaching out to caress her cheek with one fingertip.

'For me, too,' she whispered, capturing his hand and holding it against her face.

'I feel selfish, though,' he confessed.

Her grin returned. 'Don't. 'Twas me being selfish. For now when we love again, it can last and last.'

A chuckle rumbled in his chest. 'Clever girl! Yes, it can—and it will.'

More than that, he promised himself, he would make her burn and sigh and tremble on the brink until she cried his name and begged for release. Create for her a night she would never forget, one that would bind her to him forever.

He felt a wolfish grin light his face as a wave of sheer joy bubbled up from his chest. He couldn't wait to go to work. 'Your turn, madam, I believe,' he said.

'Joanna,' she corrected. 'Call me "Joanna".'

'Joanna,' he repeated reverently, thrilled to have been granted permission to use the name that sang through his dreams. Then he snagged the hem of her night rail and pulled the garment up over her head.

He caught his breath on a gasp as he looked at her for the first time, sitting proudly naked before him, smooth shoulders and dimpled arms and full, lush, rounded breasts, the dusty nipples already erect beneath his admiring gaze. Helpless before that invitation, he bent to suckle one.

Her head lolling back, she gave a shuddering sigh. Her gasping breaths and the rigid hands clutching at the bed linens urged him on as, after lavishing attention on each breast, he moved lower. Teasing her legs apart, he smoothed his hands over her legs to the satin of her inner thighs, then bent to lick the tender bud within the petalled folds at her centre, until, with a muffled cry, she shattered.

He gathered her close until her heartbeat slowed and her breathing settled…while the smooth caress of her naked skin against his body heated his flesh and soon had him once again hard and aching.

After a few minutes lying pliant in his embrace, she stretched against him and nuzzled his neck, then chuckled against his throat. 'Ah, I was correct, I see,' she said, bringing her hands up over his back and smoothing her fingers down his naked skin, beneath the gaping waistband of his breeches, to press his hardness against her.

'Correct indeed,' he affirmed, rubbing his cheek against her hair.

'Excellent,' she sighed. 'I can scarcely wait to begin again.'

And with that, she twisted beneath him, wrapped her legs around his and pressed upwards, sheathing him within the velvet softness of her body.

The feel of being within her, surrounding by her moist hot flesh, was wonderful beyond all imagining. 'No more waiting,' he promised, and drove himself deep.

Chapter Seventeen

Hours later, Joanna woke filled with a wonderful sense of euphoria. Despite not actually claiming sleep until the early hours of the morning, she felt brimming over with energy and enthusiasm.

How could she be anything but energised after a night of lovemaking as tender, passionate, inventive and satisfying as anything she could have imagined? Daydreams paled beside the reality of being with her Ned, who had fulfiled her hope for a reprise of their lovemaking several times over.

He'd brought the sensual appetite that had slumbered since her husband's death to full awakening—and she'd revelled in every moment. Perhaps, she thought with a sudden touch of anxiety, a bit too much. She hoped she hadn't shocked him by her shameless initiative and bold demands.

Though she'd pleasured him as thoroughly as he'd pleasured her. And, ah, how well he'd done that! With his mouth, his tongue, his fingers, his stroking member, he'd brought her again and again to the ecstasy of release.

She couldn't wait to do it all over again tonight.

She uttered a dreamy sigh at the thought, before the warmth of the sun coming through the windows suddenly penetrated her abstraction and she sat bolt upright, peering at the time on the mantel clock. Over her drowsy protest, Ned had left her bed about an hour before first light. The household had almost surely finished breakfast by now, so he must have asked Mrs Winston not to rouse her.

Embarrassment came and went in a quick hot wave. In a household this small, she knew the secrets of the night were unlikely to last long. If Mrs Winston—and the other servants—weren't already aware of their night-time revels, the maid who laundered these tangled sheets would soon alert them.

Sighing, she shook her head, then winced at the twinge of pain. If the household learned of the liaison, so be it. She was no longer a young virgin of good birth looking for a husband, but a servant without a reputation to protect, a mature woman who knew what she wanted and wasn't afraid to ask for it.

She loved Ned Greaves. It was silly and pointless to turn missish now about the prospect of the rest of the household knowing it.

The little fear darted into her heart again that their night together might have irreparably damaged their friendship. Firmly she squelched it. Too late now to worry about the consequences of her bold action.

Besides, if she didn't scramble out of bed and get herself downstairs quickly, she would miss him before he left to attend to the day's work.

Some fifteen minutes later, cheeks flushed with effort, she hurried into the breakfast room—and stopped short, both surprised and delighted to see him still seated at the table. Her cheeks flushed even hotter after Myles gave her a rare welcoming nod—followed by broad wink that confirmed the secret was out.

She suppressed an inward sigh. At least if she were known to have acted the wanton, it appeared the staff approved her choice.

But her agitation faded when she gazed into the face of the man who'd risen as she walked in. On his countenance she saw the same radiant joy that she knew illumed hers.

They must have greeted each other, though her dazzled mind heard none of the polite pleasantries. She only knew he sprang up to escort her to the sideboard, hovering beside her as if he were as eager as she was to be near again. He helped her choose food she didn't remember eating, after which Myles filled her cup with coffee she didn't recall tasting, winking at her again before he finally removed himself. At last, they were alone.

Ned reached for her hand and kissed the fingers.

'Thank you,' he said softly. 'My beautiful Joanna.'

'I should rather thank you, my wonderful…inventive…skilful…untiring Ned,' she replied, delighting as his expression changed from surprise to pleasure to an embarrassed pride at her praise.

He assisted her to her feet and walked her towards the door. 'I must go to town this morning and see about arranging Barksdale's arraignment, then question as many as possible of the witnesses. The Assizes are to meet shortly, but I'll send word to see if I can speed up the process by having a judge come here immediately to conduct a hearing. The men of Blenhem and Hazelwick are respectful of the law, but I don't want to test their patience by keeping the villain too long in gaol—or allow any of his cohorts to slip away. Though I hope all the danger has passed, will you indulge me and stay here today?'

'Will you indulge me?'

'If I can,' he answered, a tenderness in his face that sent a soaring thrill of delight through her as he halted beside her on the threshold.

'Kiss me, then!' she demanded.

Readily he bent his head. As he cupped her face in his

hands, she prolonged what had begun as a sweetly tender exchange by slipping her tongue between his pliant lips and thrusting deep inside. After a startled instant, his hands clenched, then slipped down to grasp her shoulders, as his tongue met hers, sliding, suckling, tasting, until her blood fired to boiling and she pressed herself against him, exulting at the hardness straining against his breeches.

With a groan, he gently pushed her away. 'Vixen! If I don't stop immediately, I'll be lost, and I must go to Hazelwick…though all I want to do is carry you back to my chamber and resume what we discontinued in the early light of dawn.'

'Why don't we?' she suggested with a wicked smile as she trailed a finger down his chest.

With another groan, he captured her finger before it could descend to its ultimate destination. 'You'll be the death of me, you heartless wench!' he scolded her with a chuckle. 'And I must warn you, I shall punish very severely tonight…several times over. Little as I wish it, though, to Hazelwick I must go.'

She knew it was naughty of her to tease him…yet her heart exulted at the regret evident in his voice. It was quite obvious that, despite the serious obligations calling him, he was finding choosing duty over pleasure extremely difficult.

But he wouldn't be her darling, wonderful, honourable Ned if he weren't guaranteed always to place duty first, regardless of his own desires.

'Besides,' he continued, giving her fingertips another kiss before releasing them, 'I'm trying mightily to maintain at least a semblance of discretion. When Myles sniggered as I walked into the breakfast room this morning, my first thought was I must have tied my neckcloth awry—a very great possibility, since my thoughts were so occupied by memories of a certain lady that I was scarcely aware of putting on my garments.' With a wry grimace, Ned sighed. 'He laughed outright when I checked it in the glass. I fear he suspects our attachment.'

'He gave me a knowing wink,' she admitted.

Ned's face sobered. 'That concerns me. I shall be most displeased if any of the staff says or does anything slighting towards you because of my…imprudence last night.'

'It wasn't imprudent,' she said at once. 'It was wonderful.'

That half-pleased, half-embarrassed smile lit his face again, touching her heart with how greedily he soaked up her praise. Obviously no lady had ever voiced appreciation for his lover's skills as eloquently as she should have!

Joanna was thrilled the task had fallen to her—and it would, she vowed to herself, henceforth remain hers alone, now and forever!

Unless, after a few weeks or months of an agreeable liaison, he sent her away. Once again she rejected the thought, firmly refusing to allow anything to dim today's joy.

Meanwhile, Ned repeated, 'I must go now, I'm afraid. I hope to uncover enough evidence to guarantee a conviction against Barksdale, not just for holding you captive, but for plotting, if not himself setting, the mill fire and for being the leader of the Spencean group at the Hart and Hare.'

'I wish you the best of luck. If my testimony can assist in that effort, I shall be happy to offer it.'

He gave her hand another squeeze. 'Thank you. I expect to be back by late afternoon. And if all unfolds as I hope it will, I shall have something very important to tell you. Something even more important to ask. Will you wait for me?'

Could he mean what she thought he meant? Bubbles of joy and excitement fizzled in her veins like champagne uncorked. She bobbed her head eagerly, not minding the pain such an action set off. 'I will wait forever,' she vowed.

He chuckled. 'Both I, and my very overheated imagination, sincerely hope it won't take that long.' Darting a look down the hallway to make sure none of the household was in view, he planted a quick kiss on her cheek. 'Until later, then—my sweet darling.'

He gave her a broad smile and strode off.

Smiling too, she watched him walk down the hallway to the front door. With a giggle, she hurried to the morning room to give him a little wave from the window when he turned towards the house before accepting the groom's leg up on his horse. She continued to watch until he rode out of sight, before wandering back into the hallway.

Where she stopped abruptly after almost colliding with Mrs Winston.

'I was coming to see how my patient did.' Looking her up and down, the older lady smiled. 'I can see you are doing quite well. No matter how much that head might hurt!'

Though Joanna blushed, she was too bursting with happiness to mind that the housekeeper obviously knew about her liaison. 'I'm very well indeed, thank you!' Then to the housekeeper's surprise, she grabbed the woman's hands, laughing, and twirled her in a circle.

Shaking her head at her, Mrs Winston pulled her hands away. 'Goodness, you'll make me dizzy! As he made you, I see.' With an arch smile, she murmured, 'A fine, big, strapping lad, is he? Made the stars fall for you all night, I'll wager!'

'You cannot imagine!' Joanna affirmed with a sigh.

Mrs Winston laughed. 'Though 'tis years since I lost my man and took up housekeeping, I can still imagine. Go on with you into the morning room. I promised Mr Greaves I'd brew you some herbal tea and check your bruises…though I suspect he's already provided the best possible medicine a woman could wish for to cure a bump on the head, eh?'

Wrapping her arms around herself, Joanna smiled after the departing housekeeper. She was Ned's lady now and apparently everyone knew it. Though in the back of her mind, the remnants of her genteel upbringing fretted at the fact that their relationship was already so widely known, she couldn't, wouldn't regret last night. Better to concentrate on the much more exciting question of what Ned was coming back to tell—and ask—her.

Might he solicit her hand in marriage?

'Twas what she desired above all things—but she would never push him to it. Still, Ned Greaves was an honourable man through and through. One who'd already expressed his concern about her reputation among the staff, a man who was unlikely to trifle with a woman whom he knew had earned the respect of her fellows and the whole community. One who was to become the schoolteacher for that community.

Though she could do little now to advance his career, perhaps it was possible that an ambitious young man of vast talents might still consider it advantageous to wed a woman who'd been a gentleman's daughter and a gentleman's wife. Though her exalted former in-laws—and her even more exalted cousin Lord Englemere—would probably look down on her for allying herself with a man they and their society would unquestionably view as vastly beneath them.

She shrugged. Since her in-laws had done nothing to enable their son's widow to maintain her status, she wasn't about to start worrying about their opinion—nor that of the *ton*. Despite their link by blood, she'd never belonged to the exclusive social world that embraced Lord Englemere.

Not for the first time, she wondered exactly what was the social background of the man she could so easily envision marrying. He'd told her nothing of his past, which led her to suspect it was far from exalted.

Perhaps he showed such a ready sympathy for Davie because he, too, was an orphan. Given his placement in Lord Englemere's service, he might even be the illegitimate son of a lord, who'd educated his by-blow and sent him off with references to work for the class to which he was connected by blood, but could never enter.

What would her vicar father think of her allying herself to such a man? Reproving herself for the unexpected flash of dismay engendered by the thought, she told herself tartly that Papa would receive it better than the intelligence that his daughter had lured a man to lie with her out of wedlock.

But what did it matter what her family or society thought, as long as they were both happy? For herself, she knew without doubt she could happily spend the rest of her days as Ned Greaves's wife.

How easily she could picture their life together. She, teaching and nurturing children at school. Him, rebuilding the stocking mill, helping farmers tend their fields through the autumn, then gathering in perhaps the best harvest Blenhem had seen in many years. Obtaining a good price for their crops, guaranteeing a bounty to last through the winter.

Working with Davie too, who, she felt sure, would learn quickly. By next autumn he might even be ready to obtain a tutor to prepare him for university, if Ned could persuade his lofty patron Lord Englemere to sponsor the boy. Which, of course, he would. Her amazing, sensual, wonderful Ned could do anything!

Ah, to think of reuniting after a hard day's work every night to kiss and touch and love, greedily drowning in the exquisite sensations he created in her.

Only one cloud obscured her vision of bliss. Though her condition had allowed her to boldly seduce Ned without worry of consequences, if they wed and the doctors in India were correct, she would never be able to give him a son.

But she'd not think of that now, any more than she would listen to the vile whispers of doubt that hinted the information he wished to share and the question he meant to ask would have nothing to do with marriage.

She couldn't bear to consider it…because even if he dashed her hopes and offered her *carte blanche*, she wasn't sure she'd have the strength to refuse him.

So she simply *wouldn't* consider it. Hugging her joy close, she danced down the hall to the morning room.

Chapter Eighteen

Late that evening, over a tankard of the Hart and Hare's finest ale, Ned sat at the desk in a small upstairs bedchamber, reviewing notes taken during the day. It had helped his quest for information that news of Barksdale's imprisonment had spread rapidly, leading many townspeople and local farmers to come peer through the bars at the prisoner, as if he were a beast in the Tower of London.

Though the analogy ended there. Unlike those rather pathetic, caged animals who had lost the instincts of the wild, even in confinement, Barksdale remained dangerous.

Many of the visitors, informed by the constable that Ned was gathering testimony, had subsequently come to visit him at the Hart and Hare. While understanding their honesty might lead them into difficulties, shocked by the mill fire and the subsequent attack upon Mrs Merrill, a gratifying number of men involved in the radical group had come forward to testify.

Barksdale himself, since his original outburst at the schoolhouse, had maintained an aloof silence, making no reply to the gawkers who questioned or taunted him. Given the damning evidence he'd gathered from the witnesses, Ned hoped perhaps to extract a confession from the man his Nottingham and Manchester allies had unanimously described as the planner and fomenter of local unrest. Though as evidence of Barksdale's ruthless character continued to build, Ned realised such a hardened villain was unlikely to oblige.

However, so many witnesses had been eager to speak that by late afternoon Ned realised he would need to remain overnight at the Hart and Hare if he wished to record all of it, a decision reinforced when he received a reply to the urgent missive he'd sent early that morning. Rather to Ned's relief, since he held such a low opinion of the man, Squire Abernathy, the local magistrate, was away in London. Given the gravity of the offenses alleged against Barksdale and the fact that some of them had taken place in other parishes, a magistrate from the adjacent county had agreed to ride over and conduct a hearing on the morrow.

His last conference with an unemployed mill worker had ended just half an hour previous. Confident now that Barksdale would not be able to escape the tightening noose of incriminating evidence the man himself had fashioned, Ned at last let his thoughts return to the tantalising object that, despite the urgency of his task, had been teasing at the edges of his mind all day—Joanna.

He'd felt gloriously, rapturously happy as he rode off this morning after returning Joanna one last wave. He'd given his frisky mount his head, letting the animal gallop and laughing in joyous abandon as the horse cleared the fence into the front pasture, then the stone wall by the gatehouse to the Hazelwick Lane. He could hardly wait to finish this business and return to Joanna—*his* beautiful, witty, sensual Joanna.

He'd begun his interrogations on fire with enthusiasm to track down every witness to the incidents at the mill and the school, then to closely question the Nottingham journeyman and all the men Mary had tagged as members of the group that met at Hart and Hare. His excitement and impatience had only heightened after he learned the hearing would be held tomorrow. Perhaps by noon, he could see this business finished for good and all.

Ned certainly hoped so. He felt as if he'd been marking time all his life, waiting to find Joanna and begin anew, embarking together into a future filled with more richness and delight than he'd dared believe possible.

As he envisioned her lovely face, his heart swelled in his chest with the same exuberant impatience his mount had shown in taking the obstacles. How he longed to see her again!

But he'd have to wait until tomorrow. After realising he would need to remain in town overnight, Ned had penned the household a hasty note informing them of the delay and requesting that they come to Hazelwick in the morning for the hearing—and bring Davie. He'd need Joanna to describe how she'd been detained against her will and threatened at pistol-point. Though Davie was not of age to give evidence, Ned wished him to be available if the magistrate wanted to question him about the events Tanner and the other witnesses would present.

He longed for her, but as he looked around the small bare inn chamber, he also felt a small measure of relief. Now that he had tasted her sweetness, it would be difficult indeed to restrain himself. He wasn't sure he would have been able to resist the temptation of spending the night in Joanna's bed if he'd returned to Blenhem. She'd proved last night how easily her allure could crumble his will to resist.

He was serious about his concern in exposing her to gossip and possible censure. Despite his parting remark this morning, he intended to stiffen his resolve and refrain from dallying with her again until she was legally his wife.

Oh, that it might be soon! Especially after last night, he couldn't wait to reveal all he'd been forced to hide and proceed with her on an honest footing.

Still, an underlying uneasiness stirred at the prospect. She was bound to be incensed at first that he'd kept the truth from her for so long. Still, surely after he laid all the facts before her, she'd understand why he'd felt the deception had been necessary?

At least, he hoped so. If she remained angry, he'd simply have to find some way to allay her disapproval. He would not even entertain the thought of what he would do if the unthinkable happened and she refused him. After she'd fulfilled his most extravagant fantasies last night, he couldn't envision a life without her wit, competence and industry at his side by day and her sensual fire in his arms by night.

Once Barksdale had been arraigned and bound over for trial—please heaven, let it be tomorrow!—he could take the first steps on the road to claiming that life.

Despite his lack of sleep the previous night and the anticipation of settling the business of Barksdale on the morrow, Ned slept poorly. Finally, after tossing and turning most of night, pale light illumined the windows, announcing the dawn of what would probably be the most important day of his life.

The common room at the inn being the largest public space in Hazelwick, the hearing was to be held there. Going downstairs for an early breakfast, Ned discovered a crowd was already gathering. Turning away cordially the volley of questions and speculations fired at him, he invited all interested parties to stay for the hearing, where they might hear the witnesses speak and watch the evidence presented.

By the time he returned after going up to his chamber to gather his notes, the makeshift courtroom was full to overflowing. Among the assembly he saw Mary, Jesse protectively at her side, and nodded. He'd already assured her yesterday he did not intend to call on her unless absolutely necessary.

As his pocket watch ticked closer to the hour they could expect the magistrate to arrive, Ned saw Davie escorting

Joanna into the room. Ned had time only to send her a brilliant smile of greeting before, in a sudden silence broken by a
few jeers and mutterings, the constable led Barksdale in.

The prisoner seemed neither cowed by the hostile recep-
tion nor as coolly impassive as he'd been yesterday. Indeed,
to Ned's surprise, he raised his bound hands and waved for
silence, his expression genial.

'Hear me, good people,' he called out, his resonant voice
easily carrying through the packed room.

'Hear you gag at the end of a rope!' someone shouted.

'If that is my fate, so be it,' he called again, 'but let me
speak now.' Again he held out his hands for silence, radiating
such a sense of confidence and authority that, startled, reluctant, the assembly fell into an uneasy quiet broken only by a
few mutters.

'As you know, I lived among you for a number of years—'
he waved his hands again to calm the eruption of comments
that remark incited '—and I admit, I've not always seen eye
to eye with some of you. If I left hard feelings or harm, I'm
sorry for it. But you know me well. You know how resolute I
am, how once I give my word, I keep it.'

The whole group was silent now, their attention riveted on
the bound man addressing them. Barksdale was a born public
speaker, Ned thought, marvelling at the sheer skill and strength
of personality with which he controlled a hostile room. Ned
could easily see him standing beside the radical Drummond,
exhorting the spinners and weavers of Manchester to set off
on their hunger walk to London, the ill-fated 'March of the
Blanketeers' that had taken place just this past March.

How tragic a man of such gifts and tenacity had not har-
nessed his talents in a nobler cause! Ned thought as Barksdale continued, 'This late business was unpleasant, but just a
misunderstanding. No one was seriously injured. I'm prepared
to abandon my efforts to effect a change for the better here

and go my own way, leaving you to whatever limited assistance Mr Greaves can offer you.'

'Go your way? When pigs fly!' someone shouted.

'Nay, you'll stand before the judge!' another cried.

Barksdale seemed neither frightened nor affronted. Instead, he simply stood shaking his head, a pitying look on his face.

'It would not be wise to stand me before a judge, good people of Hazelwick and Blenhem. I see among you in this very group many who know why. If I am put under oath, I will be forced to name names and bring the pitiless light of the law glaring upon your neighbours…husbands…brothers. Are you willing to risk them to a system that wants to condemn and hang rather than address the injustices it visits upon the common folk?'

Ned could almost see a wave of apprehension ripple through the room. Everyone here was probably remembering last summer's riots at Loughborough, after which six men had been hanged and three transported.

So that was Barksdale's ploy, Ned realised. Blackmail the citizens with the threat of accusing as many of them as possible of involvement in his nefarious schemes so they would be cowed into letting him escape his just punishment.

Escape unscathed, after what he had done to Mary—and tried to do to Joanna? Seeing the crowd beginning to waver, outraged, Ned stepped forwards.

'Good people of Hazelwick and Blenhem,' he called, his scornful tone mocking Barksdale's address, 'you need not be afraid, as this villain would have you be, of the honest workings of the law. In testimony given by man after man among you— testimony to which even more shocking and horrifying evidence could be given by some ladies here present—the prisoner stands before you accused of heinous crimes. You must not let him intimidate you into releasing him. Do you not want to see justice served for the many abuses you suffered at *his* hands?'

Ned looked back at Barksdale. 'Threaten as you will, these people are not cowards. The hearing will go forward, and when all the evidence is presented, it is *you* who will be hanged or transported.'

As the outcries and murmurs began turning against him, Barksdale's expression lost its congenial look. His face hardening, he beckoned to Ned.

With distaste, Ned approached him. As he neared the prisoner, he could sense a ruthless desperation under the still-polite veneer.

'Be careful what you ask for, Greaves,' Barksdale said, pitching his voice under the noise of the crowd so that only Ned could hear him. 'If you force me to, I'll come forth with names you'd rather not hear, names against whom solid evidence can be produced. Names of people important to your schoolmistress sweetheart. Yes, I've seen you sniffing up her skirts. Tasty little plum, isn't she?'

Even realising Barksdale's purpose must be to goad him to fury—perhaps into striking a bound man and compromising his claim of impartiality in laying evidence before the magistrate—Ned had to call upon all his powers of control to restrain himself from taking a swing at the man.

'Your morals are as despicable as your politics,' he said contemptuously.

'Seeing the way she's eyeing you now like a vixen hot for mating, 'tis a bit hypocritical to talk about "morals",' Barksdale sneered. 'But then, the world has always allowed a different standard of conduct between the likes of me and *gentlemen* like you, hasn't it?'

Gazing into the implacable stare of his adversary, suddenly Ned realised the implications of Barksdale's last remark.

That comprehension must have registered on his face, because, with a satisfied smirk, Barksdale continued, 'So she doesn't know? Well, then, I could tell your little sweetmeat a few things about you she'd be shocked to hear, couldn't I? How well would she take the news, I wonder? So high-principled a woman, with such a strong prejudice against the ruling class.' Barksdale's voice dripped scorn. 'If you value your cosy little arrangement, you'd better encourage this rabble to let me go.'

Ned couldn't imagine how Barksdale had found out—by intercepting his letters to Nicky, perhaps? But it was clear the man knew his name—his real name—and was threatening to disclose it to distract and dismay the crowd—incidentally causing maximum damage to his bond with Joanna—unless Ned persuaded the group to let him go.

He'd already accepted that having kept his true circumstances hidden so long, especially after taking her as a lover, Joanna was bound to feel betrayed, even if he revealed the news of his true identity privately, when she might question him and vent her anger.

What would the effect be upon her of discovering that shocking truth in a public forum, where Ned had no chance to explain? Regardless, duty gave him no choice. His heart pierced by anger and regret, wondering if his next words would sound a death knell to his dreams for the future, he replied, 'I'll see you go to the noose's end and nowhere else.'

Barksdale had the gall—and supreme confidence—to smile at him. 'I suppose I should give you credit for attempting to be a good man, Ned Greaves. But you're weak—unwilling to fight for what you want. Not a weakness, fortunately, I share.'

Turning back to the crowd, Barksdale called, 'Have I your leave to go, good citizens?'

'Never,' someone shouted while several others said, 'Aye, straight to the judge!'

'So be it, then. I've tried to reason with your spokesman here, this man who urges you to place your loved ones in danger, to no avail. So let me tell you what I'll be forced to tell the judge. I'll have to say Nick Forbes—aye, Farmer Johnston, your cousin—and Tim Harris—old Granny Cuthbert's nephew—and Mark Matthews—who's kin to all you Redmans there—were the officers of the local society that met, as you know, Innkeeper Kirkbride, each night in your taproom. Jesse Russell, there, when he wasn't sighing over his frustrated passion for your local doxy, carried news for the group, along with plans to attack mills from here to Manchester—'

'Ain't never attacked none, though,' a voice broke out. 'We talked, only!'

'Aye, he's right!' another chimed in.

'You attacked this man's carriage,' Barksdale shot back. 'You, Joe Bixby, how'd you explain to your wife that shot in your shoulder from the barrel of Mr Greaves's gun?'

The room erupted as neighbour turned to neighbour, shouting and questioning. Once again Barksdale waved for silence.

'Attacking a carriage is a serious crime. Especially as a man was injured—and especially that particular carriage. 'Twas the vehicle, as you know, of a very important person, Lord Englemere. But it was carrying another individual who is more important than any of you can imagine.' With a malicious glance at Ned, he said, 'Shall I tell them how important…Mr Greaves?'

It was his last opportunity to prevent Barksdale's revelations. While his mind and heart raged at the infamy being perpetrated against him, nonetheless Ned replied evenly, 'Say what you will. The people here know how to separate truth from lies.'

'Ah, it's truth we are to have, then! So, my friends, what do you imagine the punishment might be for attacking an aristocrat? Ah, yes, 'tis not just an estate agent who stands before you, but a gentleman of title…Sir Edward Greaves, is it not? Owner of Wellspring Manor and numerous other properties in Kent, as well as a small estate right here in Derbyshire. For *in truth*, you are the owner, not just the manager, of Blenhem Hill, are you not, Sir Edward?'

Over the shocked silence in the room, Ned replied steadily, 'I am.'

Barksdale gave a crow of triumph. 'There you have it, by *Sir Edward*'s own admission! Why do you think he lived among you in disguise, my good people, hiding his very name? To lull you into complacency with superficial acts of kindness so he might trick you into admissions that could lead you to the gallows, that's why! He came here not to help, but to gather evidence. A spy bent on bringing you to ruin, like Colonel Ralph Fletcher at Westhoughton. How many twelve-year-olds will you send to the scaffold here, Sir Edward…if these good citizens allow it?'

Chapter Nineteen

Horrified, Joanna stood frozen as the crowd dissolved into chaos around her. Even in India, she'd read of the incident that had occurred during the first Luddite riots of 1812, when among those executed for mill burnings—on evidence, it turned out later, planted by government informant Colonel Ralph Fletcher—was one Abraham Charlston. A boy listed on court documents as being sixteen years of age, but described in some news accounts as only twelve, and slow for his age. He'd cried for his mother on the scaffold. Nausea coiled in her gut, making her so queasy that for a moment she had to concentrate solely on breathing slowly in and out.

When she dared think of it again, she still couldn't believe it. Ned Greaves, the man she'd ridden beside day after day, worked with hand in hand, smiled at, shared her past with— had taken into her body—was a government spy? Was that possibility any more outrageous than learning—for he'd not denied it—that he wasn't merely the estate agent, but the *owner* of Blenhem Hill?

She'd set out this morning brim full of hope and optimism. Ned had written yesterday that he'd gathered so much evidence against Barksdale that he felt confident the man would be indicted, his removal most likely bringing about an end to the unrest that had been occurring in the area. Though she'd been disappointed to learn he would not return to ask the question she'd been waiting eagerly all day to hear, she'd dreamed all night of the joy of a future together.

Only her Ned was not 'Ned' at all—but 'Sir Edward'. Wincing inwardly, she now could hardly bear to speculate what that question might have been.

Sick and distraught as she was, she still had an important role to discharge in this hearing. For the moment at least, she must master her distress and get through the rest of it with an outward display of calm.

Still concentrating on her breathing, she started reining in the rampaging emotions, with some success—until she glanced up and saw Ned's gaze fixed on her, a sorrowful, pleading look on his face. As if scalded, she looked quickly away, while anguish blasted away the fragile boundaries she'd been erecting to contain it.

Around her people pushed and shoved, shouting and arguing in a swirling din that seemed to suck up all the space and air in the room. Her heart a splintering pain in her chest, she felt faint, dizzy, unable to suck in a breath. Panic prickled her skin and she was seized by the urge to bolt out of the door, into the sweet, fresh air outside, away from all this tumult— and heartbreak.

As if from a far distance, she heard Davie's voice at her ear. 'Are you all right, ma'am?'

Joanna had to suppress the impulse to laugh hysterically. All right? How could she be 'all right' when her whole world had just shattered, leaving her no longer sure who or what she was?

The pounding of hooves and the neighing of horses from without brought a stillness to the room. It must be the magistrate and his party arriving, she realised.

With a frantic glance towards the door that gave the lie to

his outwardly confident demeanour, Barksdale cried, "Tis the moment to decide, citizens. Let me go…or see your sons, brothers and husbands face the gallows of an uncaring, ungrateful government!'

'No one will face the gallows who is not guilty of some grievous wrong,' Sir Edward countered. 'In Hazelwick, that will mean first, and probably only, the man who *organised* the attack on my carriage. The man who actually set fire to the mill. The man who took Mrs Merrill hostage and threatened to shoot her. This man—Jake Barksdale. Surely you will not allow him to go free!'

The crowd had quieted again during Sir Edward's impassioned address. Looking around, Joanna watched the faces of the men pondering that question, Barksdale's fate hanging in the balance.

Then a man shouted, 'Aye, he starved my kin! Let him pay for his crimes.' 'Turned my widowed sister off her farm!' another cried. 'Led my poor Joe astray!' Mrs Bixby added.

While a growing volume of outcries affirmed the group's decision, the door opened. The judge checked on the threshold, pausing in surprise at the turmoil within.

Slipping past the constable, Barksdale ran for the back exit. After him in a flash, Sir Edward seized him by the shoulders and held on, absorbing the kicks and desperate swinging blows from the man's bound hands until several others hurried over to help him subdue the prisoner. They dragged him, struggling, back into the centre of the room.

'What's this commotion?' the magistrate demanded. 'I'll have an orderly assembly at this hearing, not a shouting rabble!'

'It's not a commotion, sir,' Sir Edward replied, 'but the thwarting of an attempt at escape. An escape, I'm sure, that you will never countenance once we lay the evidence before you.' Gesturing to the crowd, he said, 'Shall we let the hearing begin, gentlemen?'

As the crowd ceased its jostling and murmuring to settle into place, the magistrate took his seat and the hearing started. Too sick and dazed to hear much of it, Joanna concentrated simply on remaining in place and breathing evenly to keep nausea at bay until she could present her testimony and escape.

Whether Ned—nay, Sir Edward—felt satisfaction or triumph about the accumulating body of evidence against Barksdale, Joanna didn't know. As much as possible, she tried to tune out the sound of his voice as he introduced the various witnesses—and she simply couldn't bear to look him in the face.

At last the magistrate called her name. Quickly and succinctly, she presented her story and answered his few questions. She could feel Ned's—no, Sir Edward's—gaze on her throughout, but resolutely resisted the temptation to turn towards him and discover if contrition still filled his eyes.

It took all the strength she could summon just to keep her thoughts and emotions suppressed and distance herself from what had occurred in this room so she could survive the proceedings with her dignity intact.

The moment the magistrate nodded a dismissal to her, she seized Davie's arm and pulled him after her out of the room. Her hands were shaking, she noted with detachment, as she fought off another wave of nausea.

'Davie, I must return to the manor,' she told him urgently.

'Now?' he asked, his eyes widening. 'But they haven't finished giving testimony yet! Don't you want to see ol' Barksdale get back his own? And how 'bout Mr Greaves—Sir Edward, I mean—being a toff all that while and us never knowing!'

'Imagine,' she said drily. Thank heavens Davie could not know why the news was of such dire import to her. And of course the boy would want to stay. He might still be called on, and the shocking events of this day probably made it the most exciting of his life.

'Can you ride back with Myles and Mrs Weston, then?' she asked. 'I'll go now and take the gig.'

He agreed with alacrity before his eyes narrowed. 'Sure you'll be all right, driving yerself back? No offence, ma'am, but you ain't looking so good. I can understand, though, after Barksdale hurt and threatened you like he done, must sicken you to have to be in the same room with 'im. I kin drive you back, if'n you want me to.'

Once again, Joanna had to hold back an hysterical outburst of mirth. If he only knew it was not her attacker, but her rescuer who caused her to feel so ill! But grateful for Davie's erroneous assumption—and hoping the other residents of Hazelwick and Blenhem had reached the same conclusion about her sudden departure from the hearing—Joanna had no intention of enlightening him.

'No, I shall be all right. Go on,' she urged. 'You don't want to miss anything important.'

With a nod, the boy loped off again. Joanna was heading on trembling legs towards the gig when someone called her name. Looking over her shoulder, she saw Mrs Winston hurrying towards her.

'Mrs Merrill, if you are returning to Blenhem Manor, might I ride with you?'

Joanna really didn't want any company…but perhaps the woman's presence would keep at bay a little longer the dire questions she must ask herself and the onslaught of emotions the answers to them would entail. Long enough for her to recover from her shock at least at little, so that she might deal with all of this more rationally.

For deal with it she must, and immediately. Before Ned—Sir Edward—Greaves returned to Blenhem Manor.

His manor, she thought, another sick wave of distress sweeping through her.

'Of course, ma'am,' she returned the only possible answer.

But her hopes of blocking out the questions and allowing her emotions to calm during the drive back were swiftly dashed when it became evident that Mrs Winston was almost as agitated as Joanna. She had scarcely manoeuvred the gig out of the crowd of tethered horses and vehicles when Mrs Winston burst out, 'Whatever are we to do about the shocking news?'

Joanna thought about returning some remark about Barksdale's iniquities, but she knew that was not the shock to which the housekeeper was referring—nor did she expect such a diversion would work. Giving in to the inevitable, she replied reluctantly, 'It was…unexpected.'

'Oh, indeed! What is to become of us? When I recall some of the things I've said and done to Mr Greaves, who is not a "mister" at all, but master of Blenhem Hill! I declare, when he confirmed that fact, I feared for a moment I might swoon!'

Joanna could readily understand the lady's reaction. Before she could reply, Mrs Winston continued, 'Of course, he always did have that air of quality about him. But his manners was so easy and unassuming, I just never imagined… Dear me, how many times I must have insulted him, teasing and joking with him as if I were his equal! Myles, too! Oh, I just know he shall turn us all off without a character for our effrontery!' Had the housekeeper not needed to clutch at the rail to keep her seat in the bouncing gig, Joanna thought the woman would have wrung her hands.

She, too, had treated him as an equal, Joanna thought grimly. Nay, worse—as a 'gentleman's widow' she'd sometimes even fancied herself above him. As recently as yesterday, she recalled now with chagrin, she'd wondered if, so reticent he'd been to talk about his family, he might be illegitimate!

She cringed now at the thought, her fingers jerking at the reins and making the horse shy. Humiliation washing through her, she quickly controlled him.

But worse was to come. Looking up at her suddenly, Mrs Winston said, 'You didn't know, either—did you?'

'No,' she confessed through clenched teeth.

The housekeeper put a sympathetic hand on her arm. 'Oh, you poor dear. Mine is nothing to the shock you must have suffered!'

Her blush deepening, feeling ill all over again, Joanna recalled Myles's knowing wink, Mrs Winston's arch remarks when she'd come down to breakfast yesterday, all dreamy-eyed, her infatuation obvious to anyone in the household to witness. How she wished now she had behaved with more discretion!

Would they all now think her a nobleman's doxy?

How ironic, she thought bitterly, to have run half the length of England only to willingly become what she'd fled Selbourne Abbey to escape!

And so it continued until they reached Blenhem manor, the housekeeper recalling and lamenting each idle word or careless action to which Sir Edward might have taken offence. Too sick and weary to try to either reassure the woman or attempt to give her thoughts a different, more cheerful direction, Joanna simply endured the chatter, adding no more to the conversation than an occasional non-committal murmur.

She had a pounding head as well as a queasy stomach by the time they finally reached Blenhem, where she thankfully dropped off her passenger before turning the gig over to a groom. Swiftly, before news of the shocking developments in Hazelwick could be spread to the servants who'd remained at the manor, she hurried to her chamber and locked the door.

For the next few minutes, she simply gave in to the violence of the emotions she'd been restraining since the news had first been revealed. Throwing herself on the bed, she wept with humiliation, disappointment and grief for the loss of the dream that, the facts now indicated, had been impossible from the beginning.

At length, the storm of emotion passed. After drying her eyes, she went to sit at her desk.

Weeping accomplished nothing. What was she to do?

Her heart argued that 'Sir Edward' was the same 'Ned' she'd grown to know and love. That before condemning him for misleading, lying to and betraying her, she must allow him to explain the reasons behind the vast deception he'd perpetrated upon everyone at Blenhem Hill.

But memories, other bleaker memories, crowded in, telling her the reasons behind his actions didn't change the fact that the revelation of his true station in life upset the whole balance of the relationship she thought they'd established. She had memories far more extensive than those of Mrs Winston of times she had joked with him, teased him, treated him with a familiarity she would never have considered had she been aware she was addressing not a fellow estate employee, but its owner.

Indeed, she most probably would have left Blenhem Hill the day after her midnight arrival had she known the man who'd received her was 'Sir Edward' rather than estate manager Ned Greaves. She recalled the cold look of dislike on his features the moment they met. The dismaying thought struck her that it could very well have been Sir Edward, rather than her cousin Lord Englemere, who had discharged her brother!

Another wave of memories flooded her—all the times she'd argued with him about the venality of the government, of the ruling class and the aristocracy in general. She understood now why he had said so little in reply. Why he'd told her next to nothing about his childhood, upbringing, background.

Even worse, though she discounted Barksdale's contention that he'd come among them to play the spy, though she could understand why he would want to discover the reason behind the attack on his carriage, by deceiving everyone at Blenhem, he had taken advantage of the trust he'd established with the tenantry to lure them into revealing information that might well lead to severe legal repercussions. The law, as Barksdale rightly alleged, was inflexible when it came to attacks on the aristocracy and their property, punishment for such offences being swift and severe.

No, whatever relationship she thought had developed between herself and Ned Greaves was as artificial and false as the name and occupation he'd given her the night they had met.

She must leave. Though she was but a servant, the long-engrained habits of her genteel upbringing argued that it wasn't proper for her to live in the same house with him. It never had been, had she only known it.

But even as she thought about it, a protest against leaving him rose up from the depths of her being. She had known such joy this past month, found a happiness she'd never expected to experience again. She'd contentedly envisioned making Blenhem her permanent home, helping the children of the tenants, making a success of the school, assisting Davie towards a promising future.

She felt another pang. With Sir Edward as his patron, the talented boy she'd come to look upon as a sort of son didn't need *her*. The Baron could easily find the boy a much more qualified tutor, and with his connections among the aristocracy, could do far more for Davie than she could ever manage. She was grateful for that, at least.

But as she waded through the muddy bog of love and humiliation, anger and pain, a sense of betrayal and her anguish over it, an even more dismaying realisation surfaced.

Despite all that had happened today, she still wanted him. Part of her reluctance to leave, she knew, was based on the urgings of desire. It seemed her body, awakened anew to pleasure and greedy for more of it, was deaf both to reason and shame.

Knowing now who he really was, she was reasonably sure what question he had intended to ask her. It did her self-esteem little good to recall how humiliatingly easy she had made it for him to ask. Hadn't she been throwing herself at him, doing her best to tempt and seduce him, practically since her arrival? Small wonder if he thought her a plum ripe for the picking!

He wants you for more than just your body, her heart argued. What of the humour, tenderness, sense of purpose you shared? All of that was as real as your passion.

Was it real, cold reason replied—or had she only wanted to believe it so as to make the slaking of her desire more acceptable to her sense of honour? For if she were brutally honest, despite all she had learned today, if he returned this evening, persuasive and cajoling, soothing and gentling her with his touch—and then offered her *carte blanche*—she was not sure she'd be able to repulse him.

She must leave as soon as possible then, before the pleas of her heart and the demands of her body made her resolve waver. She would begin packing at once.

Fortunately, she reflected with gallows humour, she hadn't yet accumulated many belongings. A shattered heart and broken trust wouldn't take up much space in a trunk.

She had set out her few things on her bed, ready to place in a box she would borrow from Mrs Winston, when a knock sounded at the door.

'Mrs Merrill—Joanna.'

She froze, as Ned's—no, Sir Edward's—voice penetrated the study oak panel. The voice that had cried her name as she pleasured him, urged her to the brink as he plied his manhood between her legs, whispered sweet treacherous words of love in her ear as she lay spent on his chest.

'Joanna, won't you come out, please? I must talk to you.'

Chapter Twenty

Never in his life had Ned burned with such a need to do violence to another person as he had when, with agony in his breast, he had turned from watching Joanna bolt from the hearing room after giving her testimony, to see Barksdale smirking in satisfaction.

He'd clenched his hands on the chair back, struggling to hold the white-hot fire of rage fettered inside. To keep his hands from reaching for the throat of the man who'd casually, cruelly struck him what the villain knew was the most cutting blow he could deliver.

Only the perseverance developed through years of riding through icy rain, enduring the blazing heat of summer and the twenty-hour days of harvest, putting his own needs aside so as to tend first to duty, carried him through the rest of the proceedings. Though after the damning testimony of a dozen witnesses, the magistrate had no hesitation in binding Barksdale over for trial, Ned still had work remaining, for as that villain predicted, the allegations linking other men to the sedition he'd preached in these dangerous times was taken very seriously.

To the credit of the soldier's honour, if not his discretion,

Sergeant Russell had not contested Barksdale's accusations. Though he contended he had never participated in violence, he admitted he had carried messages for the group meeting at the Hart and Hare. The others had also freely confessed to their connections.

Ned had attempted to argue with the magistrate for leniency, but he'd been cut short. With one curt pronouncement, the official bound over for trial Sergeant Russell and all the other men alleged to have participated in the group, leaving the very real possibility some of them might be transported, if not hanged.

He would have to get Nicky to summon all his influence in Parliament and on the bench to avert that. There were times, he thought grimly, when being an aristocrat, even a minor one, had its benefits.

Probably not, however, according to Joanna. At the very first moment he could get away, he'd left the hearing for Blenhem, urging his horse to a gallop in his urgency to address the imperative that had consumed his heart since the moment Barksdale had revealed his name: persuading Joanna Merrill not to despise and reject him for deceiving her.

Hand still resting against the panel of her chamber door, he told himself that surely she'd at least hear him out. But as second after second ticked away and she made no reply to his appeal, fatigue and anguish filling him, he laid his head in defeat against the door frame. He was trying to decide whether or not to invade her room by force when, after a soft click, the door opened.

With reddened eyes that spoke of weeping, she flicked him the briefest of glances, as if she couldn't bear to look upon him. Pain scoured him at her distress while despair plunged his heart to his boot tips at her stiff, affronted stance and the cold disdain of her expression.

So she despised him now—not without cause. But he would never give up Joanna, his Joanna, without a fight.

'You will accompany me to the study?' he asked.

She swallowed hard and blinked back a tear—making him feel, if possible, even worse. 'I would rather not, but I suppose, to be fair, I should at least let you speak.'

Overwhelmingly grateful to be accorded that much, he stood aside to let her pass. He ached anew at how careful she was not to touch him as she walked by.

Still avoiding his gaze, she took a seat in the study, in a wing chair near the fire, across the room from her usual place on the sofa. 'Say what you will.'

In a few rapid sentences, Ned related what had happened on the way to Blenhem Hill, his concerns about the future of the estate and the tenantry and why he'd decided on subterfuge.

After he finished, she nodded politely, as if he had just offered her a proof in geometry. 'I agree it was necessary to uncover the villains responsible for the attack and the leader trying to tempt men into lawbreaking. But after we were better acquainted, why could you not have told me the truth and confided your purpose to me? Surely you couldn't think I had a part in such plans?'

'I wasn't sure at first,' he admitted. 'Your brother had just been discharged—not by me,' he added hastily, 'under less than ideal circumstances. I thought you might be part of some scheme to get him reinstated. Your actions soon convinced me otherwise. But from the sentiments you expressed about the wrongs done to men like Jesse Russell, I thought it possible you might be sympathetic to the reformers' cause.'

'You thought me capable of supporting lawbreakers?' she asked angrily. 'I see I was mistaken in believing that friendship and trust had developed between us!'

'No, you are not!' he quickly countered. 'Trust, friendship—and affection—did develop. From very early on, I never doubted your good sense and good faith. Especially not after you told me about Hampton's visit and revealed your misgivings about him and the unrest here. After that, I was only concerned that you be kept out of whatever was going on. Kept safe. You are by nature open and honest, a stranger to subterfuge. If Hampton or Russell had come by seeking news, I didn't want you to possess knowledge you might have to hide, information that, if revealed, might place you in danger.'

'I fell into danger anyway, not knowing,' she pointed out.

He'd suffered qualms of conscience about that himself. 'Along with having to deceive you, having inadvertently jeopardised your safety is my greatest regret. But surely you cannot doubt that what I feel for you, what we shared, is genuine! After we came together two nights ago—'

She thrust out her hand, cutting him off. 'Please, do not speak of that!'

'But I must speak of it. I love you, Joanna. I want you in my life, permanently. I want to marry you—'

'No! she cried, leaping to her feet, tears dripping down her cheeks. 'Don't you dare tell me that! Not now. Not when you know how easy it would be to tempt me with caresses, to lure me into coming back to your bed again and again with sweet promises of calling the banns the next week or the next, until all the world knows I'm a kept woman and 'tis no longer necessary to ply me with false promises.'

Horrified, Ned said, 'You think I would betray you so?'

She gave him a long, level look. 'Again, you mean?'

He wanted to hotly protest…but he had deceived her. Originally he had not trusted her enough to tell her the truth; later, he'd refrained from divulging it in a probably misguided attempt to safeguard her and the progress of the investigation. Those excuses sounded hollow now even in his own ears.

'Do you truly believe everything we shared was false, then?' he asked quietly.

'Yes. No—oh, I don't know! I don't know you or myself now.'

'But you *do* know me,' he argued. 'I'm the same man who

worked on the school with you. Visited the tenants to urge that their children attend it. The friend you spent hours with every evening discussing every topic under the sun. All that is different now is that you've discovered there's a bit more to my name.'

'Which makes more than a "bit" of difference! I thought we were partners—equals. That we met on common ground. You, perhaps minor gentry, like me, an estate agent, not an owner—' She halted abruptly, her eyes widening. 'One who purchased the property from Lord Englemere. But you didn't just purchase it at market… You've known him many years, you said, and held him in high esteem. Damnation, he's a close friend, isn't he?'

Though he knew the answer would likely only further incense her, there was but one reply. 'Yes,' he admitted.

She sprang up and paced the room. 'Oh, this gets better and better! How amusing you must have found it when I abused his character—and that of all aristocrats. No wonder you had so little to say in response! Which makes my behaviour even more mortifying. How could you not see me as just a lightskirt, trying to tempt a wealthy man into soliciting her services!'

Knowing he deserved her anger, Ned would tolerate much, but not that. Springing to his feet himself, he cried, 'It wasn't like that! I gave myself in love to you, as you gave yourself to me! Skewer my character if you must, but I will not allow you to sully what we shared!'

Every muscle and nerve screamed at him to seize her and pull her into an embrace, let the harmony that melded them whenever their bodies touched reinforce the truth of his words. But doubtless realising his intent, she put both hands out to fend him off.

'Don't touch me! Oh, no more, I beg you!' she cried, weeping openly now as she wrapped her hands protectively around her body. 'I c-can't bear it! I d-don't know what to think about you—or me. I need t-time.'

She took a shuddering breath, visibly trying to regain control. 'Time to determine if I can believe what you say now when you deceived me so totally before. To decide what to do next. And I cannot sort this all out with you hovering over me—all the household smirking, knowing you've been in my bed! I shall leave first thing tomorrow.'

As he opened his lips, trying to frame another protest, she added quietly, 'I shall leave and you cannot stop me. Please, if you claim to love me at all, let me go in peace.'

Let her go? The very thought set his insides churning in panic. Her leaving was the last thing in the world he wanted. If she left, how would he ever convince her to give him a second chance?

Desperately he tried to come up with some other argument to stay her. 'I can understand your imperative to leave the manor. But what of the school and its pupils? You made a promise to them. We could prepare separate quarters for you, near the school—'

'No,' she said flatly. 'Of course I have a duty to the children. After I've determined what I mean to do, I shall return, at least until another school teacher can be found. But not before a cottage for my use can be readied, which, given my experience with the school, should take some weeks.'

'What about Davie? He's been counting on you!'

That point struck home, for she looked away. 'He'll forget me,' she said, fidgeting with her skirts. 'Sir Edward can do so much more for him than I ever could.'

'He's far more attached to you than he is to me. You needn't leave while a cottage is prepared. Stay in town—at the Hart and Hare! Mr Kirkbride would be happy to offer accommodation, which the estate would fund. As far as anyone at Blenhem knows, we could say it had been the plan all along to create quarters closer to the school for the mistress.'

'Stay in town, once everyone learns of our…relationship?'

she cried. Cutting off his attempted denial of the possibility, she shot back, 'Of course the word will spread! Perhaps not initiated by Mrs Winston or Myles, but can you expect the day maid or the laundry maid to keep such delicious gossip to themselves? If I leave immediately, perhaps the news will not seem worth the repeating, especially if you give out that Barksdale's revelations propelled me to London immediately to enquire after my brother.'

Though in truth, he couldn't dispute any of her claims, every instinct urged him to find some way to hold her. 'It's never wise to make a decision when one is distraught,' he threw out in desperation. 'Leave if you feel you must, but please, Joanna, wait at least a few days. I can't bear to think of us parting with you still so angry at me.'

She looked back at him, her eyes glassy with the tears dripping down her cheeks. 'Ned, if I give in to your persuasion and stay, even for a few days, I will become known as your mistress. I will end up despising myself—and you. Please, let me go.'

If she was near the breaking point, her emotions scraped raw and bleeding, so was he. Even now, he had to restrain the strong compulsion to drive her beyond that point and force her to stay.

Ned had never before met a challenge he hadn't been able to master, circumstances that he could not, with determination and hard work and ingenuity and patience, bend to his will.

But she was right. He couldn't compel her to love him. The Joanna who had escaped Lord Masters, who'd insisted on going to the mill fire to treat the injured, who'd resisted Barksdale and nearly succeeding in escaping him, if pushed to decide right now for or against him, might well make a choice he wouldn't like.

Besides, if after she had time to reflect upon all she'd learned, she chose to believe that they had not truly created between them something beautiful, precious, and worth the effort to salvage, nothing he could do or say mattered.

Finally, he forced to his lips the hardest words he'd ever spoken. 'Go, then, if you must.'

With a sigh, she closed her eyes. 'Thank you,' she whispered.

He might have to let her go, but he didn't want to be left without any allies whatsoever who might vouch for his character. Thinking rapidly, he said, 'You spoke of going to London. Let me send you to Lord Englemere—'

'Never!' she cried, her eyes flying open as she cut off his plea. 'The man who set this whole catastrophe in motion? Englemere is the last person in England I'd wish to contact! I shall go to Greville's lawyer, who should know, if anyone does, how to reach him and the rest of my family.'

'Lord Englemere *is* your family,' Ned pointed out. 'A cousin by blood—who happens to reside at present right in London.'

She stiffened. 'I would stay with those of my own rank.'

'You would be. You're a gentleman's daughter; he a gentleman's son. Besides, you mentioned wishing to seek out your brother. Contact his lawyer, by all means, but if his solicitor is not aware of his location, Englemere can offer additional resources to help you search for him, if you wish to locate him as quickly as possible.'

Finally he'd hit upon something that distracted her. Straightening, she dashed the tears from her eyes and actually looked at him, worry replacing the distress on her face.

'You cannot imagine how alarmed I am about him! I knew I could not have been that deceived in Greville's character. Barksdale told me my brother discovered his double-dealing, and when Greville threatened to discharge him, Barksdale set up Martin to get Greville turned off first. After which, Barksdale boasted to me, he "took care" of Greville. I cannot imagine what he did, but given the vileness of Barksdale's character, I fear that he might have done Greville some grave harm.'

So Anders had finally seen the culpability of his manager, Ned thought, momentarily diverted. Perhaps the man was

worth saving. 'Barksdale threatened your brother? Lord Englemere will want to know that. Your brother is his relation, too.
If Anders was wrongfully discharged, Englemere will want
to make restitution; if Barksdale committed some offence
against your brother, he will certainly want to find him and
have him give evidence against the villain.

'Besides,' Ned continued, mining this promising vein, 'I owe
you at least your first quarter's pay, but as I mentioned after the
fire, I have little cash remaining here.' He made a wry grimace.
'I was not exaggerating about needing to approach Englemere
for a loan to rebuild the mill. If you agree to meet him, I can have
him pay you what you are owed. Let me do at least that. Once
you've spoken to him about your brother and received the wages
due, you may, of course, proceed as you wish.'

Ned knew if he could just get her to call at Stanhope House,
his friend's clever wife Sarah would find a way to persuade
her to stay. He held his breath as she weighed the argument.

'Very well,' she conceded after a moment. 'I will call on
Lord Englemere. And I will consider your explanations—I
can promise no more. Now, I believe we've said everything
that is needful.'

She drew herself up and made him a formal curtsy. 'Good
evening, Sir Edward. I must reluctantly accept passage money
to London, but please do me one final favour and do not
attempt to see me again before I leave.'

He would have to let her go without even a final embrace?
'Can we not at least shake hands and part as friends?' he
asked. Though a shake of the hand was far less than what he
wanted, he would settle for that small touch, one crumb to give
him hope that all his dreams had not been demolished this day.

Refusing to meet his imploring gaze, she shook her head
vigorously. 'It would not be…w-wise,' she replied, her voice
breaking as she stumbled towards the door.

In the face of her refusal, Ned found it hard to summon a

reply, what with the crashing and clanging and shrieking within him as want collided with need, desire and honour, dreams shattered like poorly blown glass and his hopes fell to bits as the crumbling foundation of the school had dissolved beneath his boot. Ephemeral as a sandcastle on a beach disappearing beneath a wave, the joy of the last few weeks vanished in an instant.

'A-as you wish, then,' he said at last. 'Please believe I never meant to hurt you, Joanna.' It took him one more try before he could force a farewell through his lips. 'God speed to you, my love.'

Nodding, avoiding his gaze, she fled the room.

Overwhelmed by the immensity of the disaster, Ned sank into a chair and put his head in his hands.

Standing by the window the next morning, Ned watched as a groom drove Joanna away in the gig. Though he had much to do, wondering why he was torturing himself with the sight, nonetheless he'd been compelled to delay leaving for work on the farms so he might catch one last glimpse of her.

He'd not slept all night, torn between trying to physically restrain her from leaving, pounding on her door to plead with her again, and allowing her to go unopposed as she'd wished. Eventually he'd settled on the latter.

But a future without her stretched ahead like a desert. Faced with the catastrophe of losing her for good, even desire had withered away. Just as well it had. If this ended in the total break that was entirely possible, quite likely he would never feel the sweetness of her touch again.

But, he rallied his exhausted spirits, he refused to give up yet. Since she'd offered no choice short of permanent alienation if he opposed her, he would give her time to calm down and reflect on his words. In the interim, as promised, he would refurbish a cottage for the schoolmistress's use, should she return to fulfil her obligations to the students.

If she did not... He hoped Sarah's ingenuity and Joanna's quest to discover her brother's whereabouts would keep her in London, but even if she set off to India to join her family—or if this incident had hardened the republican leanings she'd often expressed and sent her off to a new life in the Americas—he would track her down.

Ned believed with all his heart in the rareness and irreplaceable worth of the love they'd shared. He would never turn his back on that without seeing Joanna one more time. Never give up unless, when they met again, she convinced him that for her, what they'd created between them was over, something she did not value enough to wish to try to revive.

Meanwhile, during his sleepless night, he had composed and already dispatched by private courier several missives to London which, since Joanna had refused the extra money he'd left for her to travel by private vehicle, were guaranteed to arrive before she finished her journey by stage coach.

In one, he'd poured out the whole sorry situation to Sarah, begging her aid in keeping Joanna from leaving London and asking that she let Ned know when the time might be right to approach Joanna again.

A second note addressed to Nicky detailed Barksdale's threat against Greville and asked his friend to involve Bow Street and ask his contacts in the Home Office to investigate, if Joanna discovered that her brother had indeed gone missing. He also begged for Nicky's help on behalf of the men Barksdale had informed against, if it became necessary.

As the carriage carrying Joanna away from him turned out of sight around the corner, Ned left his post beside the window. Taking a deep breath, he strode towards the door.

He would go on, as he must. And between his tenacity and Sarah's cleverness, he refused to believe all was lost for good.

Chapter Twenty-One

A few days later, after a much swifter journey than the one that had taken her from Selbourne Abbey to Hazelwick, the stage coach deposited Joanna at the posting inn in London.

She'd thought upon leaving the Masters' estate that nothing could be worse than being forced from her position, disgraced and penniless. On this trip, she'd had coin enough to purchase meals and an inside seat on the coach for the whole transit, a loquacious lawyer and his giggling wife the only intrusions upon her comfort.

But though she had sufficient funds for the journey and her sojourn in the city, even the expectation of being able to finally locate her brother had not kept Joanna's spirits throughout from being lower than the mud beneath the carriage wheels.

It seemed turning your back on the man you'd just begun to believe would be your lover and companion for the rest of your days had a way of crushing all anticipation, enthusiasm and joy from your life as effectively as the coach smashed a package fallen into its path.

It was with feelings still as flattened as that packet that, soon after her arrival in the city, she engaged a jarvey to transport her from the posting inn across London to the Englemere residence on Curzon Street.

After clambering down from the vehicle a half-hour later, while the driver extracted her single trunk from the boot, Joanna stopped short, her gaze tracking upwards. The impressive classical façade of the town house surprised a jolt of emotion even from her deadened spirits.

The majestic dwelling before her exemplified the power and wealth her brother had always coveted when he talked of their cousin's good fortune in being born heir to a marquisate. And the owner of this vast demesne was the man Ned—Sir Edward—had called one of his closest friends.

Suddenly feeling almost as ill as she'd been that first moment in the Hazelwick courtroom after Barksdale had detonated his cannonball about Ned's true identity, for an instant Joanna thought of recalling the hackney.

But she'd promised she would at least call upon her exalted cousin before visiting the office of Greville's lawyer. Stiffening her spine, she walked up the steps.

Mostly likely, a marquess would not even receive someone as insignificant as a widowed cousin several times removed, she thought as she plied the door knocker. If she were admitted at all, probably some secretary or man of business would meet her to exchange the promissory note Sir Edward had sent with her for the salary she was owed, funds essential for her to hire rooms after she consulted with the lawyer about Greville's whereabouts.

Perhaps, she thought, her dull spirits brightening a bit, the lawyer might be able to tell her this very day where her brother now resided. Perhaps Barksdale had only meant to frighten and discourage her, and had in reality done nothing to harm her brother.

A footman resplendent in gilded livery and powdered wig

answered the door. Upon hearing her name, he bid her enter and beckoned her down the hall, intoning that he would inform the master of her presence.

Mutely Joanna followed the servant into an anteroom. After walking through the marble entry down a corridor decorated with classical Greek busts she suspected to be genuine, all displayed on intricately worked marquetry tables, then passing through a pedimented and pilastered doorway into a drawing room ornamented in Adamesque style, she urgently hoped she would be received by a simple secretary.

She was already awed enough by the surroundings and the footman.

But as she sat nervously pleating the skirt of her gown while she rehearsed what she meant to say to the cousin whose relation to her seemed more distant by the minute, the soft swish of the opening door was followed by the entry of a tall, golden-haired woman. Her face warmed by a smile, she hurried over to Joanna.

As Joanna wondered who this unannounced lady might be, her hands were seized by the newcomer, who raised her from the curtsy she'd automatically risen to offer. 'Mrs Merrill, how very glad I am to meet you at last! Ned—Sir Edward, our dear friend, has told us so much about you.'

Before Joanna could get her tongue to master some sort of response, the lady exclaimed, 'But here I am, rattling on like a looby! Please, take a seat! I'm Sarah Stanhope, your cousin Nicky's wife. Being presently occupied with his man of business, he sent me ahead to welcome you and will join us as soon as he is able. Ned told us when to expect you. Did you have a pleasant journey?'

As she spoke, Lady Englemere motioned to an even more impressively liveried personage who'd followed her into the room. 'Glendenning, bring tea, please? You would like some refreshment after your travels, I imagine. You must be famished

as well after so long a trip! One never eats well on a journey.
Some cakes and ham, too, if you please, Glendenning.'

'At once, your ladyship,' the servant said and withdrew.

Joanna blinked, feeling as if she'd awakened from a dream
to find herself inhabiting someone else's body. She was having
a very hard time comprehending that this lady chatting with
her as unaffectedly as the nursery maid at Selbourne Abbey,
who had greeted her with far more warmth than Mrs Winston
had managed upon her arrival at Blenhem Hill, could actually
be a Marchioness and mistress of this enormous dwelling.

At least, this time, she was not wearing a cloak and bonnet
that drooled rain all over the carpet.

But she was sure she had heard the Glendenning person,
whom she assumed must be the butler, address the blonde
woman as 'your ladyship'—so she must be...mustn't she?

Trying to sort through the other bits of intelligence
conveyed by a woman who was so different from what she
had expected of a high-born aristocrat's wife, Joanna sat down
abruptly, feeling a bit dizzy.

'You—you said you were expecting me?' she asked.

'Yes, Ned sent a message saying you were arriving by post
today. Of course, we've known about you since you came to
Blenhem and have been hoping you would pay us a visit! I
have a large family, but Nicky is an only child and values his
few relations. Ned has praised the work you've begun at
Blenhem, establishing a school for the village children and
the tenants. I do so admire you! Despite your important obligations, I hope you will be able to stay long enough that we
may get to know you.'

Ned had written to them that she was coming? Joanna felt
her cheeks go pink. What else had he said about her?

She had been prepared to have her exalted cousin ignore
entirely the sister of his disgraced former manager. Or, if he
deigned to acknowledge her, to do so coldly and grudgingly.

But hard as she searched, she couldn't read either irony or condescension into what appeared to be the sincere welcome Lady Englemere was offering her.

She hardly knew how to respond to such open warmth.

It seemed churlish to demand to see her cousin's man of business, collect the salary due her, request assistance, if necessary, in locating her brother and take her leave without even meeting 'Cousin Nicky', as she'd resolved to do while she had sounded the door knocker.

Among the jostling thoughts and impressions tumbling about in her head, another realisation fell into place like a faro ball in a slot. 'I—don't mean to stay here!' she protested, belatedly understanding Lady Englemere's implication. 'You barely know me. It would be a complete presumption!'

Her hostess's eyes widened. 'We know you are family— and that is all that matters. Oh, please say you will agree to stay with us! Knowing that your obligations must soon return you to Blenhem, 'twill be the only way we can find enough time to become as well acquainted as family should be. Besides, Ned said your brother might be in some difficulties. If so, surely it would be more convenient to remain here, so Nicky might be better able to advise and assist you? Have you any other family in London?'

'Well, no,' Joanna admitted, wondering with no little irritation if there was anything about her the prodigiously busy Sir Edward had not conveyed in the letter he'd apparently sent to arrive ahead of her.

Meanwhile, her hostess leaned over to press her hand. 'Please, do say you'll at least consider remaining with us! Ah, here is Glendenning with the tea tray.'

But when the door opened, behind the butler she heard the rapid patter of footsteps. A beautiful little boy of about two years of age burst into the room, darted around the butler and ran to Lady Englemere. 'Mama! Aubrey play with Papa's cousin?'

'Oh, dear!' the golden-haired lady exclaimed. 'Aubrey, you naughty boy!' Looking up at the butler, she said, 'I see he escaped the nursery again?'

The butler actually smiled, shocking Joanna, who felt sure the face of this august personage would crack at expressing such levity. 'The lad can smell tea and macaroons all the way up in the nursery.'

The boy's eyes brightened guilelessly. 'Mac'roons? Aubrey stay, please, Mama?' He turned to stare at Joanna with the unabashed interest of a child. 'Pretty lady! Papa's cousin?'

'Yes, dearest, Papa's cousin.'

'Come play with me?' he asked hopefully. 'Give you biggest mac'roon!' With a winning smile, he selected one and held it out to her.

'Aubrey, 'tis more polite to let the lady choose her own sweets,' his mother reproved. Turning to Joanna, Lady Englemere said, 'His fingers are probably none too clean.'

But Joanna, who always had a soft spot for a child, could never say 'no' to so bright a little face raised trustingly to hers, its owner certain of offering her a delight. Replying in the only manner possible, she said, 'Thank you, sir', and accepted the biscuit.

At that moment, a hapless nursery maid rushed into the room. 'Oh, there he be! I'm so sorry, your ladyship! I'll take him back upstairs at once.'

Consternation on his face, the child tugged on his mother's sleeve. 'Stay, please, Mama? Be gentl'man.' He hopped down from the couch, turned to Joanna and offered a very creditable bow. 'Please to meet you, ma'am.'

His mother sighed and Joanna had to suppress a chuckle. 'I suppose, if our visitor doesn't object, you may stay for macaroons. Mrs Merrill?'

Even though a bittersweet pain lanced her heart at the knowledge that no little face would ever look appealingly at her and call her 'Mama', Joanna couldn't resist his plea, no more than she'd been able to reprove her sisters after they'd committed some bit of harmless mischief when she'd had the rule of Papa's household. 'I'm pleased to meet you, too, Master Aubrey. Which macaroon would you like?'

While his mama nodded a dismissal to the nursery maid, the child selected one, then proceeded to chatter away about the metal soldiers his mother explained were his chief passion. While her hostess poured tea, somehow Joanna found herself doffing her bonnet and encouraging the child to climb up beside her on the couch. Before the pot ran dry and the macaroons had disappeared, she'd been induced to relate the story of her life to the kind lady with the turquoise eyes.

Finally, stuffed with sweets and warm tea, the boy began yawning. 'I must take Aubrey back to the nursery for his nap,' her hostess said, beckoning to the child. 'I expect Nicky will have joined you before I can return.'

'Pretty lady come, too?' Aubrey asked drowsily.

'Not now, pet. She must speak to Papa.'

'Later?' he asked. 'Show soldiers!'

'Perhaps,' his mother replied. 'Mrs Merrill has other business in London and may not be able to stay with us, though we certainly hope she will.'

The child turned back to tug at Joanna's hand. 'Please stay! Play later! Give you best soldiers. Gen'rl Blücher, too!'

Even as his mother murmured a reproof, she sent Joanna a rueful glance that said, 'How can you refuse such a request?'

She couldn't. Which was how it came about that Joanna Merrill, arriving in London determined to have as little as possible to do with the exalted cousin who had discharged her brother and never before concerned himself with her, agreed to become a guest in his home before ever meeting him or making clear any of the reasons that had brought her to his doorstep.

She was still marvelling at that fact when the door opened

and a tall, dark-haired man entered—once again, unannounced. 'Mrs Merrill,' he said, 'I apologise for my delay in receiving you. I trust my wife tended to you well, though I understand my scamp of a son interrupted your tea,' he continued, affection and pride infusing his tone as he mentioned the child. 'I'm Englemere, of course. Welcome, cousin.'

Joanna was glad that the Marquess, at least, maintained some formality. After the upheavals of the last few days, she didn't think her disordered nerves could handle addressing this impressive man, with his air of confidence and the instinctive authority of one born to high rank, as 'Nicky'.

Ned had the same indefinable air, she reflected. Why had she not noticed it? She had, of course, she recalled—only she'd seen it just as evidence of his confidence, competence and concern. Which it was. A concern that had manifested itself in his tireless efforts on behalf of the tenants and villagers at Blenhem.

Her heart turning over in a spasm of grief, she thrust the observation away. She would not think about him yet. She couldn't.

She surfaced from her memories to find Englemere gazing at her. 'I must thank you for agreeing to stay with us. I know after what happened with your brother, you have good reason to resent me. I understand there may be mitigating factors in his situation. If so, I assure you, I will certainly make corresponding restitution.'

Given what she'd observed at Blenhem, her brother might well have deserved his discharge—if only for letting Barksdale wreak his havoc unopposed. Not yet willing to concede that to Englemere, however, she replied, 'That would be fair.'

'I also understand you have a more serious concern—that Barksdale, the villain, might have actually done your brother an injury. Excuse me for proceeding without consulting you, but given the gravity of the charge, I took the liberty of contacting the office of your family's lawyer, Mr Gresham, to make enquiries. If it is agreeable with you, we will meet him tomorrow, as his assistant indicated he would be away from his office this afternoon. Although I hope Gresham will be able to reassure you about your brother's whereabouts, if necessary, we will get Bow Street involved.'

Fear for her brother momentarily displaced all the other tangled emotions in her heart. 'Do you think that will be necessary?'

'I hope not,' Englemere replied soberly. 'But we should be prepared to take the next step, if warranted.'

Overwhelmed at being stripped in short order of all her grievances against Englemere, weakly Joanna said, 'Thank you, my lord. It's very generous of you to involve yourself—especially in light of the questionable service my brother gave you.'

Englemere waved a hand dismissively. 'He's my relation, too, after all. 'Twas partly my fault, probably, in offering your brother employment in a field in which he had little expertise. Blenhem, Ned assures me, is a land in good heart that will recover in time. It's in his sure hands now, and I can think of no one better qualified to bring it back to prosperity. Even if it were not, whatever happened there was no fault of yours. But you must be tired after so long a journey. Sarah tells me your room has been prepared.'

He bowed. 'Again, let me welcome you to London and assure you how glad we are that you've agreed to be our guest. I look forward to hearing about your life in India and your observations on Ned's work at Blenhem Hill. Until dinner, then?'

He left Joanna with nothing to do but curtsy in response, while she wondered what in the world she might find to wear that would begin to meet the standards of such an elegant establishment. As she rose to her feet, Englemere rang the bell pull.

A maid appeared so swiftly she must have been stationed outside the door, awaiting the end of Joanna's conference with Englemere.

'I hope you'll enjoy your stay,' Englemere said, ushering her through the door and handing her off to the maid, who beckoned for her to follow.

'Thank you…cousin,' Joanna replied, the words still sounding strange on her tongue.

Chapter Twenty-Two

∽⧜∾

One morning a month later, Joanna sat before the looking glass in the cream-and-gold guest chamber to which the maid had shown her the day of her arrival. Pinning the last braid in place, she couldn't help but admire how well the modest but fashionable russet morning gown became her.

The garment was one of several gowns she'd recently been wheedled into allowing her cousins to purchase for her, after firmly refusing such largesse while accompanying her hostess on previous shopping forays.

She'd never intended to trespass this long upon the Stanhopes' hospitality. While unable to return a churlish response to the warmth and kindness of their welcome, she'd determined to remain at most a few days, so Englemere might assist in locating her brother and the distant cousins could become acquainted. But then Aubrey begged her to stay with him during several evenings when his parents were to go out, and Sarah always seemed to find another shop or garden or friend she wished Joanna to visit, and the investigation into her brother's whereabouts dragged on and on…

Almost without her noticing, 'a few days' had become a week, then another. Until the point that, when they stopped at Sarah's favourite mantua-maker to pick up some gowns previously commissioned while on their way to take Aubrey to the park and Sarah pressed her to consider purchasing a few for herself, she'd finally succumbed.

Joanna strongly suspected Aubrey had been coached to ask why his favourite cousin was not getting a pretty dress too. So when, along with his mama's gowns, the proprietor brought out a russet confection that the boy declared 'bootiful' and Sarah proclaimed perfectly complemented Joanna's vivid hair and green eyes, she'd not been able, this time, to refuse it.

Perhaps because after a month, she no longer thought of Lady Englemere as a Marchioness, wife of her noble cousin the Marquess, but simply as her friend Sarah. Indeed, that lofty image, which had nearly crumbled to bits during their first meeting, hadn't survived one dinner *en famille*, when they'd been joined by Sarah's younger sisters, Emily and Cecily, both to make their débuts the following Season. The sisters treated each other with a warmth and familiarity that reminded Joanna so strongly of life with her own family in India that she'd felt at once homesick and at home.

She'd learned her new friend, far from being raised amid august surroundings in the bosom of the *ton*, had grown up in genteel poverty and almost been forced to wed a villain even more despicable than Lord Masters in order to prevent her family estate from being sold at the block. Englemere, then just a good friend, had stepped in to save her by offering a marriage of convenience, which later had become a true love match.

Even if Sarah hadn't succeeded in captivating her, Aubrey, with his child's innocence and trusting heart, won her over from their first tea together. The second night of her stay, with the Englemeres engaged to dine elsewhere, he had again escaped the nursery and found his way to her chamber. Once there, he asked, with a cherubic smile no lady of tender heart could refuse, if she might read him a story. Reading to him had now become a fixture of their day, every afternoon before his nap and any evening his mama's social obligations called her away. She found caring for the child both delightful and bittersweet, satisfying even as it tore at her heart with reminders of the son she'd lost and the child now she would likely never have. Once she had thought to subsume that longing in teaching the children of the estate. But, despite her promise to return in a week to open the school, she found herself unable to do so, still incapable of facing Ned and coming to a decision about him.

She'd even grown more comfortable with her august cousin Englemere, though she wasn't sure she'd ever be able to call him 'Nicky' in the breezy way his wife and young sisters-in-law did. It had proved impossible to continue regarding him as some high dignitary after witnessing him sprawled on the nursery floor playing soldiers with his son, rolling on the carpet tussling with the shrieking child after their game, or teasing his wife, for whom his respect and affection were evident.

She also owed him a great debt of gratitude for his efforts on behalf of her brother. Her worst fears had been confirmed when they had consulted Mr Gresham and discovered the solicitor knew nothing of her brother's whereabouts. He'd received a hastily scrawled note from Greville some three months previously—which would have been approximately the time he left Blenhem Hill—saying her brother meant to call on him in London shortly. But Greville had never appeared, nor had the solicitor heard anything further from him.

Lord Englemere immediately proceeded to hire Bow Street Runners, who just a few days ago had returned both distressing and welcome news. Praise heaven, Greville was alive, but apparently had been attacked—as Davie had been—after leaving Blenhem and delivered unconscious to a press gang, awaking later to find himself the unwitting and unwilling newest member of the crew of HMS *Indefatigable*. Englemere was now pursuing contacts within the Navy department to see about obtaining Greville's release from the service.

Tightly as Joanna had tried to hang on to her prejudices, it appeared not all aristocrats were as contemptuous and uncaring of the welfare of those of lesser birth as Lady Masters and her husband's family, nor as venal and selfish as Lord Masters.

Though surely she had a vast amount of wealth available to her, Sarah was a frugal housekeeper who owned only a modest wardrobe of gowns and jewels. She was a kind, doting mother and caring sister, a loving wife, an engaging, considerate friend. By her own observation, Joanna had witnessed Englemere working long hours tending to the business of his estates and tenants, as well as attending meetings of the Lords in Parliament and taking part in the deliberation of affairs essential to England.

No wonder Ned had been able to tell her so much about government policy, obtaining news as he had from the lips of his closely involved, close friend!

She'd spent many hours this last month thinking about that gentleman. Though she'd wished at first to put everything that had occurred at Blenhem Hill out of her mind until she had recovered sufficiently from her shock and chagrin to be able to objectively review the events, somehow she found him always creeping into her thoughts.

Observation of Englemere's tireless activities reminded her of how hard Ned had worked at Blenhem, leaving the manor early every morning to ride the acreage. He'd not thought himself above rolling up his sleeves and giving the farmers a hand with their ploughing or tending their cattle or repairing thatch. He listened intently to the needs of those who approached him, offering his expertise and assistance to meet them if possible.

By now, despite the remaining hard kernel of hurt and outrage at his deception, honesty and fairness had about forced her to conclude that otherwise he'd told her the truth. On points of honour, compassion, industry, intelligence and concern for those around him, Sir Edward and the Ned she'd known were, as he claimed, the same man.

Indeed, he possessed every trait she admired—save honesty. She might admit he'd had valid reasons for the role he'd played, but she was still uneasy about the means he'd chosen to flush out the radicals at Blenhem, given the dire consequences that might yet come to those he'd deceived. Though she'd quickly dismissed as ridiculous Barksdale's contention that Sir Edward had come to Blenhem to be a government spy, in presenting himself as a man of the people, he certainly had misled the tenants of Blenhem into confiding information they would never have divulged had they known they were addressing Blenhem Hill's owner and a man of rank. She worried about what would happen to Sergeant Russell, the innkeeper Kirkbride, Davie and the dissidents who'd met at the Hart and Hare.

Nor had she yet forgiven him for deceiving *her* into believing him to be a man of her own station, lulling her into uttering sentiments about aristocrats in general and the landed class in particular that still made her cringe with embarrassment and remorse. He'd encouraged her to talk freely and she had, baring her soul to this man she'd come to believe her most intimate friend…when in truth, he'd revealed nothing about himself at all.

It was as if they'd played some lover's game, blindfolding each other and stripping down to play hide-and-seek in the dark and at the end, laughing, she'd pulled off her mask to discover that though she was naked before him, he was still fully clothed.

Neither her resentment nor her embarrassment, however, prevented her from awaking nearly every night, when her brain was too befuddled with sleep to stave them off, filled with the hungry yearnings of the body he'd reawakened to pleasure.

Yearnings that magnified the many other small things she missed about him—his smile, the little wink he had given her when they had shared an opinion or a joke, even the lock of hair she had always been tempted to brush off his forehead. All the visions and memories and needs tumbled together into a churning mass in her gut that frustrated her attempt to find peace while it tempted and cajoled her spirit to forgive him and return to begin anew.

Waiting for news of her brother had given her an excuse to linger here and postpone the decision, wavering between returning to Blenhem and expunging it from her memory for good. Between missing him and wanting him, while at the same time mistrusting the guileful harpy of lust pushing at her to return, she was left teetering in indecisiveness between the past and the future.

Learning yesterday about her brother's fate and knowing there was nothing further she could accomplish for him here removed the last excuse for her not to make a decision. She was sighing with irritation and remorse over her seeming inability to resolve the argument that circulated continuously through her mind when a knock sounded at the door.

A maid entered with a curtsy. 'There's someone here to see you, ma'am. Glendenning showed them to the back salon. From Blenhem Hill, he said they was.'

Her spirits soared and excitement made her momentarily dizzy before she realised the visitor could not be Ned. He would have been conveyed not to the small back salon, but to the grand front drawing room—or more likely, as an intimate of the family, escorted directly to join Englemere in his library or Sarah and Aubrey in the nursery.

'Tell them I'll be down directly,' she replied, wondering who might have come from Blenhem. Whoever it was, they would certainly have news of—perhaps even from—Ned. After weeks of silence, she found she was starving for information about him.

Trying to calm the flutters in her stomach, she hurried downstairs to the back salon. She stopped short on the threshold, surprised but pleased to find Sergeant Russell and Mary, the barmaid from the Hart and Hare, seated within.

'How good to see you!' she exclaimed as she entered, exchanging a curtsy with Mary and receiving a bow from the soldier. 'Especially you, Sergeant Russell. I've heard nothing of the proceedings since I left and had feared, after Barksdale's testimony, that you and the others he named might be facing severe legal repercussions. How relieved I am to discover that is not the case.'

The soldier laughed and shook his head. 'Oh, but we did get bound over—the lot of us. After hearing of the attack on Sir Edward's carriage and then the fire that destroyed Sir Edward's mill, the judge wasn't inclined to be lenient.'

'Indeed,' Mary chimed in, 'for a time, all of us in Hazelwick feared our men might be transported…or worse!'

'Sir Edward, though, worked tirelessly to free us,' the sergeant said. 'Told the judge *at the Assize Court* he believed there was no true conspiracy, just a vicious design instigated by a man bent on revenge, who played upon the distress in the countryside to persuade others to follow him. 'Twas Barksdale, he said, who planned and carried out both attacks, Barksdale who shot at the coach and set the mill fire. The rest of us were guilty of nothing more than bad judgement associating with him.'

'Sir Edward persuaded the judge of it, too,' Mary continued. 'He sentenced Forbes, Harris and Matthews, leaders of the local group, to gaol for a time and fined Mr Kirkbride for letting the group meet at the inn. As for Jesse—no lawyer could have argued more eloquently that, after the service he'd given for England and the injuries he suffered, 'twould be monstrously unjust to punish him for so slight an offence.'

The sergeant laughed. 'Perhaps Sir Edward should go into

politics! I doubt Orator Hunt himself could have swayed a crowd more effectively. In the end, the judge agreed with him on that point as well. I was released with no penalty at all.'

In his argument on behalf of the Sergeant, Ned had nearly quoted her own words to him, Joanna realised, both surprised and immensely relieved to hear of so favourable an outcome. Before she could congratulate the Sergeant, Mary said, 'But that's not all he did for Jesse—and me,' she added with a blush.

Smiling at her, the soldier took her hand. 'Sir Edward told me I needed a position worthy of my talents—and busy enough to keep me out of trouble. He also approved of my desire to settle in America. So he wrote to Lord Englemere, who has offered to employ me as the factor in his business office in the Carolinas. We're here now to work out the details of the contract. Then, as soon as we can be married, Mary and I are off to the New World to deal in timber and cotton.'

While Joanna absorbed all that information, a knock sounded at the door. 'Lord Englemere will see you in his study now, Sergeant.'

'I shall stay and talk to Mrs Merrill while you gentleman talk—if that would not be inconvenient?' Mary asked, looking to Joanna.

'Not at all. I should be delighted to catch up on all the events in Hazelwick and Blenhem. And may I offer my congratulations to you both,' she added, with a pang of both pleasure and envy at their obvious happiness.

After pressing the hand of his new fiancée, the soldier followed the butler out.

'So you're to be married!' Joanna exclaimed. 'The Sergeant once told me about the sweetheart he'd lost, but even when I saw you together at the hearing, I didn't realise it was you!' With more intense interest than she might have felt before leaving Blenhem, she said, 'How did your reconciliation come about, if you don't mind telling me?'

'Not a bit,' Mary replied. 'I know you'd never guess it—
me being the town doxy—and, yes, I was that in truth. You
wouldn't think I grew up a shy, bookish lass. I met Jesse when
he was home from the army visiting his family in Nottingham
and I was there helping my sister-in-law with a new babe. He
courted me and, just before he left, asked me to marry him.
But before we could be wed, the news came that Bonaparte
had escaped from Elbe and Jesse was recalled to his unit. I
promised to wait for him until he came back from the army.
But then…' Her face colouring, looking away, Mary briefly
related how Barksdale had attacked her, then threatened her
family with ruin to buy her silence about what he'd done.

'When Jesse came back, it was too late. I knew he'd believe
me a lightskirt who'd betrayed him. I *wanted* him to believe
it, so he'd be too angry to approach and torture me with
thinking about what might have been. After the shame of what
happened, I didn't think I deserved a man as good as Jesse.'

Mary gave her a radiant smile. 'Only look at me now,
though! We're to be married, and it's all Sir Edward's doing!
He said nothing would ever make up for what I'd suffered,
but he could offer me a new beginning. The people in Carolina
will know me only as Jesse's lady, the wife of the manager of
a prosperous business. Jesse and I can start over again, as if
all the bitter years apart never happened.'

'I'm so happy for you,' Joanna said softly, her eyes misting
over with tears. How wonderful it must be to be able to truly
begin over again!

Mary hesitated, then said, 'May I say something else,
though it is not my place to do so?'

'Of course,' Joanna replied, curious about what else the girl
might reveal.

'Sir Edward works hard—harder than ever since you left.
But he always looks so sad. It's obvious he cares a great deal
for you. That there was something between you.'

Joanna felt her face flame. 'Do people say I'm his doxy?'

Mary stared at her. 'His doxy? No! He told everyone that Barksdale had threatened your brother and you came to London to find out what happened to him. You mean you and he...?'

Cursing herself, Joanna reflected that though she was relieved to discover she wasn't a byword in Hazelwick, it would have been more prudent not to have given herself away.

Before she could decide how to answer, Mary chuckled. 'Don't worry, you can certainly trust me, of all people, to keep your secret! Everyone knows Sir Edward is sweet on you, but no one knows exactly how you feel about him. Now that...oh, my!' she exclaimed, her widening eyes indicating she'd just stumbled to the heart of the matter. 'You were lovers and you didn't know his true identity?'

'No,' she said grimly.

Mary nodded slowly. 'I can see discovering that must have been...upsetting.'

'Indeed,' Joanna replied drily.

'You felt betrayed...humiliated, even?'

Wishing now she had never encouraged her visitor's frankness, wanting to end the conversation and move on to other matters, Joanna said, 'Yes, all of that. Though 'tis no matter now.'

'And that's why you've stayed away so long.'

'Only partly,' she hedged. 'I've been awaiting word about my brother, who was indeed attacked by Barksdale.' But she knew, if she were completely honest, that the search for Greville had only been an excuse to delay coming to terms with what she meant to do about Ned Greaves.

'I'm sure Sir Edward had his reasons for deceiving you. All things are possible if you really love someone. Imagine, Jesse managed to forgive me, after all I'd done! Sir Edward told Jesse that if he loved me, we owed it to each other to try to begin again. That love, true love, is a rare, precious thing worth working for. Worth forgiving for.'

'Sir Edward said that?' Joanna echoed faintly.

Mary nodded. 'Mrs Merrill, I've never met a finer man, save for my Jesse, of course! If you truly care for him, why not come back to Blenhem and see if there's a chance for you to start over, too?'

Before Joanna could frame an answer, a footman entered. 'Lord Englemere asks that you join him and Sergeant Russell in the study now, miss.'

Mary jumped up. 'I must go, then. So nice to talk to you, Mrs Merrill. You'll think on it, won't you?'

Joanna nodded. 'I will. Good luck to you both, and congratulations.'

Mary paused on the threshold to wink at her. 'Good luck to you, too, ma'am.'

Chapter Twenty-Three

B ack in the privacy of her chamber, Joanna reviewed all the startling and gratifying bits of information she'd just learned.

First and foremost, she exulted that the men of Blenhem would not suffer for having been lured into following Barksdale's lead. What Sir Edward had done was wonderful, bringing all his powers of persuasion to bear to induce the judge to release them.

Using all his influence, too. If Sir Edward had deceived the people in his charge, he had also defended and protected them in a time of grave danger, wielding power a mere Ned Greaves could not have summoned.

Perhaps that fact mitigated his want of honesty in dealing with them. She had to admit that taking on the identity he had chosen had allowed him to gather information to solve the crimes that he probably wouldn't have been able to uncover if he'd arrived at Blenhem under his true name.

And if she acquitted him of that fault…perhaps Sir Edward truly did possess all the virtues she'd seen in her Ned.

Relieved as she felt on that point, she wasn't sure their relationship was salvageable. She was still uncomfortable with the deception he had perpetrated against *her*. Embarrassed at the presumption, assumptions, ignorant speculations she'd been lured into uttering, of baring her soul while he concealed his. Recalling some of their conversations, she blushed anew in chagrin, even as the thought of seeing him now, after what Mary had told her, made it ten times more difficult to restrain the yearning that had been building in her for more than a month.

A light knock at the door startled her from her reflections. As she looked up, Sarah peeped in. 'Have you a moment to chat?'

'Yes, of course. Please come in,' she replied, curious about what her hostess wanted. The busy Sarah seldom sought her out in her chamber in the middle of the day.

'Did you have an enjoyable time with the people from Blenhem?' Sarah asked as she took a seat.

'Yes, thank you.'

'Isn't it wonderful news about the Sergeant and the others! Ned has outdone himself this time, getting them released, which in these troublesome times was no easy matter. I'm sure you've read about the horrors of men, probably only poor and deluded like these, stirred up by some radical, who paid with their lives for their indiscretion.'

'I have, and it was well done of him,' she replied, a little surprised at the rush of pride she felt for him.

Sarah hesitated. 'I've tried not to say anything, though it was obvious there has been some…attachment between you. I know you must have been angered that he did not take you into his confidence. But have you ever considered the problem as he would have viewed it? If he had confided in you before the plotters were uncovered, would you have been able to support the ruse, knowing the truth, yet hiding it from everyone?'

Stay at the manor, pretending he was just 'Ned', a fellow employee, an equal partner? Dissemble before Jesse or 'Mr Hampton' about his true identity, if pressed?

There was no doubt the answer to the first question was a

resounding negative. Uncomfortable as she was with distorting the truth, she would probably have had difficulty concealing his identity, had she chosen to remain at Blenhem after he confessed it. 'It would not have been easy,' she conceded.

'You must see Ned couldn't reveal the truth until he accomplished what was necessary to uncover the dangerous agitator who had been spreading unrest through the countryside. Despite his deception, it wasn't Ned who placed them in danger—but Barksdale. It was Ned who saved them, though—quite brilliantly, I might add.'

Despite the tumultuous emotions churning in her, Joanna had to smile. 'You are quite eloquent yourself! Did he write you a speech to deliver along with the other news he sent?'

Sarah smiled back. 'No, that was my speech, based on what I know of events. Would you like to know what he did write?'

The indignation she'd felt upon first learning he'd sent Sarah a report about her revived. 'Yes, I believe I would,' she replied with some heat.

'Since he never precisely directed me to keep it secret— and since I think it will help you better understand his sentiments—I shall read it to you, then.'

Drawing a letter from her sleeve, she unfolded it and began. '"Sarah, dear friend, I am relying on you in my direst, most desperate moment. I've met the woman I've been waiting for all my life, Joanna Merrill, about whom I've written to you before. But as you might expect for one who's always been cow-handed in matters involving females, I've made a complete muck of it. Just when I was at the point of confessing to her all my hopes and dreams, the truth of my identity was revealed in a fashion designed to make me appear in the worst possible light. Though it was not what I wanted, I was forced to accede to her wishes and let her leave Blenhem.

'"I can only thank a merciful heaven I was at least able to persuade her to come to you. I now place my hopes and dreams, my very future, in your hands. I rely on your ingenuity and discretion in prevailing upon her to stay with you until her anger cools, that she might be induced to allow me a second chance. While she remains with you, please offer your tenderest care, my friend, to the dearest delight of my heart.

"'I cannot ask you to boast to her of my character, for you know my faults too well. But do assure her, if you can, of my steadfast and faithful heart. If, in the end, she no longer believes in the love we shared and chooses another way, please assist her as much as is in your power, knowing my heart goes with her.'"

For a moment after Sarah finished reading, they both sat silent.

The simple beauty of his words—and the unmistakable sincerity of his expression—touched something deep within Joanna, a harmonic chord that set off a resonant response in her own heart and senses.

While she remained mute, too overwhelmed to speak, Sarah said quietly, 'Ned has been one of my husband's dearest friends for years. Like all of us, he is a flawed mortal who makes errors in judgement. But love does not always go smoothly, even when sincere and true. My own marriage began as a bargain: Nicky would rescue my family's estate; I would be a compliant wife who made no demands. He'd kept a beautiful mistress for several years before we married, and I told myself I must reconcile myself to that fact. As I grew to love him, I could not—though as it turned out, he had broken with her just before we married. But jealousy and misunderstanding almost destroyed our love before it fully began. We had to fight to save it. But true love is always worth fighting for.'

Sarah reached over to pat Joanna's hand. 'I know he hurt and disappointed you. But if you truly loved him as Ned, won't you give Sir Edward a second chance?'

Handing Joanna his letter, Sarah stood up. 'There, I'm done

with meddling. As Ned said in his letter, it's not for me to persuade, but for you to act according to the truth you discover within your own heart. I shall see you at dinner, I expect.'

After Joanna, still too full of emotion to be coherent, murmured an affirmative, Sarah walked out. Joanna remained seated, trying to bring some order to the thoughts swirling in her brain: joy over the Blenhem men's release, relief and approval at Ned's part in arranging it, admiration for his further assistance to Sergeant Russell, awe tinged with a bit of shame for how harshly she'd used him after learning of the special compassion he'd shown Mary.

And then there were those tender, selfless words of love he'd written about her. Carefully smoothing out the letter, she read it through several times.

By the time she finished, the turmoil of indecision that plagued her was gone. A sense of peace and purpose filling her, she knew clearly what she must do.

Ned Greaves—Sir Edward Greaves—was indeed the man she'd first thought him. A man she'd fallen in love with. A man she still loved. What was a bit of embarrassment compared to the wonder of that?

She'd already given him her heart. Surely she possessed the character to offer him forgiveness and the courage to see if their love could move beyond deception and disappointment into a relationship founded on honesty and trust? Excitement lifting her spirits, the joy she'd thought lost forever began trickling back into her needy soul as anticipation of his touch sent a surge of longing through her needy senses.

Jumping up, she headed for the wardrobe. Time to get busy! She would set off for Blenhem at first light tomorrow, and, thanks to her friend Sarah, this time she had more to pack.

Several days later, Ned sat at his desk in the study in the late evening, trying to finish totalling several long columns of figures. After losing track for the fourth time, he threw the pen down in disgust.

It was no use. He'd been rising early, eating little, driving himself without rest as he rode about the estate inspecting fields, directing ploughing, assisting repairs to cottages. He'd even pulled off his coat and lent his hands and his back to Tanner and his amused crew of stoneworkers as they renovated the cottage that was to be the schoolmistress's dwelling—a building he hoped with every fibre of his being would never be put to its intended use.

Ned wanted Joanna back—but with him. In his house. In his bed. As his wife.

But no matter how much he punished his body with relentless work, sleep eluded him. Hope, longings and recollections tumbled about within his angry, anguished, grieving mind, robbing him of peace and rest.

Unable to face the sight of a bed that inflamed so many needs and brought back so many exquisite, anguished memories, he'd taken to remaining in the study, dozing when he could on the sofa.

After weeks without adequate sleep, he now went through his days in a weary haze. He'd had to keep special guard over his tongue of late to avoid letting the constant fatigue and the wretched uncertainty about his future spill over into sharp and impatient speech.

Especially with Mrs Winston, who'd been distraught over her supposed 'disrespect' during his tenure as Ned Greaves, behaviour for which she'd apologized several times over. Despite his reassurance that he valued her services too much to ever turn her off, the poor housekeeper still flinched if he so much as frowned in her direction.

The problem was, he admitted, staring in disgust down at the muddle of figures in the ledger, he couldn't ride hard enough to escape loneliness or fast enough to outdistance the fear that

pierced his gut, sharp as the stubble of wheat left in the field
after the scythe. He might fill his days from early dawn until
well past midnight, trying to blot out the harrowing possibility
that he'd lost Joanna for good, only to be brought up short, like
a colt on a training lead, by some unexpected jerk of memory.

A child's query about school beginning would bring back
to vivid immediacy the image of her silhouetted in the door
of the schoolroom. Mrs Winston's serving a chutney relish
with the meat course would recall her expressive face and
velvet voice relating stories about life in India.

The inquiries by everyone from the innkeeper Kirkbride to
Granny Cuthbert to Davie about when they could expect her
back drew a rapier of doubt across the already bleeding
anguish of his soul over whether she would ever return.

Was the continuing enquiry over her brother all that kept
her there? Once that was completed, would she come back
and give them another chance?

Suddenly furious, he jumped up, ledger in hand. He was
but a second from tossing it into the fire when rational
thought returned.

Fingers trembling, he set the ledger back on the desk and
raked his hands through his hair. He couldn't go on like this
any longer, uncertain and unknowing, poised between hope
and despair.

He'd given her more than a month to reflect and reconsider.
If she would not return to Blenhem, he must go to London
and discover what her decision would be. Know now whether
or not hope was dead and he must somehow reconcile himself
to a future without her.

If she felt honour-bound to return and finish out her
teacher's contract, but not return to him, he might have to
leave Blenhem. He didn't think he could stand knowing she
was near, knowing she could never be his.

He gave a scornful laugh. Who was he trying to fool? He

didn't think he was capable of simply letting her go. Not without trying, with all the tenacity and persistence he possessed, to woo her back.

He'd pack a bag and leave for London at first light. Just the thought of taking some action to escape from the terrible agony of waiting made his spirits lift.

Feeling the first flickers of enthusiasm since he'd watched Joanna ride away from Blenhem, Ned strode to the door, heading for the bedchamber he hadn't visited for days. As he placed his fingers on the latch, however, suddenly it opened and Myles walked in, almost colliding with him.

'Excuse me, Sir Edward,' the butler exclaimed.

'What the devil are you doing still up?' Ned said. 'I'll snuff out the candles. Get yourself off to bed!'

'Yes, Sir Edward. But first I must tell you that though the hour is very late, there is an importunate Young Person to see you.'

Before Ned could gather his wits, in a rustle of skirts, Joanna—his Joanna—walked around the butler and curtsied to him.

'Sir Edward, excuse me for intruding upon you so late. At least this time I came in a carriage, so I am not dripping on your carpet.'

Staring at her in disbelief, Ned couldn't seem to get his tongue to work. He'd wanted her, longed for her, dreamt of her return for so long, he wasn't sure the woman before him was real, not just a vision conjured up by desperate imagining.

He realised suddenly that she was holding out a hand to him. 'Are you not even going to offer me a greeting?'

Behind her, Myles, swallowing a grin, cleared his throat loudly. 'Shall I bring wine, Sir Edward?'

Still in a daze, Ned nodded.

The door shut behind the butler. While she stood smiling at him, Ned remained rooted to the spot, seemingly unable to speak to her or move.

Hope and dread, need and joy had his mind in muddles and his insides churning. All he wanted was to take two giant strides, seize her in his arms, bury his face in her hair and never let go.

But that might very well not be what she wanted.

He tried to reassemble his rattled wits and summon some semblance of civility. Not trusting himself to touch even her hand, he waved her to the sofa. 'Welcome, Mrs Merrill. Won't you sit by the fire and warm yourself?'

Nodding, she swept by him, enveloping him as she passed in that unique, spicy scent he loved so well. After closing his eyes for an instant to savour it, he said, 'Am I allowed to say how very, very glad I am to see you?'

After seating herself on the sofa, she looked back at him. 'You may indeed. For I am very, very glad to see you, too.'

Trying to control a wild surge of hope, Ned took a seat in the wing chair, wanting her so much he didn't dare place himself any closer. Glad to his toenails that she was here, in his study, smiling at him.

Myles returned with a full decanter and bowed himself out. His hands shook as Ned poured her a glass, memories spilling over him of all the evenings they'd spent here. How he hoped to make more!

'Since you've returned, I trust the enquiry you've been conducting into your brother's disappearance has finally had results?'

'Yes, the Runners located him. He's been impressed into the British navy—quite a change for a Wellington army man. Since he has already seen service as a soldier, Lord Englemere is hopeful he may be able to obtain a discharge when Greville's ship next makes port. At least I know he is alive, and where. But that is not the reason I returned.'

'It isn't?' Ned asked, trying to restrain another surge of hope.

'No. I wanted to thank you for allowing me time to think

and not trying to force me into a hasty decision. If you had, by the way, I would most certainly have rejected you, rejected your offer to contact the Stanhopes. And thereby missed the chance to meet a lovely lady who has become a dear friend, missed getting to know her adorable son. Forfeited also the chance to obtain Englemere's assistance in locating my brother, which has proved invaluable, for without his connections, I cannot imagine how long it would have taken to find Greville. I wanted to thank you for obtaining the release of Sergeant Russell and the other men. For your kindness to me—and your rescue, for which I never adequately expressed my appreciation.'

Glad of her approval, but beginning to feel embarrassed, Ned waved a hand. 'No need to thank me, especially not for that.'

'Oh, I believe there is. But that is not yet the complete litany of things for which I'm grateful. I've left the best, most important for last. Don't you want to know what it is?'

Not daring to speak, Ned nodded.

'Though I still feel embarrassed when I think how I blathered on to you, casting insults at the aristocracy along with nuggets about my past, I do understand now why you felt you had to conceal your identity. How once the deception had begun, it became more and more difficult to reveal it.'

I understand. Could there be two sweeter words in the language? Ned wondered, gladness and relief cascading through him. If she understood, he could hope that one day she might forgive.

'You mustn't feel constrained about having offered your honest opinions,' Ned replied. 'I was enlightened, never offended. And…it was hard. So many times I was tempted to reveal the truth. I wish I had…that last night.'

Nodding, she blushed. 'So do I.'

'Would it have made a difference?'

'I don't know. All I know is it doesn't matter now. I've

come to realise that it took a man of great courage to allow
Barksdale to reveal the truth at the hearing, at a moment when
such a revelation would be interpreted at its worst. A man of
great character to put his standing and honour behind supporting the people of Blenhem; a man of eloquence and passion
to argue for their release to the judge. All of which confirmed
what I already knew in my heart, that I will no longer let
chagrin and embarrassment prevent me from confessing.
Finally, I want to thank you for being the man I love with all
my soul, the man I want to spend the rest of my life with. Ned
Greaves, Sir Edward, whatever your name, if you still want
me, I am yours.'

He had her in his arms before she'd finished the last
syllable. Clutching her tightly, he rubbed his face against the
silk of her hair, savouring the feel, the scent of her. The
warmth and fire of her in his arms.

'All I want is you, Joanna. I was so afraid I'd lost you forever.
So we may begin again? You'll allow me to court you?'

He felt the tremor of her laughter. 'Heavens, no! We are
well beyond courting, don't you think? Besides—' she hesitated, pushing him back gently as a shadow passed over her
eyes '—I must remind you the physicians in India believed it
unlikely, after I lost my child, that I would ever conceive
again. A gentleman will want an heir, so you mustn't think it
necessary to offer marriage—'

'Nonsense!' Ned cried, joy and excitement licking in his
veins along with hotter, more carnal desires. 'I'll have no
other woman as my wife. Besides, physicians are not infalli-
ble. In this instance—' he gave her a devilish wink '—I shall
be inspired to try very hard to prove them wrong. So, let us
call the banns! In the interim, do you wish to stay at the
cottage or the Hart and Hare? I want everything to be right
and proper this time.'

Leaning back in the circle of his arms, she studied his face for a long moment. 'You are very sure you want to marry me, regardless?'

He nodded. 'With all my heart.'

Two tears glittered at the corners of her eyes before she dashed them away. 'I should try harder to dissuade you…but sinner that I am, I cannot. By all means, let us call the banns. Aside from that, however,' she continued, her tone turning sultry, 'I don't want "proper" now any more than I did one magnificent night over a month ago.'

Lips parted invitingly, she walked her fingers up his chest and traced his lips. 'Won't you allow me to stay *here*…and thank you "properly"?' she murmured. 'From this night forward, for the rest of our lives?'

Joy and the tingling, tempting touch of her fingers almost paralysed his ability to answer. 'Tonight, and the rest of our lives,' he said hoarsely. Bending to give her a swift, savage promise of a kiss, he lifted her in his arms, blew out the candles and carried her from the room.

* * * * *

*Celebrate 60 years of pure reading pleasure
with Harlequin®!*

To commemorate the event, Silhouette Special Edition
invites you to Ashley O'Ballivan's bed-and-breakfast in
the small town of Stone Creek. The beautiful innkeeper
will have her hands full caring for her old flame Jack
McCall. He's on the run and recovering from a mysterious illness, but that won't stop him from trying to win
Ashley back.

*Enjoy an exclusive glimpse of Linda Lael Miller's
AT HOME IN STONE CREEK
Available in November 2009
from Silhouette Special Edition®.*

The helicopter swung abruptly sideways in a dizzying arch, setting Jack McCall's fever-ravaged brain spinning.

His friend's voice sounded tinny, coming through the earphones. "You belong in a hospital," he said. "Not some backwater bed-and-breakfast."

All Jack really knew about the virus raging through his system was that it wasn't contagious, and there was no known treatment for it besides a lot of rest and quiet. "I don't like hospitals," he responded, hoping he sounded like his normal self. "They're full of sick people."

Vince Griffin chuckled but it was a dry sound, rough at the edges. "What's in Stone Creek, Arizona?" he asked. "Besides a whole lot of nothin'?"

Ashley O'Ballivan was in Stone Creek, and she was a whole lot of somethin', but Jack had neither the strength nor the inclination to explain. After the way he'd ducked out six months before, he didn't expect a welcome, knew he didn't deserve one. But Ashley, being Ashley, would take him in whatever her misgivings.

He had to get to Ashley; he'd be all right.

He closed his eyes, letting the fever swallow him.

There was no telling how much time had passed when he became aware of the chopper blades slowing overhead. Dimly, he saw the private ambulance waiting on the airfield outside of Stone Creek; it seemed that twilight had descended.

Jack sighed with relief. His clothes felt clammy against his flesh. His teeth began to chatter as two figures unloaded a gurney from the back of the ambulance and waited for the blades to stop.

"Great," Vince remarked, unsnapping his seat belt. "Those two look like volunteers, not real EMTs."

The chopper bounced sickeningly on its runners, and Vince, with a shake of his head, pushed open his door and jumped to the ground, head down.

Jack waited, wondering if he'd be able to stand on his own. After fumbling unsuccessfully with the buckle on his seat belt, he decided not.

When it was safe the EMTs approached, following Vince, who opened Jack's door.

His old friend Tanner Quinn stepped around Vince, his grin not quite reaching his eyes.

"You look like hell warmed over," he told Jack cheerfully.

"Since when are you an EMT?" Jack retorted.

Tanner reached in, wedged a shoulder under Jack's right arm and hauled him out of the chopper. His knees immediately buckled, and Vince stepped up, supporting him on the other side.

"In a place like Stone Creek," Tanner replied, "everybody helps out."

They reached the wheeled gurney, and Jack found himself on his back.

Tanner and the second man strapped him down, a process that brought back a few bad memories.

"Is there even a hospital in this place?" Vince asked irritably from somewhere in the night.

"There's a pretty good clinic over in Indian Rock," Tanner answered easily, "and it isn't far to Flagstaff." He paused to help his buddy hoist Jack and the gurney into the back of the ambulance. "You're in good hands, Jack. My wife is the best veterinarian in the state."

Jack laughed raggedly at that.

Vince muttered a curse.

Tanner climbed into the back beside him, perched on some kind of fold-down seat. The other man shut the doors.

"You in any pain?" Tanner said as his partner climbed into the driver's seat and started the engine.

"No." Jack looked up at his oldest and closest friend and wished he'd listened to Vince. Ever since he'd come down with the virus—a week after snatching a five-year-old girl back from her non-custodial parent, a small-time Colombian drug dealer—he hadn't been able to think about anyone or anything but Ashley. When he *could* think, anyway.

Now, in one of the first clearheaded moments he'd experienced since checking himself out of Bethesda the day before, he realized he might be making a major mistake. Not by facing Ashley—he owed her that much and a lot more. No, he could be putting her in danger, putting Tanner and his daughter and his pregnant wife in danger, too.

"I shouldn't have come here," he said, keeping his voice low.

Tanner shook his head, his jaw clamped down hard as though he was irritated by Jack's statement.

"This is where you belong," Tanner insisted. "If you'd had sense enough to know that six months ago, old buddy, when you bailed on Ashley without so much as a fare-thee-well, you wouldn't be in this mess."

Ashley. The name had run through his mind a million times in those six months, but hearing somebody say it out loud was like having a fist close around his insides and squeeze hard.

Jack couldn't speak.

Tanner didn't press for further conversation.

The ambulance bumped over country roads, finally hitting smooth blacktop.

"Here we are," Tanner said. "Ashley's place."

* * * * *

Will Jack be able to patch things up with Ashley,
or will his past put the woman he loves in harm's way?

Find out in
AT HOME IN STONE CREEK
by Linda Lael Miller
Available November 2009
from Silhouette Special Edition®.

This November,
Silhouette Special Edition®
brings you

NEW YORK TIMES
BESTSELLING AUTHOR

LINDA LAEL
MILLER

At Home in
Stone Creek

Available in November
wherever books are sold.

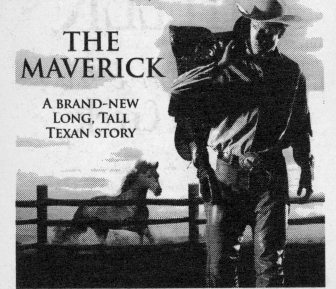

Silhouette Desire

FROM *NEW YORK TIMES* BESTSELLING AUTHOR

DIANA PALMER

THE MAVERICK

A BRAND-NEW LONG, TALL TEXAN STORY

Visit Silhouette Books at www.eHarlequin.com

SD76982

REQUEST YOUR FREE BOOKS!

Harlequin® Historical
Historical Romantic Adventure!

2 FREE NOVELS PLUS 2 FREE GIFTS!

YES! Please send me 2 FREE Harlequin® Historical novels and my 2 FREE gifts (gifts are worth about $10). After receiving them, if I don't wish to receive any more books, I can return the shipping statement marked "cancel". If I don't cancel, I will receive 6 brand-new novels every month and be billed just $4.94 per book in the U.S. or $5.49 per book in Canada. That's a savings of 20% off the cover price! It's quite a bargain! Shipping and handling is just 50¢ per book.* I understand that accepting the 2 free books and gifts places me under no obligation to buy anything. I can always return a shipment and cancel at any time. Even if I never buy another book, the two free books and gifts are mine to keep forever.

246 HDN EYS3 349 HDN EYTF

Name _____ (PLEASE PRINT) _____

Address _____ Apt. # _____

City _____ State/Prov. _____ Zip/Postal Code _____

Signature (if under 18, a parent or guardian must sign)

Mail to the **Harlequin Reader Service:**
IN U.S.A.: P.O. Box 1867, Buffalo, NY 14240-1867
IN CANADA: P.O. Box 609, Fort Erie, Ontario L2A 5X3

Not valid to current subscribers of Harlequin Historical books.

Want to try two free books from another line?
Call 1-800-873-8635 or visit www.morefreebooks.com.

* Terms and prices subject to change without notice. Prices do not include applicable taxes. Sales tax applicable in N.Y. Canadian residents will be charged applicable provincial taxes and GST. Offer not valid in Quebec. This offer is limited to one order per household. All orders subject to approval. Credit or debit balances in a customer's account(s) may be offset by any other outstanding balance owed by or to the customer. Please allow 4 to 6 weeks for delivery. Offer available while quantities last.

Your Privacy: Harlequin Books is committed to protecting your privacy. Our Privacy Policy is available online at www.eHarlequin.com or upon request from the Reader Service. From time to time we make our lists of customers available to reputable third parties who may have a product or service of interest to you. If you would prefer we not share your name and address, please check here. ☐

HARLEQUIN® HISTORICAL:
Where love is timeless

The Winter Queen
AMANDA MCCABE

Lady-in-waiting to Queen Elizabeth,
Lady Rosamund Ramsay lives at the heart
of glittering court life. Charming Dutch
merchant Anton Gustavson is a great favorite
among the English ladies—but only Rosamund
has captured his interest! Anton knows just
how to woo Rosamund, and it will be a
Christmas season she will never forget….

Available November 2009
wherever books are sold.

COMING NEXT MONTH FROM

HARLEQUIN®
HISTORICAL

Available October 27, 2009

• **A REGENCY CHRISTMAS**
by **Lyn Stone, Carla Kelly, Gail Ranstrom**
(Regency)
'Tis the season for romance! Share the promise of Yuletide with a
helping of festivity, family, warmth and passion....

• **ALASKAN RENEGADE**
by **Kate Bridges**
(Western)
Victoria Windhaven is shocked to discover that her bodyguard on
her dangerous journey through the Alaskan wilderness is none other
than Brant MacQuaid—a man she'd never wanted to see again! But
rugged bounty hunter Brant soon becomes the one man Victoria finds
impossible to resist, and in the confines of their stagecoach their
passion quickly escalates....

• **THE RAKE'S WICKED PROPOSAL**
by **Carole Mortimer**
(Regency)
Lucian St. Claire, one of the wickedest rakes around, needs an
heir—so it's time to choose a wife! High-spirited Grace Hetherington
is definitely not the spouse he wants, yet there's something irresistible
about her.... And when they're caught in a rather compromising
situation, he has no choice but to make her his convenient bride!

• **THE WINTER QUEEN**
by **Amanda McCabe**
(Elizabethan)
Lady-in-waiting to Queen Elizabeth, Lady Rosamund Ramsay lives
at the heart of glittering court life, though she never quite feels
fulfilled.... Charming Dutch merchant Anton Gustavson is a great
favorite among the English ladies—but only Rosamund has captured
his interest! Anton knows just how to woo Rosamund, and it will be a
Christmas season she will never forget....